THE ASYLUM

FOR

WAYWARD VICTORIAN

GIRLS

A NOVEL

EMILIE AUTUMN

The Asylum Emporium:
help@asylumemporium.com

Publisher's Note: This is a work of fiction. Names, characters, places, and incidents are a product of the author's imagination. Locales and public names are sometimes used for atmospheric purposes. Any resemblance to actual people, living or dead, or to businesses, companies, events, institutions, or locales is completely coincidental.

The Asylum for Wayward Victorian Girls / Emilie Autumn. – 4th ed.
ISBN 9780998990927

Contents

hospital entry 1: suicide watch

It was the dog who found me.

I heard him crying outside the bathroom door, but the sound seemed very far away.

I wasn't there anymore.

I was lying in a field of tall, soft grass—tall enough to hide me from anyone who came looking.

The grass moved around me, but there was no sound; I felt a soft blanket of tree-filtered sunlight wash over me, and I wanted to sleep forever.

I felt no fear, no panic; I felt relieved . . . relieved that I had made my decision and gone through with it, and now there was nothing left to do but wait and lay, wait and lay, wait and lay . . .

All my highs and lows, ups and downs, *TO BEs* or *NOT TO BEs*, were over at last.

I had no regrets.

I was at peace, and this was a sensation I hadn't known until that moment.

I was at peace . . .

I was at peace . . .

I was at peace . . .

Then, there were arms lifting me up, voices screaming in my ears, and I was being shaken violently while hydrogen peroxide was poured down my throat. There was no sunlight, no grass—just a dirty bathroom floor, and all I wanted was to go back to sleep.

I am standing in the back of the line at the Emergency Room, and I feel like a fraud.

I'm not bleeding.

I can walk.

I've been bribed.

I would never have come willingly had I not been threatened with the immediate cutoff of my psychiatric medication. And, just as a breakup is something that should never be done by phone, neither is being informed that you need to go to the insane asylum.

But it was.

Shrink: I can't see you anymore until you check yourself into a mental hospital.

Me: What? Why?

Shrink: Because the moment you tell me that you attempted suicide, I have no choice but to insist that you be kept under watch a minimum of seventy-two hours.

Me: Under watch? By whom? I don't need to be watched. I need my drugs.

Shrink: Then you'd better get yourself to the hospital today. I can't refill your prescriptions after what you've done. I legally can't.

Me: Wait . . . just wait . . . you asked me how I was doing, and I told you. I told you because I thought I was supposed to be honest with you. I thought you were the *one person* that it was safe to be honest with. But it's beginning to sound like you're the only one I really needed to lie to.

Shrink: Emilie, you're an extremely intelligent and talented young woman, but you are also very, very sick, and you need to be in a place where you can get better.

Me: Please . . . can't I just come in and talk to you? Show you that I'm all right? I mean, I'm not *crazy* . . . at least, not in the way this looks like. There are real reasons, *valid* reasons why I did this to myself, and, you know what, Doctor? I stand by them. I believe anyone could have done the same in my place.

Shrink: No, you can't come in to see me. Or, rather, you can, but if you do, you won't need a ride home because there will be an ambulance waiting to take you directly from my office to the hospital.

Me: So, basically, you are refusing to give me my bipolar medication until I agree to check myself into, what, a psych ward? Even though we both know that, within forty-eight hours, I will be a suicidal lunatic running into the street in the hopes of getting hit by at least one car if I *don't* get the drugs? If I say "no, I'm not going," are *you* comfortable with that out-come?

Shrink: Look, Emilie, I think that being under this kind of supervised care is exactly what you need right now.

Me: Dear god . . . only seventy-two hours?

Shrink: Seventy-two hours . . . minimum.

Me: No. No, this is not going to work . . . I have shows coming up. Fuck, I have an album to finish . . .

Shrink: Then you'd better check yourself in this morning.

"Why are you here?" snaps a woman in minty-green scrubs, and sounding a smidgeon impatient about it. She is approaching me with a clipboard, and I assume she's coming to ask what the hell I think I'm doing here, and why I look like I've just come from a costume ball, and why I have a heart painted on my right cheek, and why I am wearing boots with skulls on them because it's bloody morbid and dying people shouldn't see things like that and—

"I'm suicidal," I announce.

Oh my.

I sounded almost *proud* about that.

And I'm *smiling*. God, maybe I do belong here.

The nurse looks as though she doesn't believe me, and I don't blame her. I'll try again.

"What I mean is, I tried to kill myself, so my doctor cut off my medication. He said I have to get it from you now."

I don't think I've ever sounded so absurd in my life. However, this does the trick, and the nurse marches me right past the front of the line and into a tiny examination room where another nurse tucked safely behind a desk orders me to sit down.

Nurse: Family history of bipolar disorder?

Me: Yes.

Nurse: Family history of suicide?

Me: Yes. But that's not why—

Nurse: Ever hear voices?

Me: I hear you.

Nurse: Voices in your head? That nobody else hears?

Me: I did when I was little. Every night, in fact, for years. But not anymore.

Nurse: Ever been abused?

Me: How do you mean?

Nurse: Sexually?

Me: Is rape abuse?

Nurse: Rape is abuse.

Me: That's nice. I thought it was just something men did.

Nurse: Ever been pregnant?

Me: Yes.

Nurse: Are you pregnant right now?

Me: No.

Nurse: When did you stop being pregnant?

Me: Last week.

She raises her eyes from the form she's been filling out, and I can feel her judgment—the judgment I suspect I had better become accustomed to, because I know that it will never go away.

Me: It wasn't my fault. I was on the pill, but my bipolar medication cancels out the pill and my doctor never felt this worth mentioning to me. It wasn't safe to keep—

Nurse: You have any family?

Me: No.

Having completed her form, the nurse now takes my vitals without responding at all to what I've just told her.

Me: Aren't you going to ask me why I did it?

Nurse: Did what?

Me: Took all my sleeping pills at once.

Nurse: No.

A plastic hospital bracelet is slapped onto my wrist, and, fancy that! It already has my name on it.

Patient: Autumn, Emilie

Age: 27

Everything done, I would have thought I'd be off to a hospital bed or tied up to a pole perhaps, but, alas, it's into the waiting room for me. There is something slightly dangerous in the air, the patrolling armed guards are staring at me with questionable intent, and, if I'm honest, I don't feel that my new plastic bracelet is giving me the "street cred" I'd hoped it might.

I've been given a form of my own to fill out, so I take my clipboard and choose a torn vinyl chair in the middle of the room, having learned the hard way that a room's more remote edges are the worst place one can be.

I can explain: If you want to be safe, walk in the middle of the street.

I'm not joking.

You've been told to look both ways before crossing, that the sidewalk is your friend, right?

Wrong.

I've spent years walking sidewalks at night, because that's what people do who haven't got money for the bus. I've glanced around myself in the darkness, silent, frantic, and I saw the men following me, creeping out of alleyways, attempting to goad me into speaking to them then shouting obscenities at me when I wouldn't, and I suddenly realized that the only place left to go was the middle of the street.

But why would I risk it?

Because the odds are in my favor.

In the States, someone is killed in a car accident on average every 12.5 minutes, while a female is raped on average every 2.5 minutes. Even when factoring in that, *one*, I am generously including *all* vehicle-related accidents and not just those involving pedestrians, and, *two*, that the vast majority of rapes still go unreported because the victim is well aware that she *will* be blamed for the crime, I think my logic in this case speaks for itself. And, thus, this is now the way I live my life: out in the open, in the middle of everything, because the middle of the street is actually the safest place to walk.

Faced with the dauntingly vague and unsympathetic form field labeled "PRESENTING PROBLEM," I print:

Suicidal, unable to function reliably in everyday life.

An appropriately robotic description of an unspeakably painful condition. I cannot function reliably.

I am wearing an antique pink Victorian glove on my left hand; my writing hand is gloved in black-and-white stripes. It is warm, but I prefer to keep my hands covered whenever I can. I do not like to touch things.

I am in my bed, in my room, in the Emergency Ward, and my stockings are all I have left.

Before being left alone, I was put through three comprehensive security checks, each by a different guard. While I had no idea that taking all of my sleeping pills would reduce me to the status of common criminal in the eyes of the state, I certainly feel much less suicidal now that three men with guns have gone through my underwear.

This is the checklist of what I brought with me to the hospital:

1. Several books (I had figured that, in between all of the marvelously beneficial treatments I would be privileged to, there might be some down time.)

2. My notebooks (If I cannot relentlessly document my surroundings as though I were witnessing life from somewhere up on the ceiling, I tend to go a bit loony . . . shocking, I know.)

3. Pens/pencils (In order not only to write but also to sketch properly, I require both.)

4. Cell phone (Do you really think I'm coming to a place like this without being able to call for backup?)

5. Two changes of clothes (If we have had the pleasure of even the briefest acquaintanceship, then you'll know that this is conservative, to put it politely.)

6. Basic toiletries (Hairbrush, toothbrush, lip gloss, etc.)

7. The clothes on my back (Long black coat, long black dress, gloves, boots, black rubber bracelets, striped stockings.)

This is the checklist of what I was allowed to keep with me at the hospital:

1. ~~Several books~~
2. ~~My notebooks~~
3. ~~Pens/pencils~~
4. ~~Cell phone~~
5. ~~Two changes of clothes~~
6. ~~Basic toiletries~~
7. The clothes on my back (~~Long black coat, long black dress, gloves, boots, black rubber bracelets~~, *striped stockings*.)

I'm not stupid.

I know exactly what's going on, and I'm not fighting it. If I have to go through this, I will glean from it any small benefit I can receive.

I will not fight this.

Bring it on.

Bring on the cure.

Bring on the fucking happy.

I'm committed.

State of California - Health and Human Services Agency

INVOLUNTARY PATIENT ADVISEMENT
(TO BE READ AND GIVEN TO THE PATIENT AT TIME OF ADMISSION)

Confidential Patient Information
See W&I Code Section 53
HIPAA Privacy Rule 45 C.F.R. Se

Name of Facility ▉▉▉▉▉▉▉

▉▉▉▉▉▉ Neuropsychiatric Hospital

Patient's Name ▉▉▉▉▉▉▉▉▉▉▉▉

wrong *already*

Section 5157 (c) and (d) of the Welfare and Institutions Code requires that each person admitted
evaluation be given specific information orally and in writing, and a record of the advisement
in the medical record.

please listen

My name is ▉▉▉▉▉▉▉   My position here is ___ M.D.

to me

You are being placed in this psychiatric facility because it is the opinion of the professional staff
result of a mental disorder you are: check applicable

they are not listening

☒ Dangerous to yourself
☐ Dangerous to others
☐ Gravely Disabled (unable
for your own food clothing

document specific evidence which substantiates reason for hold):

We feel this is true because ___ you are depressed and suicidal, have
a plan to overdose,

You will be held for a period of up to 72 hours. This does include weekends or holidays.

Your 72-hour period will begin: ▉▉▉▉▉▉ 2 pm
(Time and Date)

Your 72-hour evaluation and treatment period will end at: ▉▉▉▉▉▉ 2 pm
(Time and Date)

NO! I don't have a plan,

During these 72 hours you will be evaluated by the hospital staff, and the treatment you receive may inc
medications. It is possible for you to be released before the end of the 72 hours, but if the professional
decide that you need continued treatment, you can be held for a longer period of time. If you are held lo
the 72 hours, you have the right to a lawyer and a qualified interpreter and a hearing before a judge. If
unable to pay for the lawyer then one will be provided free.

it already did

The law presumes you to be competent regardless of whether you have been evaluated or treated for
mental disorder as a voluntary or involuntary patient.

just listen

ad cause for Incomplete Advisement

Signature
to RLL
Date

hospital entry 2: the red crayon

I know I said only a moment ago that I would cooperate and trust in the wisdom of the medical community, but I was perhaps a bit hasty.

When my things were taken, the staff had assured me that they would be brought back to me as soon as I was "settled." Now that I am naked beneath a flimsy gown that doesn't close (why do they call it a "gown"? Is it sarcasm?), and lying in a gurney (like a metal slab but less comfortable) with shallow railing on the sides (to keep me from jumping out?), I find that I've been lied to.

I am in a solitary room in the Emergency Ward, and my door must be kept wide open at all times. I have the option of either complete darkness or the harsh fluorescent lighting that triggers my migraines. Scratch that last—there are no choices; upon asking for the light to be turned off, I am told that the guards need to be able to see into my room.

One of these guards crosses my doorway every few minutes to make sure that I haven't hung myself with my own hair. I ask him when I will be given my things back, and the anxiety rises in my ulcer-ridden stomach when he tells me, indifferently, that I won't.

"But, if I can't have my cell phone, how will anybody know where I am? How will they know I'm all right?"

"You can't use your phone down here."

This argument is somewhat desperate on my part since I know that there is no one within a thousand miles who would come to visit me, let alone break me out if I couldn't take it anymore. But what if something horrible happens to me? What if I need to call 911? Oh, wait . . . I'm already *at* 911.

"What about my books? My pencils?"

"You can't have pencils in here."

"Pens! I have pens!"

"Can't have pens either, Miss."

"How in the bloody hell can I hurt myself with a *pen*? Seriously now. I can't have *one* pen? It's fucking felt tip!"

The guard shakes his head.

"Nothing longer than it is wide, is that it?"

Slight chuckle.

"Just about."

"Look, I'm going to go crazy in here . . . wrong word . . . I need just *one* book, and that's it. I promise you, Sir, I am going to go completely and utterly mad if I can't at least read. Give me a manual on CPR or *something*!"

I am shamelessly appealing to the guard's workload, assuming that he wouldn't want to be in here restraining yet another lunatic if he didn't have to, but, upon examining his physique, I determine that restraining lunatics is probably what he was bred for.

"Can't you at least ask a nurse for me? I'd do it myself but you won't let me out of this thing."

The guard walks away, and I find that my heart is pounding. I have no privacy. I have no contact with the world outside. I have nothing to do except rot under these buzzing fluorescent lights in disgrace, unable to think with all of the screaming, the chaos, the absolute bedlam (pun intended) being rolled back and forth on stretchers outside my door. No one has come to talk to me, nor has the book I begged for been delivered, and I know now that I am in the wrong place. I am not a patient; I am a prisoner. And what's more criminal? Taking all of your sleeping pills at once, or sending a suicidal girl to a place like this?

I suspect it must be late evening by now, though I have no real way of knowing. Multiple doctors have come in over the course of the day to ask me how I ended up here, and I wonder that they do not share this information with each other. Or perhaps they do and I'm simply being tested for consistency. In any case, I refine my story a bit each time I tell it, because, not only do I realize that I am confusing them, I'm exhausting myself, and, frankly, I'm tired of hearing my own voice. No one has asked me if I need anything. I'm not allowed to get out of this bed, but I know that I need water, and I still have nothing to do but try not to cry as I wonder how my life went so wrong. No, I will not cry. I have not cried since leaving Planned Parenthood seven days ago, bleeding, barely able to stagger, the old white man with his Jesus cross and cardboard sign bellowing in my face, spitting, calling me a whore, and, even then, I was ashamed of my tears.

At last, a nurse arrives, and I ask *her* if I can have my books back. It is clear that neither she nor anyone else received my request of hours ago, but nothing surprises me anymore, and I resume my begging.

Some time later, she returns with a large plastic bag branded with the hospital's logo and containing all of my belongings, as if to taunt me with its entire contents when, as she now informs me, I may keep but a single item. I select one of my favorite history books on the resurgence of the bubonic plague in the nineteenth century. Then, in my most heartrending—or so I hope—tone, I ask the nurse if I couldn't keep just *one* of my notebooks and pens as well. She refuses, adding that I'm not even supposed to have the book—I should be resting, not reading.

Seeing that none of my charms could ever hope to penetrate this soulless shell of a woman no doubt hardened by years of attending to violent or, worse, annoying patients, I surrender.

I unpin my hair, shaking the flaming red strands (*flaming*, did you like that? A little dramatic, but effective, no?) from two twisted coils perched atop my head like mouse ears, then smooth it back, attempting to look more dignified than I feel.

Changing my mind, I decide to leave it loose; I even tangle it a bit so that I appear half as crazy as I'm being treated. I imagine that this is what Ophelia looked like—sane but crazy, crazy but sane.

The nurse makes one final pass around the room, checking for hidden pens, shoelaces, and other deadly weapons, and I smear the painted heart upon my right cheek, black and red coming away on the back of my hand.

"If one is not allowed to read, write, communicate with anyone, or even walk around one's own room, what, then, is one supposed to do here?"

The nurse comes to my bedside and snatches up the hairpins lying in my lap before turning to leave. She glances back at me from the doorway.

"Sleep," she says.

My first night in the Emergency Ward, and, in the antiseptic glow of the bustling hallway outside, I can see that the night staff is a bit younger than the day-shifters. Figures. Who would want the graveyard shift if they had the seniority to choose otherwise? And why is it called the "graveyard" shift anyway?

Is that a throwback to Victorian times when cemetery staff would watch over the freshly buried bodies at night to prevent grave robbers from digging them up? Are *we* the freshly buried bodies?

In any case, the attitude of the night staff is a bit softer as well; they haven't yet had the time to become harsh.

A young nurse with an Alice band and quiet, brown eyes comes to administer my sleeping pills (really?) as well as another handful of drugs (a few extra as I am now in such a state of anxiety that my entire body is trembling uncontrollably). I ask this new nurse, "girl to girl," if there is *anything* I can write with—anything at all on the premises that I could be allowed. She looks doubtful, yes, but I can't let this opportunity slip, so I exclaim, "A Sharpie! What about a Sharpie? I couldn't possibly do anything dangerous with that, could I?"

The young nurse's brow furrows and I see that she has not altogether ruled it out. "I'll go check."

I fall back upon my pillowless bed and exhale for the first time in months. It is only one breath, and I know it won't last, but I want just one selfish moment to bask in the warmth of someone doing something nice for me.

A few breaths later and my nurse is back, a grin puffing her freckled cheeks. She holds up for my inspection a single red crayon. I burst out laughing, and, once I start, I can't stop.

"So *this* is what it's come to!" I gasp, through hysterical tears.

"I couldn't find a Sharpie," says my nurse, "but I did find this crayon from one of the children's rooms. Will it be useful at all?"

Snatching the crayon from her hand before she can change her mind, I tell her it's perfect.

And it is.

Because I'm writing all of this down in the margins of my book about the plague, and everyone knows . . . EVERYONE KNOWS . . . that you can't erase crayon.

hospital entry 3: the bed

Early-morning vitals having been taken, and another handful of pills having been choked down, I am again left alone.

Having made it through my first night with a bit of drug-induced sleep, I am feeling just as miserable, but slightly less anxious. Or is that just the fight in me dying? In any case, it doesn't last, because, when a doctor appears in my doorway and informs me that I will be stuck down here in the Emergency Ward for a few days more while they wait for a bed to open up in the Psych Ward upstairs, the panic sets in again.

"So, I won't actually be 'treated' until I can be moved upstairs, which means that my seventy-two-hour watch won't start until *that* day?"

"Yes, that's what we're looking at right now."

That's what we're looking at right now.

"But I was forced to come here on the condition that it was seventy-two hours, with good behavior. Nobody told me that I'd be waiting for god knows how long before my time card is punched. Besides, it's not *my* fault that you don't have a room. Somebody should have told me that ahead of time—if not *before* I showed up, then as soon as I checked in, or, at the very least, before my fucking ride took off."

"We can't legally discharge you once you've checked in, so there's absolutely nothing we can do until a bed opens up."

I am really starting to not like this phrase "until a *bed* opens up," or, "as soon as a *bed* opens up," or, "there are no *beds* available right now." It's creepy, and it implies that the only thing I'm really here for is a *bed*, that the *bed* is the treatment, that I am here to lie down and stay down like a lobotomized fucking invalid, and I'm not liking this one bit. I'm starting to shake again. I move to sit up in my gurney, and the thin sheet they call a "blanket" falls away from my left thigh. I quickly cover the cuts with my hand.

"I can't quite process this," I say, unable to give up until I either get my way or receive an answer that I can understand. "I didn't hurt anyone but myself, which, as far as I'm concerned, is *my right to do*, but, see, now that I've said *that*, you'll probably add more days onto my sentence, right?"

"Ms. Autumn—"

"*I didn't hurt anyone else.* I've done everything I was told. The deal is not at *all* what I was led to believe, and now you're telling me that I am here indefinitely? Have I been tricked?"

"No, you haven't been tricked. This is the way it works, Emilie. For everybody. And, judging by your behavior, I'd say this is exactly where you should be right n—"

"If I can't leave," I interrupt, "can somebody come and get me?"

"No," he flatly says, walking toward the door.

"What if I promise to come back? I'll sign something! I'll come back when you have a fucking *bed* free!"

The doctor exits my room and I hear his footsteps travel down the hall, away from me and my pleas.

It is at this moment that I know my freedom is gone.

hospital entry 4: voices

Walls are thin here, and all doors are as wide open as mine. I can hear everything. I am surrounded. A shrieking, swearing crack addict has been delivered to the ER, and I take it as a personal attack when the nurses roll her into the cell right next to mine. Don't they know that you ought not to put someone who throws terrifying tantrums next to the suicidal girl?

In the cell to my other side, a young man is being restrained; he won't stop screaming, and is physically threatening the staff when they get too close. This is just what the voices in my head sounded like when I was a child . . .

How long until I snap?

Or have I already?

My cellmates may have taken a lot of drugs, but I tried to kill myself. Which is more insane?

Every hour (I'm counting seconds to count minutes to count . . .), a new doctor will enter my room and ask me if I'm still feeling like "hurting myself."

I can't take this question seriously anymore.

hospital entry 5: dr. sharp

During the interminable days that have gone by, I am forgotten by all but the chief resident psychiatrist, Dr. Sharp. When he arrived to examine me on my second afternoon here, I couldn't keep from giggling as we shook hands.

"What?" he asked, looking almost offended.

"Oh, nothing, just your name, in a place like this . . . it's right out of a movie . . . I'm sorry, I've just realized that I'm in the insane asylum and everything that isn't funny at all suddenly *is*. Like at weddings and funerals, you know?"

"Ah, I get it," said he. "Well, the truth is that I'm not the one doing the *pricking* around here—I deal more with the . . ."

At this, he tapped his fingertips to his head, twirling his forefinger in the international symbol for "crazy," which I thought was overstepping the boundaries just a wee bit, but then what *are* the boundaries in a place like this? I suppose that, if there are any, they are erected by the doctors and not the patients, so there.

I wasn't laughing anymore, so Dr. Sharp took a step closer to my bed, speaking intimately as though we were old friends and I wasn't crazy at all.

"Besides," he said, "just between you and me, I was never comfortable with the whole 'injection' thing . . . I'm not really into blood."

As he said this last, the doctor touched his hand to my arm, playfully pretending to administer an injection. Instinctively, I pulled my knees to my chest—not in modesty but because, if Dr. Sharp was afraid of blood, then he would surely not wish to see the scarlet lines covering my thighs—lines I'd carved with tools ranging from razor blades to safety pins.

Remarkably, no one has yet noticed the cuts, but then I still wear my inexplicably allowed striped stockings, and they are tall enough to hide most of my self-inflicted wounds. Most.

I have begun to feel somehow protected by my leg-wear. I am reminded of a true accounting of a young girl in the nineteenth century who was the victim of a serial killer. The villain lured the girl up to the attic of her own house where he raped (how original) and murdered her, then set the house on fire in order to destroy the evidence. The strange bit was that, the next day, the house was burned to bits, as was the girl's body, with the exception of her legs, which remained completely unmarred beneath her striped stockings. No explanation could be found for this bizarre phenomenon, but, due to this physical evidence, the killer was caught and hanged. I would very much like to have those stockings.

hospital entry 6: watched

Every time Dr. Sharp enters my room, my stomach clenches involuntarily, and I find myself pulling my gown more tightly around my body.

There is something . . . wrong . . . about him.

His general strangeness of comportment, his noiseless arrivals, his prolonged visits . . .

In fact, he's watching me right now, from just outside my room, as I write these words in crayon over the text of my precious book because I have already filled the margins. He is always watching me. And he thinks I don't know, but I know. I always know.

I can smell him.

I've become so nervous that I don't feel hunger anymore, and have stopped eating. My body is now eating itself.

The stale white bread I am given is not going to waste, however; twice now have I spotted what I believe to be a rat scurrying about my room when the lights go out, and I have been tossing breadcrumbs into the corner in the hope that it will stay with me.

hospital entry 7: checking

Tonight, I woke to find Dr. Sharp standing over my bed, his face bent down so close to mine that I could feel his breath. When I opened my eyes, he explained that he had been walking by and thought he'd check on me.

Now, there's "checking on me" as in *suicide watch*, and then there's "checking on me" in a tight t-shirt and jeans instead of his doctor's uniform, crouching down against the wall and asking me to tell him about my dreams, tell him about my life, tell him about my *madness*, tell him about the things I'm studying in my books, things which he claims to find "fascinating." And, in one brief explosion of intelligence, I know exactly what's going on.

Upon my next supervised trip to the bathroom, I study myself in the tiny, cracked mirror in the hope of spotting some feature—*something* in my physical appearance—that could be remotely alluring, so that I can wipe it out.

I find nothing.

hospital entry 8: found

So! I am to be taken upstairs within the hour, though there is one *wee* complication. I will be going, nay, not to Ward A, the ward for mere suicidal depressives and drug addicts, but to the *other* ward, Ward B, the ward reserved for honest-to-god violent lunatics. And why? Because Ward B has a bed free.

One of the nurses had popped in to deliver the happy news— "Aren't you excited?"—followed by the good Dr. Sharp, who is looking strangely smug.

He steps up to my bedside and, without a word, hands me a folded sheet of paper. He hovers over me as I open it, and I see something more unexpected, more *shocking*, than anything I ever could have imagined: I see the lyrics to one of my own songs, "Marry Me." A true vaudevillian, I generally live by the "never let 'em see you sweat" philosophy, and, as such, have a ready answer for anything, anytime, anywhere. Right now, I've got nothing.

"Aha," I manage. "This is my song . . ."

I fall silent.

I have no idea how to respond to this.

Dr. Sharp figured out who I was. He tracked me down. He found my website ("**www.emilieautumn.com**, that's you, isn't it?").

He dug through it extensively, which I know because the lyrics to this particular song are hidden within the site; they are not available to the casual visitor.

My mind races, the rat in the maze.

Dr. Sharp is looking as though he had uncovered some marvelous secret and now ought to be rewarded.

"I really liked it," he says. "You're a great writer, an incredible violinist, and your voice is . . . *intoxicating*. But I do have to ask you . . ."

And here, the doctor takes the paper from my trembling hands, and a red pen from his own breast pocket.

"Am I mistaken, or is this," he circles one of the lines, "*a sexual metaphor*?"

"Obviously," I say, trying desperately not to sound alarmed.

"I thought so," he says, self-satisfied. "And what about *this* line?"

"Yep, that too. Honestly though, Doctor, the entire song is a sexual metaphor, and not a very positive one, as you may have realized. It's no secret. That's kind of the point."

"That's impressive, Emilie," he says. "You're very . . . clever."

Traffic in the hallway is increasing and my wheelchair has arrived. Dr. Sharp hurriedly thrusts the paper into my hands as though he is afraid to be seen with it, but I hand it back to him.

"I don't need it," I tell him. "It's *my* song."

"Oh, right, of course," he says, flustered.

Dr. Sharp stuffs the paper into his pocket, its sexual metaphors circled in red ink for all to see. He goes to the door, then turns back to fix his eyes upon me, collected once again, sure of himself.

"You know, Emilie, I've been thinking a lot about your case, and, well, there's something I'm pondering that I probably shouldn't be telling you, but it's up to you if you'd like to know it or not."

I tell him that he may as well just say what he has to say since he's already set me up to wonder at it if he doesn't.

"Well, I was thinking that, perhaps, along with being bipolar, you might also have something called 'borderline personality disorder.' It's a condition that stems back to your childhood, and would explain why you have these fragmented parts of yourself that don't quite . . . fit together. You know how broken you are."

I ask Dr. Sharp if that means I'm schizo just to see what he says, but here's the truth: I know exactly what borderline

personality disorder is, and I also know that I don't have it. A passing nurse tells me that it's time to go, and, as I crawl down from my Emergency Ward gurney for the last time, Dr. Sharp finally says what he has *really* come to say.

"I do have a private practice, and I could *possibly* find some time for you, outside of this hospital. Let me help you, Emilie. Let me fix you."

Well.

There it is then.

That old familiar self-loathing wells up inside of me, and I feel sick.

I am a fucking fool for trusting this man enough to tell him a single thing about my brain and the person attached to it. I detest myself for ever believing he was here to help me. I hate that he is in control and I am the mental patient, and that, even *were* I willing to go through the process of reporting him and, inevitably, being called a liar and watching what little is left of my life being publicly ripped to shreds, Dr. Sharp is the department head—there is no one above him for me to go to.

And so I say "thank you," and he is gone.

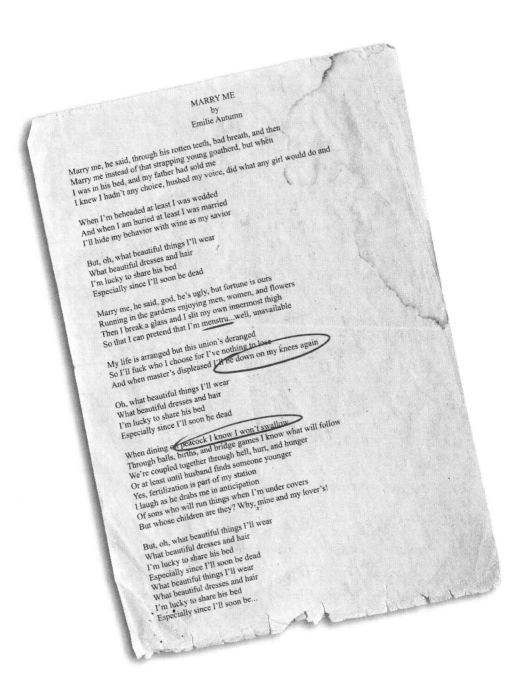

MARRY ME
by
Emilie Autumn

Marry me, he said, through his rotten teeth, bad breath, and then
Marry me instead of that strapping young goatherd, but when
I was in his bed, and my father had sold me
I knew I hadn't any choice, hushed my voice, did what any girl would do and

When I'm beheaded at least I was wedded
And when I am buried at least I was married
I'll hide my behavior with wine as my savior

But, oh, what beautiful things I'll wear
What beautiful dresses and hair
I'm lucky to share his bed
Especially since I'll soon be dead

Marry me, he said, god, he's ugly, but fortune is ours
Running in the gardens enjoying men, women, and flowers
Then I break a glass and I slit my own innermost thigh
So that I can pretend that I'm menstru...well, unavailable

My life is arranged but this union's deranged
So I'll fuck who I choose for I've nothing to lose
And when master's displeased I'll be down on my knees again

Oh, what beautiful things I'll wear
What beautiful dresses and hair
I'm lucky to share his bed
Especially since I'll soon be dead

When dining on peacock I know I won't swallow
Through balls, births, and bridge games I know what will follow
We're coupled together through hell, hurt, and hunger
Or at least until husband finds someone younger
Yes, fertilization is part of my station
I laugh as he drabs me in anticipation
Of sons who will run things when I'm under covers
But whose children are they? Why, mine and my lover's!

But, oh, what beautiful things I'll wear
What beautiful dresses and hair
I'm lucky to share his bed
Especially since I'll soon be dead
What beautiful things I'll wear
What beautiful dresses and hair
I'm lucky to share his bed
Especially since I'll soon be...

hospital entry 9: ward b

"Nope, not allowed," barked the guard as he pushed me roughly back down into the wheelchair I was struggling to remove myself from. I felt ridiculous; embarrassed—an overgrown child. I would gladly have walked upon my own two stocking feet. Why must I be treated as an invalid? What is the reasoning? Because I'm sad, I must be controlled? But no one will answer me, and so I quit asking. After a lengthy trip through the building marked by stops and starts and elevators taking me up to the very top, top, top of the hospital, I was at last rolled past the double doors—heavy black iron, and painted in white with these welcoming words:

PSYCH WARD

Yes. They actually do call it that.

In the center of the Psych Ward stands a single booth like a watchtower, encased entirely in glass windows that appear to be bulletproof. Nurses and other staff members, engaged in their coffee-drenched gossip, loiter inside of this protective chamber. I note that there is no such structure for the

protection of the inmates in what, I am truly astonished to find, is a shared male/female ward.

A morbidly obese "counselor" (is this summer camp?) grasps my arm and pulls me from the wheelchair. She leads me to a dingy area that is introduced to me as the Dining Room. Shoving me into an orange plastic chair, the counselor sits opposite, and I am ready for my inquisition. I will try, I tell myself, to make it quicker this time; I've had enough practice by now to know that telling the whole story never helps, and only confuses the brilliant minds that are in charge of the health of mine.

It doesn't matter.

Even my edited version appears to have a few too many twists and turns for the counselor. She glazes over, and I force myself to stop talking.

After making notes, she gives me a two-sentence summary of "what she is hearing from me." She's so way off it's almost funny, and proves that she either wasn't listening at all, or she knows I'm crazy and so it doesn't matter what the problem is just so long as I am here under lock and key of the state.

I am shown into a large room at the end of a long hall and behind two more industrial iron doors that look as though they ought to open out onto some back alley where a dumpster awaits housing hungry rodents. This room is to be my sleeping quarters.

The room itself is stark and cold, a sterile cell filled with numerous beds, bars covering the small, high windows. I must truly be a horrible, dangerous, psychotic person who should never be allowed contact with civilized society, for I have actually succeeded in getting myself thrown into prison.

And it *is* a prison.

It looks like a prison, it smells like a prison, and it all makes sense: *Attempted suicide is attempted murder. I committed a crime. And I am here to be punished.*

hospital entry 10: on to you

I would like to think that Dr. Sharp performs bedside service for every patient he sends to Maximum Security, but the startled expressions etched into the sickly faces of the nurses exiting my room as he enters indicate that he does not.

My intruder picks up the book set upon my hard, thin mattress, the one about the plague, and flips through the pages—the pages I've filled with red wax.

"I'm on to you," he says, too coy for his age. "You're here to do research. You're writing a book."

Oh . . . my . . . god.

I have crawled through the very depths of hell on my fucking knees, enduring horrors which I don't even dare write upon this page; I have suffered through so much that it had become unbearable, and, finally, as a simple act of mercy, I attempted to take my own life, a choice I sincerely regret the failure of. Now, I endure the judgment and the stigma that follows, and will continue to follow me for the rest of my days upon this earth. For anyone to even *suggest*, as a joke or otherwise, that I committed myself to a mental hospital needlessly, and, worst of all, for the sake of "research," is unfathomable. For a doctor, a psychiatrist whose job it is to get me through this mess alive, it is simply criminal.

A nurse arrives to inform me that I will be required to dine with the rest of the patients tonight, and Dr. Sharp makes his prompt departure, confirming my suspicion that *he is not supposed to be here.*

hospital entry 11: dinnertime

What am I doing here?

I am humiliated—a shred of a person.

I am looked at just like everybody else in the Maximum Security Psych Ward. The staff has received no memo telling them that I am only here because there wasn't room in Ward A; as far as they are concerned, I am a violent lunatic, and, as such, deserve to be in this prison—society's revenge upon the unhappy.

An alarm screams through the stale air, scraping my ears with static. This is the dinner bell.

We inmates creep from every corner of the building, some of us looking as though we are walking to our deaths, others looking too far-gone to know the difference. Entering the Dining Room, I observe the procedure: Wait quietly at the cheap plastic table of your choice (and choose wisely, or else . . .) until the grizzled cafeteria mistress calls your name, then go to the hole in the wall and pick up your tray.

The broken tables are crammed with lunatics who may or may not have remembered to tie their hospital gowns closed, and I choose a seat in the corner by the half-smashed-in piano and next to an older lady called Violet who mutters to herself constantly, and seems ever on the verge of exploding. A behemothic man lumbers toward us—a hulk of a beast with a substantial hump rising from his back. As I am occupied in calculations of just how easy it would be for him to snap my neck without even trying, the man reaches my table and begins to lower his tray. Without warning, Violet begins to scream at him. She starts off quietly, but with all the intensity of an erupting volcano.

"How *dare* you sit down without asking! *Get away, get away, GET AWAY!!!*"

Bingo.

Here sits a woman who has *obviously* been sexually traumatized, a fact that was suggested when she first introduced herself to me, adding, "Platonic. *That means no sex.*" I assured her that she was safe with me. But the wardens? Not so much. They clearly haven't diagnosed her profound issues with males being in her physical space. They haven't diagnosed mine either.

With a grunt, the giant backs away, and Violet stops shrieking. No one on duty comes to find out what went wrong. In fact, the other inmates barely raise their heads, and it seems as though the incident has been noticed by no one but myself. As if nothing had happened, Violet resumes her dinner, which consists primarily of a paper plate overflowing with canned corn kernels.

I still haven't been called up to retrieve my tray of god only knows what, and, surveying the menagerie of motley creatures devouring their scraps, I appear to be the only one left.

Just as I think I've escaped unnoticed, the cafeteria lady mispronounces my name and slams a bright orange tray down upon the metal shelf. On said tray is a soggy paper plate piled with microwaved spaghetti to be eaten with—get this—a plastic spoon. Have you ever tried eating spaghetti with a plastic spoon? If you weren't crazy before, you will be after that.

I'm trying.

I'm trying.

I'm trying.

My mouth is dry and I can't seem to manufacture enough saliva to get even a bit of white bread down my throat; it's sticking in my mouth and I think of how Jimi Hendrix died. I feel someone watching me, and I know it's Dr. Sharp.

My throat still burns from the hydrogen peroxide . . .

hospital entry 12: the first note

After my first night in the real live Psych Ward, I have new details to recount:

I am frequently awakened in the night by the sound of my fellow inmates sneaking about, fiddling with electrical outlets, crawling like giant spiders across the empty beds and up the walls as I pull my stiff blanket up to my eyes, staring out into the blackness, barely able to make out the shapes of the night creepers so that I can jump out of my brick-hard plastic-covered bed and start running if they come near my corner.

But, where could I go?

The staff secures the doors *from the outside* during the night. I suppose that, snug in their bulletproof sanctuary, they don't want to be bothered, so they leave us locked up to fend for ourselves. They can then take an extended coffee and cigarette break, knowing that we're not going anywhere. I wonder if they can hear us scream? I hope they can. I hope they can. I hope they care.

Upon rising, we are ordered to assemble in the Day Room. There, we line up to be weighed and are given our first round of pills. I wonder how the nurses are absolutely certain to give each inmate the correct medication, and not mix one's up with another's. Scanning the room, we all look so sedated and lost—

it probably wouldn't matter what we swallowed just so long as it keeps us quiet for a few more hours, until the next dose. I am given four pills that I do not recognize, and one that I do: the birth-control pill. *Why?*

At breakfast, I attempt to sample the gray eggs upon my paper plate. I'm sincerely trying—I really am—but I simply can't do it. My digestive system has shut down, and the drugs have made me sick. I do hide a bit of bread in my stocking though, because I've seen the rat again.

Having returned our trays, we are left to our own devices. There is not a single square inch of blank space remaining in my book about the plague, so I leave the Day Room and walk across the hall to the glass chamber where the staff is busying themselves for the morning shift. I lean my forehead against the pane, and, speaking through a small opening just like the ones in banks and movie theaters, I ask a nurse if she would let me have my notebook. Emerging from her sanctuary, the nurse leads me down the hall to a locked closet, swinging a key from a long chain as if she were proud of it.

As she turns the key in the lock, she tells me that I will be allowed the use of my notebook during the day *if* I promise to return it at night, and not to let it out of my sight during the hours I have it with me.

"I don't understand."

"The spiral binding" she says, clearly annoyed with my stupidity. "It's a metal wire."

Rolling my eyes (not advisable, by the way), I assure her that I do not intend to kill myself with my own notebook, but her concern is not for me; if one of the other inmates were to get hold of it, what then? I think to propose that this danger could be easily prevented by the separation of my sleeping quarters from those who made a habit of digging into other people's things, but decide against it—there is no suggestion box in the Psych Ward.

The door open, the nurse reaches into the dark and pulls a string. A single bulb dimly illuminates three walls lined with small wooden compartments. I see my boots with the skulls peeking out from an upper compartment, and reach into it before the nurse can stop me. As I slide out my long lusted after notebook, a slip of paper falls from between the pages; I bend to pick it up. Folded in quarters, it appears a bit weathered—wrinkled, and nearly transparent. I can see writing through the backside of the sheet, but I don't recognize the note, and am about to open it when the nurse, who has been standing over me and scrutinizing my every move, coughs audibly—an obvious demonstration of impatience. I tuck the paper back between the pages of my notebook, and both the nurse and I exit the closet.

Several hours have passed and I have been watched constantly, leaving me no opportunity to study the note. My stomach flutters nervously, but I don't know why. It is surely some scrap of my own that I had forgotten . . . lyrics, or a half-finished poem.

Finally, I am able to sneak away from group exercise (this is where we are all lined up and herded around the barbed-wire-enclosed roof of the hospital), and find a nurse to let me into the locked bathroom. I know I don't have much time. Shutting myself inside a stall, I unfold the paper:

. . . and when I looked out, I saw that we were heading fast upon a series of iron gates set in stone, wickedly arched, and crowned with tall spikes of erratically varying height. But what unnerved me completely lay beyond the gates: a pair of wooden doors—massive, pointed peak towering over us even from afar. Bar-crossed and studded with heavy bolts,

the doors were set in a great stone wall protecting whatever waited inside.

So paralyzed was I by the sight before me that I did not notice we had already driven past the first of the three spiked gates guarding access to the door beyond until I heard it crashing to a close behind us. A short drive onwards and we were at the second gate. I turned to see the barricades we had passed clanging shut, one after the other, by power of unseen hands or simply through habit, more accustomed were they to being closed than open.

The wind screamed round the carriage; the wheels rattled, and, as the third iron gate loomed before us, a bird, something like a raven yet a great deal larger, soared overhead, emitting a harsh, metallic shriek into the raging sky. It circled above the ever-approaching gate, sharp spikes gleaming in the pummeling rain.

Galloping onwards at a reckless pace, I heard the muffled squeals of what sounded like a swarm of insects, but, peering from the carriage window, I saw instead a great pack of rodents—sleek, furry bodies skimming the earth, leaping over one another, obsidian eyes sparkling. A quivering mass, they swam over the cobblestones like one creature—squid's ink spilling into the sea and infecting it with deep black within seconds. How they were able to keep pace with the horses mystified me, and when the swarm dispersed and shot on ahead of us, the rats darted through the spokes of the carriage wheels and round the horses' hammering hooves, yet were never trampled. Breathlessly, I watched them as they melted together again and slipped beneath the gate to the other side like a gush of dark water—the tide coming in.

It was all so ghastly . . . so sickeningly enthralling; my body convulsed in a trembling wave—a heady blend of horror and wild anticipation.

And then!

The final gate crashed to a close, and we reached the ultimate precipice at last.

The doors began to open.

There was an awful grinding of metal, a clashing of loosened chains, and, with the sky seeming to come down round us, it appeared: the Asylum.

From the Asylum for Wayward Victorian Girls,

Emily (with a 'y')

The alarm is ringing for dinner, and I know it will soon be time to return my notebook. Folding the note, I tuck it into the top of my right stocking and walk down the hall toward the Dining Room. I'm late.

hospital entry 13: the forgotten floor

Why am I still here?

My seventy-two hours were up days ago. I've been told that I am to wait for something, though what that means exactly I do not know. Treatment, I suppose, someone to come and "counsel" me, to teach me some life techniques I can use to try and be happier. Perhaps the staff is waiting for me to look non-suicidal. Perhaps they are waiting for me to gain weight. Perhaps they are actually waiting for me to *start* acting crazy, because surely I couldn't recover until I could admit that I was nuts in the first place, which, incidentally, I do—I just don't act it out as the staff expects me to.

Or perhaps they just forgot about me, in the same way that the doctors at Planned Parenthood did just weeks before when they administered the excruciating pill that starts the abortion process then stuck me in a tiny closet and forgot about me for five hours before coming back to perform the actual operation—five hours which I passed convulsing in pain, needles stuck in my veins and taped to my arms, the fluids they are meant to convey having long run out, my innards burning me alive.

And, if I ask questions, one of the wardens will speak to me very slowly as though I were not only a child but also a mentally disabled one, which, I suppose, is exactly what I am.

The funny thing about mental hospitals is that they strip away any remaining reason you have to live, but deny you the means to do anything about it. It is fascinating to me that a suicide attempt, by default, *legally* lands you into the asylum, the psych ward, the loony bin, the nut house—call it what you will, it's all the same. Perhaps you are crazy, perhaps you are not, but I do not believe that, *in itself alone*, attempting suicide proves anything at all about your mental state, save that, upon weighing the merits of living and dying, you found that one outweighed the other.

Is this crazy?

I see nothing insane about it at all.

Socially unacceptable to be sure, but not mad.

Asylum Letter No. II

Having something to write with at last, I hereby declare that I am, and have always been, of sound mind. In demonstration of this fact, I will tell my story and state my case—the case I shall never have the opportunity to present:

I was born to Irish parents in the part of London where only the poorest of the paupers make their homes. Having known no other way of living, I was far from unhappy; I had learnt to cook and sew, and spent most of my waking hours watching over my younger sisters. Sometimes I believe I have remembrances of my older sister, but I am not certain, for I was only an infant when she died. In any event, my parents never spoke of her, and, for fear of upsetting them, neither did I.

Late at night, I would amuse myself by picking out notes upon my absent grandfather's weather-beaten violin, which was hung, together with its sadly warped and nearly hairless bow, upon the peeling wall in the room I shared with my sisters. My father had succumbed to the drink, a common tragedy in those parts where opium and alcohol offer the most uncomplicated escape from overcrowding and immense poverty, and he usually stayed out well into the morning, which was quite satisfactory to us all.

Being in the possession of a memory for music, and able to reproduce most melodies upon first hearing, I would teach myself to play the tunes I heard in the streets—mostly folk songs from the lands of our ancestors: Ireland, of course, but also Scotland, and even some from India, for we were all immigrants here.

Now and again, my father would permit me to follow him to the tavern, where, standing upon a table, I would play to the drunken delight of the raucous men and their painted ladies. The more boisterous of the company would sing along to the jolly drinking songs, whilst the older men would weep silently as I played the slow and mournful ballads of the homelands they would never see again. But as marked as the effect of my music upon this varied audience, the effect upon my self was thrice as exquisite, for to share the fruit of my fingers was to share a bit of my small soul and eased a pain I carried with me always—the pain of a heart born into this world ready stocked with more love than I imagined I would ever be allowed to give.

One night, as the snow piled up against the frosted panes, a man in a tall grey hat entered the tavern as I was engaged in playing one of those haunting ballads of old. I quit my song as he selected a corner to stand in; the company stared at the intruder, all except my father who was quite in his cups (the degree to which was in no small part my very own fault, for his payment for my performance was a loose tap when he liked). The stranger requested, in a language more refined than any I had yet heard, that I continue, and so I did, afeared to disobey. As my final note faded, the man did not applaud as the others did, and I felt I must have played very poorly to the distinguished ear of such a grand gentleman.

Having wrapped my violin in its bit of red cloth, I held it tightly to my chest as I went to sit upon my little stool behind the bar, thoroughly shamed. The man with the tall grey hat walked towards me, and, despite the fire and the heat of crowded bodies, I felt cold.

'Your hair, little one . . . I've seen this colour before . . .' he said, taking one of my red curls between his fingers. 'To whom do you belong?'

I did not understand his meaning.

'Who amongst this company is your father, my girl?'

My voice sounded strange to my own ears as I answered.

'Him sitting with that lady in the corner . . . Sir.'

Without reply, the man moved towards the table I had pointed to. Approaching my father, the stranger spoke to him in a low timbre; I could not make out his words. For a moment, I thought my father seemed to recognize the man, but I must have been wrong for they did not shake hands. A few more words were exchanged, and my father nodded his head; the man turned and left the tavern with a flourish of his long grey coat.

As we trudged homewards some hours past, my father did not speak to me, but then he usually did not; I cannot say why it seemed strange at this time more than any other, and yet, it did.

Later, as I lay in bed with my sisters, I heard my parents on the other side of the parchment-thin wall. My stomach tightened; their nocturnal fighting was a common enough occurrence, but I had never hardened my nerves to it, much as I had tried. Unable to shut out the noise, I listened as I always did. Tonight was different—there were no raised voices; they spoke in hushed tones, and I could only divine hints of their conversation.

'He has promised a sum such as we could live on for a year or more,' said my father.

'Not if you drink it away this time, we couldn't. But, be that what it is, there are too many of us. Tell him . . . tell him we accept,' said my mother.

The next morning, the man with the tall grey hat knocked upon our door. Through my cracked window, I had seen him stepping lightly through the filthy snow as though it melted a clean path at his command, and was overcome yet again with that singular chill I had felt as he approached me the night before. I hid in my room, but, upon hearing the jingle of coins, I understood everything.

My mother came to find me and told me to follow; she did not look into my eyes. I took my beloved instrument from its nail and wrapped it in the red cloth; I knew, as much as I have ever known anything, that I would not have the opportunity to come back for it.

'You have, again, made a very wise decision,' said the man to my parents. 'She will be well cared for, and will, as before, receive the very finest education in music, and in all things befitting a young lady.'

As my mother left the room, my father gave a low and clumsy bow, something I had never seen him do. The man in the tall grey hat took me away, and nobody said goodbye. I was five years old.

From the Asylum for Wayward Victorian Girls,

Emily (with a 'y')

Asylum Letter No. III

Upon arriving at the Unfortunate Girls' Musical Conservatoire, I was given my first proper dress, and a new violin. Though it did not have the soul of my grandfather's, it was a worthy instrument indeed, and must have been quite expensive.

The man who had taken me from my family was, in fact, the Headmaster of the Conservatoire. When he was not traveling to recruit new pupils, our Headmaster entertained his guests—always richly attired gentlemen—guiding them on tours of the facilities and hosting recitals wherein we would play for the strangers he invited.

During the years that followed, I was educated alongside close upon one hundred girls of varying age, all seemingly orphans or castaways like myself, and I came to know a great deal about a great many things, but mostly about music. Though none of us were particularly fond of the restrictive nature of our existence within the Conservatoire, we took our lessons and became rather fine young ladies with a mastery of our chosen instruments that most men upon the world's stages could hardly compare with.

We were exceedingly privileged girls, or so we were frequently told, for, though the studies were grueling and left time for little else, the greatest reward imaginable awaited us:

We were promised that, if we all worked very, very hard, we would grow up to become celebrated musicians, performing in golden theatres and crystal palaces for kings and queens. It was this dream that we clung to through the slaps upon the hand from our Music Masters when we played out of tune, the austere coldness of the Headmaster and Mistress, and the complete absence of both love and life outside, for which we were starved.

There were joys, however. Each afternoon at four o'clock, we would pause our practice and assemble in the Drawing Room for tea.

Though we were modestly brought up, and firmly trained to watch our figures so that we could compress our developing waists into mercilessly boned corsets (we were made even to sleep in these wretched devices, can you imagine?), our cook was a kindly old creature who delighted us with buttered crumpets, sugared scones, and cherry-studded cakes when our masters' eyes were directed elsewhere.

And then, there was the tea. My near-forgotten mother had often steeped leaves by the same name, but the resulting brew was pale and flavourless in comparison. The foreign distilment I now enjoyed was dark, rich, and tasted of elegance and civility; I knew no greater pleasure than pouring my drop of milk into a delicate china cup so thin as to be nearly transparent, then infusing the liquid with steaming amber and watching the two disparate elements blend into the dusky brown that soothed the lonely soul and calmed the shattered nerves following a particularly trying lesson with the Music Master.

Whilst we all shared a common pedigree, having been removed abruptly from families who badly needed the money that was offered them in exchange for their daughters, one amongst my fellow pupils quickly became my constant companion, and this was Sachiko.

A cellist, Sachiko was from the Orient, though she did not know exactly wherein, having been sold at such a tender age that she could not remember; for reasons unknown to us, the staff took great pains to conceal details of our histories prior to admission.

Sachiko was always up for a sneak-about at nights, thieving bits of cake left out in the Drawing Room, then tugging me along to the attic where the portraits were kept. As often as we dared, we would leaf through the albums bursting with painted miniatures of hundreds, possibly even thousands, of girls, supposing these beauties to be former pupils—though some seemed awfully young to have completed their studies—gone on to grace the concert halls of a world we had only been told of. Together we passed many a blithesome hour sighing over the magnificent gowns, the exquisitely arranged hair, and imagining the glamorous lives these young ladies must now be enjoying, all the while dreaming of the day when we could join them.

Much to our mutual delight, Sachiko and I were assigned to share sleeping quarters in my fifth year at the Conservatoire. Late at night, when we had talked our voices dry, she would produce the bits of cake and lumps of sugar she had managed to pilfer, and we would lick our sticky fingers and play Mozart duets as quietly as we could until the sun came up. Though our incessant giggling often earned us reprimand, alerting the Headmistress to our being quite awake when we ought not to be, I would never have changed a moment of our time together. Alone, we were timid and nervous things, but, together, we blossomed.

One bleak February night as the bare branches scraped at our chamber windows, Sachiko revealed the flask of sherry she had pinched from her Music Master's study as he was retrieving a volume of Bach Sonatas from the Library. We were quivering with all the excitement of that which is forbidden— we had never tasted sherry, you see. We crept from our beds and scurried on tiptoe down the hall, past the Headmistress's quarters where a sliver of gold bleeding from beneath the door indicated that she had not yet retired, and up the steep and narrow staircase leading to the attic.

Once settled, Sachiko uncorked the sherry and bravely swigged it straight from the flask, pulling a wretched face as she swallowed. Impressed, I grasped the flask from her hand and sipped it myself; a bout of coughing ensued, but another taste of the liquor seemed to be the remedy. A few swills later and we were again turning through the portraits, comparing the ladies' charms, and I daresay being a bit louder about it than we ought.

Spotting a new volume, we lifted the velvet cover and soon began to recognize students we had known well, and who had only recently left the school. It was strange to see them dressed so richly, and displaying their bare shoulders and arms, but we supposed that all great ladies of London must favour such fashions.

Reaching the final page, we were struck silent. The very last portrait was of Sachiko. There was no mistaking it—her name was printed above the painting. Though she was draped in a kimono she had never herself worn, and posed upon an entirely unfamiliar settee, the likeness was perfect.

I quietly closed the book and put it back where I had found it. Leaving behind the remainder of the sherry, we descended the stairs and found our way back to our room without a word between us.

Sachiko crawled into her little bed and turned towards the wall. I blew out the candle, then got into the bed beside her.

We both wept that night; contrary to all logic, we had assumed that we would be leaving the Conservatoire at the same time.

From the Asylum for Wayward Victorian Girls,

Emily (with a 'y')

Asylum Letter No. IV

And so it came—the following day, a foggy Sunday in the February of my seventeenth year: the worst day of my life.

Sachiko and I had risen and dressed cheerfully enough, neither of us mentioning what had taken place the night before. It was as though we shared an understanding that, if we did not speak of it, it might blot itself from our history.

Then, shortly after breakfast, Sachiko was escorted into the Headmaster's study, and I knew in my heart what was coming. I waited outside the door for her to emerge, and, when she did, her face was streaming with tears and she could not speak. She fell into my arms, and I did my best to comfort her, vowing that I would practice twice as hard so that I could follow her, and that, soon, we would be the darlings of Europe, performing our Mozart duets for royalty.

As she packed her few belongings, I made Sachiko promise to write at her very first opportunity, for I would not rest until I had assurances of her well-being. Of course, I also desired to know what lay ahead for myself.

My efforts to lift her spirits succeeded sufficiently for her to show at last a dash of excitement at her impending journey, and her enthusiasm made my heart lighter as well. By the time the coach arrived, we had managed to convince each other that this was, in fact, a blessed day, and that it was to mark the first real variation in our lives. I would follow her presently, of course I would . . . it was simply a matter of time.

The footman came for her trunk, and my dearest friend was called outside and away from me. We kissed each other good-bye, and she was gone.

From the Asylum for Wayward Victorian Girls,

Emily (with a 'y')

Asylum Letter No. V

The empty bed in my room was quickly occupied by another pupil. I knew it was vile of me, but I resented her sleeping in Sachiko's bed, and putting her things in Sachiko's cabinet, and so I made no attempt to befriend her, and for this I remain sincerely ashamed. Instead, I directed all of my attention towards my studies, and, to the delight of my Music Master, worked more diligently than ever, practicing tedious arpeggios, études, and countless concertos until my fingers were raw.

Weeks crept by, then months, and still I had not heard from Sachiko. I had taken up the habit of loitering near the Conservatoire's entrance at the post's usual hour; thus was I there to snatch my letter directly from the postman's hands at last, scampering away before he had opportunity to object. The missive bore no return address, but I knew from whom it came.

Back in my room, I tore open the envelope and unfolded the enclosed parchment. Scrawled in a reddish smear were only two words:

At that very moment, the Headmistress seized the letter from my trembling hands. She grasped my arm and rushed me down the hall towards the Headmaster's study. There, the being who will forever be known to me as the man with the tall grey hat was waiting, though he took no apparent pleasure in my arrival, for his lined face was hard as stone as he informed me that I would be taken that very afternoon to the city in preparation for my debut.

Ought I to have been happy? Perhaps. But I could not be.

I returned to my room to find a small trunk already packed, my two violins in their cases beside it.

Although Sachiko had been my closest companion, I had made a good many friends during my time at the Unfortunate Girls' Musical Conservatoire. My schoolmates stood in the doorway and waved their hands as the horses lifted their hooves and wheeled me away. Some of the girls even shed tears, and, for that, I loved them more than ever.

From the Asylum for . . . oh, *bother*! Enough of these for-malities, Diary; you know who I am, and I must conserve my pencil lead . . .

Asylum Letter No. VI

Inside the coach, I was met by a man with the wrinkled face of a prune and almost as much charm. Clad in butler's livery, he passed his drooping eyes over me, yet spoke not a word, and I hoped that his dour exterior was no indication of the sort of household I was to visit. Desperate for clues to my immediate future, I summoned the courage to inquire as to our destination.

'You are being brought to Bainbridge . . . the estate of your new Master,' answered the man, his vacant face to the window.

I experienced a striking pang of anxiety, but steadied myself.

'*Master*? I don't understand you, Sir. Why should I have a master?'

The man would not look at me, and turned his eyes down to peruse a bundle of papers he held upon his lap.

'Begging your pardon, Sir, for I can see your papers absorb you entirely at the moment, but I must trouble you with my question once more. I have departed from the Conservatoire to begin my career as a performing musician. I am no longer a pupil, and, thus, should have no master. Is this not correct?'

Again, my escort made no reply, and for three hours more we drove in awkward silence.

At last, we reached London, and the willow-lined drive that was my introduction to Bainbridge.

Asylum Letter No. VII

The estate was a sprawling structure set atop a cliff directly above the bank of what I would later learn was the river Thames. Ornate, even garish, this vulgar display of wealth was decorated lavishly in the Baroque style, crowded with stone columns, curling ornaments, and gilded angels, naked and grinning.

My traveling companion led me to the mansion's entrance, where I was calmed slightly by the appearance of a young, auburn-haired housemaid. The butler then took his leave of me, not surprisingly without a farewell.

Still overwhelmed with apprehension, I stood unmoving in the foyer, violin case in either hand.

'Come on, then, Miss,' she said, taking up my trunk.

I followed the maid up a grand and circular staircase, then down a long corridor with lofty, frescoed ceilings and several doors to either side. Walking close behind, I saw that she bore what appeared to be burn marks upon her neck—long red lacerations where the skin was peeling.

Stopping suddenly, she opened a door to the right and led me into a richly furnished chamber, the centerpiece of which was a magnificent, canopied bed draped with gold-embroidered gauze. Upon the walls hung several large paintings of a most peculiar sort; I did not like to look at them, and, as indicated by her downcast eyes, neither did the maid.

'I'm to tell you to please stay in your room, Miss. You may unpack your things if you like, but you're not to come out.'

She curtseyed quickly and turned to leave, but I called her back.

'Please, couldn't you stay for a little while?'

'I'm afraid I cannot, Miss . . . the Master would be upset.'

Again, that word.

'The Master? But how would he know?'

'He knows everything.'

Her parting words frightened me more than a little, and for a long time I sat perched upon the edge of the bed, too afraid to inspect my surroundings.

At last, my native curiosity revived itself and I rose to walk about the room, skimming through books, picking up trinkets then setting them down again, hoping to find some object that would hint at what sort of place I had come to.

Against my will, my eyes swept across the paintings. That directly opposite the bed featured a demonic satyr in the act of tearing the clothing from a half-naked young girl.

I cried out in surprise. The satyr's eyes had been replaced by holes cut into the canvas, and through one of these holes stared a glittering blue eye.

Upon my involuntary outburst, the eye disappeared, but it was all too much; I curled up behind the bed curtains and shook from head to toe until I lost consciousness from sheer exhaustion.

Asylum Letter No. VIII

I could not say how many hours had passed, but when the housemaid came to rouse me, it was dark out.

'Miss,' she said, softly, 'I'm very sorry to wake you, but I am to tell you that the Master will see you tonight. I will help you to prepare yourself.'

The maid opened a wardrobe, revealing several gowns in rich colours and fine fabrics. She selected a cream silk with lace and ribbons adorning the short, puffed sleeves; after handing me a pair of freshly pressed undergarments and tightening my corset, she helped me into the dress. It was a beautiful gown, but I felt over-conscious of my exposed flesh, my neck and shoulders more bare to the world than they ever had been. It occurred to me then that I had not been measured for any new dresses, but, as this one fit me precisely, I supposed that one of my own had been sent to be copied in advance.

My assistant worked noiselessly, often pausing as though she were listening for something. I could stand the silence no longer.

'What is your name?'

'Anne, Miss.'

'Mine is Emily. With a "y", you know.'

'I know, Miss.'

'And where did you live before you came to this house?'

Anne did not answer.

'Anne?'

'I lived where you lived, Miss.'

'Really? At the Conservatoire, you mean?'

'Yes, at the Conservatoire. I was a pupil there as a child, before your time.'

'How queer! And what was your instrument there?'

'Violin, Miss . . . the Master has an especial preference for violinists . . . but I don't play anymore.'

'Why ever not? Oh, Anne! You must play one of mine! I wouldn't mind a bit. In fact, I insist upon it.'

In my enthusiasm, I had turned my body, wresting the laces of the stiffly boned bodice from Anne's fingers. She gathered them again and pulled them tight, giving me a jolt.

'I am a maid now, Miss. I aspire to nothing more.'

'But how did you come to be such? Did you not leave the Conservatoire for the stage, as I have?'

'I suppose that, in a way, I did. But I failed.'

She paused.

'You will not fail as I did. The Master's been asking for you for quite a long time now, and, had there not been others bidding as well, I daresay you would have come sooner.'

'Others? Anne, I really don't see . . .'

My throat had gone dry as if in defiance of the questions I wished to ask.

'Anne,' I lowered my voice, 'Anne, I must ask you something, though I hardly know how, it is so strange. After you left me earlier, I saw something in the painting there . . . that awful one with the satyr—'

Anne dropped the pins she had been using to fasten tiny white flowers to my hair, which she had dressed very prettily indeed in long, loose curls.

'Miss, we must go to the Music Room at once.'

She spoke curtly, seemingly frightened as she bade me fetch my instrument. I sensed Anne's disapproval as I chose my weather-beaten friend over its better, for she stared at the violin with the most peculiar expression, but I was unsettled and felt it would bring me strength.

We walked briskly down the long corridor and into an oak-paneled room hung heavily with velvet curtains in the deepest scarlet I had ever seen. It was there that Anne left me.

Asylum Letter No. IX

The Music Room was as lovely as it was ostentatious, with several intricately carved chairs placed in clusters round a magnificently crafted harpsichord, the lid of which was raised and painted inside with ladies in a pastoral scene. It is true that the pianoforte is more in the fashion these days, but many still prefer the percussive element of the older instrument.

Entirely immersed in my inspection of the lid (for I had noticed that the ladies pictured were quite without clothing), I was startled by footsteps close behind me. I spun round to find myself facing a tall man with the fairest hair imaginable and only one eye. A grey velvet patch covered the spot where his left eye ought to have been; his right was a piercing, icy blue.

'Greetings, my pet, and welcome to Bainbridge,' said the man, with a ceremonious bow. 'I am the Count de Rothsberg. I have been to your Conservatoire to watch you play many times.'

I thought it odd that he used the word 'watch' instead of 'hear', but then, English was not his native language—his speech was coloured with something foreign . . . German?

'I am pleased to see you grace my Music Room at last. Though, you're looking rather pale . . . Never mind, I daresay

I like you pale. You were not meant to be an *English rose*, as they call it here. But, you are not nervous, are you?'

I did not answer. The Count had raised his hand to my face, his long white fingers lifting my chin and turning my head slowly from side to side.

'I trust your fingers are as nimble as ever?'

I managed a small nod.

'Your skill with the bow . . .' he said, 'quite . . . what is the word . . . *intoxicating.*'

His words were not unkind, yet I did not like to be touched, and my skin shivered in protest as I retreated a step. The Count smiled, exposing sharp, irregular teeth.

'You see, my pet, *ma petite fille, mein kleines Mädchen*, it has been my fondest wish that you should make Bainbridge *your* home, as well as mine. All I ask is that you play exclusively for me, and my occasional guest, of course.'

'My home?' I faltered, speaking for the first time. 'I'm afraid I do not . . .'

With false courage, I began again.

'I do thank you for your generous offer, Sir, but I do not intend to establish a permanent residence, as I believe my professional obligations will restrict me to travel for quite some time.'

The Count began to laugh, very quietly at first.

'I've been chosen . . . I have been trained, Sir, for . . .'

As he continued to laugh, I could no longer remember what exactly I had been trained for.

'All those years of education and they really do teach you *nothing* . . . it's almost cruel, isn't it? Come now, be a good girl and play us a bit of Bach . . . one of the slower Sonatas, perhaps?'

Seating himself in the corner, the Count waited silently for me to begin. I knew instinctively that this was a man to be obeyed, and so, despite every desire to do otherwise, I lifted the violin to my chin and began to play. Several bars passed my fingers and my wooden companion did indeed seem to stay my nerves, as I knew it would, as it always had.

A soft sigh issued from the Count's corner. Still playing, I glanced towards him; his one eye was closed, and his body swayed slightly in his chair, causing the wooden legs to creak. Though he was partially obscured by the furniture surrounding him, I could clearly see that his breeches had come undone . . . my bow slipped from my fingers.

Opening his eye, the Count shouted at me to continue, his feigned courtesy having dissolved completely. So startled was I that my cherished instrument slipped from my hands and fell to the floor with a clatter, cracking the body; the wound may as well have been my own.

'Pick up your instrument and play, you stupid bitch!'

I stood for a moment, staring at the Count in disbelief. Then, I turned and ran from the room, scalding tears of indignation, disgust, and, from a new, shadowy place that had been born within me that night, shame in my womanhood, streaming down my cheeks.

I ran back the way I had come, but was soon lost in the maze of corridors. The gaslights had not yet been lit, and so it was without warning that I ran directly into Anne, nearly sending us both toppling to the floor.

Raising her candle, Anne put a finger to her lips. She opened a narrow door in the wall and pulled me in after her, quickly shutting it behind us. The flame faintly illuminated a closet just barely large enough for us both. I tried to speak, but Anne clapped her hand over my mouth. She put her ear to the door. Hearing nothing but the pounding of our own hearts, Anne set down her candle. She held my soiled face between her hands and steadied me with her green eyes so like my own.

'You must listen to me, sister.'

'Where am I?' I whispered.

'It will never again be as bad as this first night. I promise you.'

'How can you know that?'

She did not answer.

'I have to go back, Anne . . . and you'll come too! When they hear what's happened, where I've been taken, what a grave mistake has been made . . . I must write a letter! Yes, I'll write a letter, and someone will come . . . someone will come—they *must*!'

My frantic movements had caused the dying flame to sputter out, leaving us in complete darkness.

'Anne . . . Anne . . . oh, how do I leave this place?'

'You don't.'

At that moment, the door flew open and there stood the Count in his shirtsleeves. The angles of his chiseled face were lit from below by the candelabrum he carried.

'Rats in the cupboard again?' he sneered.

He extended the candelabrum until a flame singed a lock of Anne's hair, hissing like a cat as it did so. The Count reached his other hand into the closet and seized my arm, dragging me out with a force I was unable to fight. Digging into his shirtfront, he produced a golden key hanging from a chain about his neck.

'We shall keep *this* rat in her trap tonight,' he said, before slamming the door shut and locking it with Anne inside.

I could hear her screaming and thrashing against the door as the Count pulled me down the corridor and back to my chamber.

Once within, the Count lifted me violently from the floor where I had fallen, only to send me back just as rapidly with a sharp blow to my face. And this was but a prelude of what was to come . . .

Asylum Letter No. X

When I opened my eyes the following dawn, my body was bruised and broken, and I was lying in a tangled mass of blood and torn fabric.

There was a faint tapping at the door, then Anne crept in, carrying a pile of rags and a bucket of steaming water. She had wrapped a kerchief round her neck, but still I could see more of the angry burn marks I had noticed upon my arrival.

Without a word, Anne helped me to my feet, then wrapped me in a clean white dressing gown and put me to bed. I lay still and watched as she made a valiant attempt to mop up the blood, scrubbing the stained wood with all the strength her pale arms could muster, but the floor was beyond repair. Stopping her work, Anne set down the brush and buried her face in her hands.

'Anne . . .' I choked forth, reaching towards her. 'What is happening?'

She turned to me, meeting my eyes at last.

'Can you still not see it?'

I breathed the word 'no', but sound did not follow. Anne rose from her knees; as she did so, something within her skirts scraped against the floor. Wiping her tears with the back of her hand, her fingertips then fluttered to her under-fed waist where she began to tug at the fabric of her blouse, lifting it higher until I could quite clearly see the corset beneath, and something else . . . From her waistband, Anne drew my bow—the violin bow I had dropped in the Music Room the night before—and brought it to me with a strange reverence, the offering of a sacred object, a prayer for forgiveness.

Her voice trembled. 'I'm so sorry about the . . . the . . . he smashed it all up . . . I couldn't . . . I know how much it meant . . .'

And as I curled my bleeding fingers round the slender stick of wood, more powerful than its delicate dimensions should allow, my vision went dark and from somewhere in the farthest corner of my brain came a blinding flash, a piercing pang, and knowledge.

I saw the shiny buttons on the waistcoats of the endless string of strange men who would visit the Conservatoire. I saw the sunlight on the day I had asked the Headmistress my surname, and of how I was slapped and told that my name was Emily and nothing more. (In response to her statement, my fellow pupils and I organized our own little rebellion, calling one another by some identifying element of our Christian names as a means of establishing at least the illusion of individuality within an organization that regularly reminded us that we had none—I was *Emily with a 'y'*.) And, finally, I saw Sachiko. Only too late could I interpret the chilling instruction written in her own blood. The pretty pictures I had engraved upon my mind over the long years—dreams I had depended upon simply to survive from one day to the next—all had faded over the course of a single night, leaving only despair in their place.

Twining our aching arms round one another, Anne told me all she knew of the world we now inhabited—a world I could scarcely comprehend, and was utterly unprepared for.

Through interactions with the numerous girls who had been brought to Bainbridge before myself, Anne had learnt that the

Conservatoire was hardly the only institution of its kind; there were several such establishments throughout the country and beyond, catering to the varied tastes and preferences of the men who funded them.

Anne was delivered to Bainbridge just as I had been, but she had disappointed both her new master and her old tutors by her excessive nervousness when asked to perform; her fingers would turn to ice, and every note she had ever learnt would flee her memory. Her inability to delight the Count and his clique rendered her worthless to him, despite her physical attributes, for she possessed an angelic face punctuated by a light frost of freckles, eyes a changeable green, pale and graceful limbs, and a great expanse of fire-red hair quite the same color as mine. Our close resemblance had not eluded us, though I did not suppose myself nearly so pretty.

Naturally, the Count had demanded the return of his payment for Anne, but had kept her anyway; it seems he was in need of an upstairs housemaid, and so Anne was thrust into the role of enslaved domestic servant.

She had watched closely for any opportunity to escape, but the Count had fitted every door and every window within his estate with double-sided locks that would open only by the turn of one Master Key, and this he always wore about his neck, even whilst he slept.

Once, and once only, had Anne glimpsed her chance at freedom: Upon her arrival at Bainbridge, a pair of identical twin girls occupied one of the innumerable chambers. Painfully shy, they rarely spoke, and so their origins were a mystery, their nocturnal screaming being the only evidence by which Anne could be certain they had tongues at all. When first obtained, it was expected that Anne would take on her share of the torture, but, when she failed to amuse, she became less of a target for not only the Count's passions, but his furies as well. Thus fueled by disappointment in his faulty purchase, the Count fell upon the twins doubly hard.

In the Banquet Hall one morning, Anne had begun to clear the wreckage from the previous evening's debauchery when she heard a sound like dripping water—slow, yet persistent. She moved about the room in search of the source, but could find nothing. Then, a drop of liquid splashed upon her cheek. She touched her face, then studied her fingertips. Red. Anne looked up to see one of the twins hanging directly above, suspended from her feet at a distance nearly six meters in the air. Bruises alone covered her nakedness, and long gashes reached from her childish hips to her chest, as though a pack of madmen had sought to slash the unripe womanhood right out of her. Blood had pooled below the pitiable wretch, droplets of which were still trickling from the tips of her silver-blond hair.

That afternoon, when the corpse was being tossed into its beggar's box, Anne observed a patch upon the dead girl's skull where the blood-streaked tresses had been cropped close. The lid nailed shut at last, Anne watched from the peephole in the front door as the little coffin was loaded into the undertaker's cart like nothing more than another day's rubbish.

Feeling faint, Anne leant against the door and felt it give way; the impossible had at last occurred—the entrance to Bainbridge had been left *unlocked*.

If she were to move quickly, she could easily overtake the cart before it passed the gates. With luck, she could leap upon it and conceal herself between the coffins. She could reach the city. She could have a second chance. But Anne never left the house.

Anne explained that she considered herself responsible for the child's death—a sentiment I admired but did not agree with—and, thus, owed her own life to the surviving sister who had not only fallen into a state of severe shock at the loss of her twin and sole companion, but was also in even greater danger now that she was the only one left.

As it happened, Anne had little opportunity to console the girl, for, upon delivering the tea that very evening, she found the child's room empty. Anne returned the tray to the kitchen only to discover the Count himself slumped over in a servant's chair; a visiting doctor changed a soiled bandage upon his face, which looked as though a very important piece had been cut out of it.

Later on, the butler, the same who had been my escort to Bainbridge, was able to verify that one of the good carving knives had gone missing, but the Count would make no explanation of his injury to the doctor, nor to any of the staff. Instead, he took to his quarters, and, upon emerging, sported the eye patch that he was, from that day to this, never seen without.

For months after, below-stairs gossip speculated that it was the missing twin herself who had wounded the Count, though how she could have managed it was never reckoned. All suspicion aside, the girl was not seen again, and Anne, like the rest of the servants, believed her dead.

In the years since, Anne had never again sought her escape, still carrying with her the guilt of mistaken responsibility. I was glad to have her with me, yet I would rather she had run when she could.

Exhausted from talking, we had both fallen into a light slumber when I was stirred by footsteps in the corridor. The knob slowly turned. Anne leapt from the bed, scurrying to the mantelpiece where she fell to dusting the ornaments with the corner of her apron. The baby angels, the porcelain dolls, all lace and rosy cheeks . . . I was clearly not the first young lady to have occupied what I now knew was a chamber of torture.

The Count did not speak, but moved towards the bed, an insidious sneer framing the pointed teeth I had become intimately acquainted with the night before. He wore his riding costume and smelled of the outdoors. Over his left eye—or, rather, where his left eye used to be—was a new patch made of crimson silk.

The Count arranged himself upon the edge of the bed; gingerly did he remove one of his gloves before sliding his long-nailed thumb between my lips, then down my neck to my chest. I cringed and turned away. Rising without a word, he flung himself into an armchair opposite me.

'Emily, my pet, I have come to congratulate you. Your debut performance began a bit doubtfully, it is true, but it ended very well indeed. I am significantly pleased with you, though I do suggest you learn to better control your nerves.'

At this, the Count directed his gaze towards Anne, who stood with her back to us. A gaudy cherub she had been intently polishing fell to the ground, the glass shattering. I shut my eyes tight to trap the tears that rose beneath my swollen lids.

'I am expecting a sizeable assembly of guests this evening. I have lured the gentlemen to Bainbridge with intelligence of my new prodigy's arrival, and they are most desirous of seeing you perform. I shall expect you delectably attired and prepared to amuse us after we dine.'

To the astonishment of both the Count and myself, it was Anne who burst out in protest.

'Please, Sir,' she begged, 'could she not have a day at least to recover? She's not yet well, Sir . . . you'll kill her . . .'

The Count softly laughed and rose from his chair.

'Your concern for your new playmate is most touching, Anne. Now, raise yourself and come to me.'

From inside his shirtfront, the Count again produced the Master Key of Bainbridge. Replacing the glove on his right hand, he held the key to a flaming taper, turning it over several times. As he did so, Anne mechanically tilted her head to one side, exposing her fragile neck already marked by scars and unhealed gashes. I, too, had become oddly transfixed by the Count's steady movements, by the dancing of the flame, seemingly exultant in its task, and by the way the golden key gleamed ever brighter as it warmed.

Finally, the Count lifted his key to Anne's neck and pressed it deep into her flesh. Her delicate skin hissed and popped beneath the metal, and my hand felt beneath the bedsheets, searching, seeking something I had nearly forgotten was there . . .

Quietly I crawled from the bed as the Count moved to punish Anne with a second burn. I approached slowly. When I was near enough, I shoved Anne aside, sending her reeling, jolted from her trance.

'Step away from her, Emily, and learn your place,' he commanded me.

'You will not touch her again' I growled, in a voice that was never mine before that moment. 'You will not touch me again.'

Advancing towards me, the Count began to laugh and this is when my right arm lashed out from behind and struck him across the face with the violin bow. A wide gash now ran from his ear to the corner of his mouth, splitting his face in two. A length of the bow, which had snapped upon the impact, now jutted from his cheek where it was embedded.

Upon his roar, Anne ran at the Count from behind and struck him in the back of the head with a heavy volume of erotic 'art'. The Count stumbled forwards; he had me by the arm, but I managed to claw at his face with my free hand, tearing away his eye patch. The gaping socket was surrounded by thick white scars resembling writhing maggots. Shrieking, the Count recoiled and covered his ghastly visage, his vanity allowing us the moment we needed to open the chamber door.

Through the corridors we ran, flying down the magnificent staircase to the foyer with our enemy fast behind us.

Halfway down the steps that Anne and I had descended not an instant before, the Count paused upon the landing to seize an ironwork candlestick, thick, dripping tapers still alight. He launched the object towards us; I was struck, a sharp edge of metal slicing into my shoulder. Boiling wax shot through the air, spattering onto my right cheek and burning me badly.

Stunned, I nearly fell, but when Anne shouted my name and tossed me an elaborately carved stone phallus, I managed to catch it in one hand and send it flying towards the Count's head. *Success!* He tumbled down the remaining stairs, lying motionless at the bottom, his forehead bleeding profusely.

My wits recovered, I reached the front doors at last, but Anne had tripped over one of the Count's hunting hounds, a barking pack of which had come to join the merriment.

'It's locked!' I shouted back to Anne.

The Count's legs twitched and I knew that he was not yet dead.

Anne struggled to her knees and crawled over to where the Count's body lay; tearing open his shirt, she located the Master Key. His eye fluttered open, and he groaned weakly. Balling her fist, Anne pounded it directly into the Count's face; his eye closed once again. One final tug and the chain snapped.

Anne slid the key across the polished floor towards me; stopping it with my foot, I snatched it up, turned it in the lock, then ran back to Anne, pulling her through the door behind me just as the Count staggered to his feet.

The entrance to Bainbridge faced the river. Anne pointed to an obscured path leading down from the garden to the rocks below; from there, we could climb the five metres to the dock, gaining entrance to the bridge leading from the bank beneath us to the city of London upon the other side of the Thames.

Our bare feet were scored raw by the time we reached the dock. Frantic neighing sounded from the bluff of Bainbridge above; we turned to see the black silhouette of a figure on horseback, menacing before the setting sun, the sky ablaze with its dying burst. The Count had spotted us, and would be close behind within minutes.

'Don't look, just run!' shouted Anne.

The bridge was tremendously tall, rising in a steady arc; lampposts marked the points where supporting columns plunged down into the water, creating a series of arches wide enough for the boats to pass through. The sun seemed to be sinking faster than nature could possibly allow, and I felt as though time were speeding along at thrice its usual pace. The darkness devoured us. We had nearly reached the median, and would soon behold our destination.

Hooves pounded the stones behind us, and the baying of the hounds grew ever louder. The Count had boarded the bridge, and he was not alone; his expected guests had arrived. All were mounted, charging towards us in a frenzied horde, the leaders carrying flaming torches to light their way.

Finally, we passed the apex, then stopped short. The town sparkled exquisitely, an enchanted faerieland we had risked our lives to join, but we would never reach it. The opposite end of the bridge was impassable, blocked entirely by a temporary barricade, the debris of masonry under repair.

With no cause to run further, we darted to the side of the bridge, peering over the ledge into the blackness below; the air was cold, the water surely colder. The moon was high now, extending across the river a path of light to us, as if to offer another way . . .

The water lapped softly at the pillars.

'*Come home*,' it whispered.

Turning to Anne, I believed she had heard it too.

A peculiar calm washed over me, and I was no longer afraid.

'Can you swim?' I asked Anne.

'No,' she answered, distantly. 'But I wasn't going to.'

'Neither was I,' I said.

We embraced each other like sisters; we did not speak again.

Asylum Letter No. XI

I was roused by the clang of church bells. Judging by their number, it was early morning. I lay flat upon my back, my body stiff and cold. Gazing upwards, I could see the spire of a cathedral towering overhead. My hands explored the ground round me—grass, damp earth. In the air hung the smell of rot. I knew I was not dead and in Heaven, for, if I were, surely I would not continue to feel such physical pain as I yet did. And besides, suicides don't go to Heaven, do they?

I raised my head; dozens of bodies were laid out upon wooden planks just like the board beneath me. They were all female, and they were all dead. At the opposite end of the yard, two men carried the body of a girl freshly plucked from the river, her face blue, her soaked garments watering the grass below; without regard, the men tossed her onto an empty plank, and her limp body hit the ground with a dull, wet thud.

Having managed to stand upright, I surveyed my surroundings. The dead women were of vastly varying age; they lay in diverse states of undress, most in soiled and still wet rags, some completely naked. A gaggle of schoolboys gathered outside the churchyard gates, pelting the dead girls with pebbles, and howling over the naked ones. *Would little girls*

75

have done so? I wondered. I gave thanks that I was still in my dressing gown, torn and bloodied as it was.

From the twisted necks of the dead hung wooden plaques crudely painted with the word:

My interest was then captured by a queer old man who was absorbed in the mixing of a pot of plaster. I watched as he spread a thin layer upon whichever of the lifeless faces he fancied, then removed it once the plaster had dried.

'Ah, so it's you, then! Pity you're not dead, isn't it?' said the old man.

'A pity it may be,' said I, bewildered, 'though it seems a bit rash to decide just yet.'

The old man heartily laughed, then resumed his work.

'Incidentally,' I said, 'what on Earth do you do with . . . oh, never mind, I don't wish to know.'

The old man looked hard at my face.

'I don't suppose you'd be willing . . . no, no, no, it wouldn't do, too much life in those features . . . though you might do well without that mark upon your cheek there . . . now, how's a girl get herself a sore that shape?'

'What shape?' I asked.

'Why, it's a perfect heart, that's what it is.'

I touched the spot but could only feel the sting. The plaster man lifted the dried mask from the girl before him. Anne was a ghastly grey, her fiery braids still pinned neatly round her pretty head. A curious sort of smile curled her blue lips, as though she kept a secret that the rest of us would never know, and I was not sad for her. Anne had succeeded where I had failed, and she was free whilst the confines of this world were still mine.

'No, Sir,' said I, kneeling in the dirt beside Anne's body. 'You've already captured the most beautiful face in all of nature . . . you don't need mine.'

Presently, I noticed the Master Key of Bainbridge, still wound upon its broken chain about my wrist. I thought first to leave it with Anne, to be buried with her in whatever pauper's grave she was to rest in, but decided against it; should the scavengers come, the key would only be nabbed, and I did not like to think of it back in the hands of a criminal of any sort.

I would keep the key, I resolved at last, and wear it upon my person always, as a remembrance of Anne and of the freedom she had given me.

'Did you know this poor child then?' the old man asked.

'Anne? A little. She saved my life.'

And she had. Her intervention was the key to my escape, and I promised her that I would make my second chance count.

I left the churchyard behind, and joined the mob upon the streets of London.

Asylum Letter No. XII

I fought my way through the crowd. I was not at all certain of my destination, and I knew that I would be wise to think of shelter and a place to pass the coming night, but I wanted only to get as far away from Bainbridge as possible. Even now, someone could be hunting for me.

By noon, the encompassing fog had given way to a light rain; I was shivering, soaked, and painfully hungry. I became aware of footsteps behind me. I struggled to convince myself that I was merely imagining, for there were dozens of people traversing the same route as I; why should there not be footsteps? Still, I felt myself walking a good deal more briskly, and, before I realised it, I was running.

The sky was nearly black now, and the air had turned dangerously cold. Passing a darkened alleyway between two dwellings, I spotted a small barrel fire surrounded by a haggard band of beggars. Approaching, I took the liberty of warming my hands over the meager flames. An ancient and toothless crone took pity upon me and removed the tattered, scarlet shawl from her shoulders, but a little man with mud embedded in his whiskers took offense at my presence, and he chased me from the alley before I could return the shawl.

Ill from the salt water I had swallowed, I turned my face to the sky, opening my mouth wide to taste the rain that poured down ever more heavily as the night settled in. Entering a swarming marketplace, I began to look at the awning-covered baker's cart with a different eye. I waited until the merchant was attending to a proper customer, then plucked a toasty, brown bun from a heaping bushelful, hiding it beneath my borrowed shawl.

The bun's rightful owner never witnessed my fledgling attempt at thievery, but a young police constable did. Taking hold of me, he looked closely at my face, and, after a moment, told me to be good and follow him to the station, adding that, if I did as he bade me, he would let me keep the bun I had and give me another besides. Supposing that anywhere I might end up with a police constable was quite as good as anywhere I might end up on my own, I ate most indelicately as the constable herded me through the streets.

Upon reaching the station, I was led inside and unceremoniously shoved into a cell. Should such a fuss be carried out for all the petty thieves in London, the prisons would have been bursting.

Hearing voices in the corridor, I raised myself to see a tall female figure attired from head to toe in a heavy charcoal-grey crepe, as though she were in perpetual mourning. By her side stood the young constable who had brought me to the station. The woman in grey produced a small portrait from her handbag, much like those in the attic of the Conservatoire; she seemed to be comparing its subject with myself.

'It's her, isn't it, Madam?' asked the constable, eagerly.

'You were quite correct to alert us, Constable,' the woman replied, snapping the portrait shut, her gaze fastened still upon myself rather than at the young man who begged her attention. 'You shall be rewarded for your powers of perception.'

The woman's voice struck me as a knife cutting through the air round her; her features were concealed beneath a veil sheer as smoke, as well as the shadows cast by the bonnet bearing the severed wings of some unfortunate bird. Only a hint of her left cheekbone and a twisted corner of her tight lips were visible to me, though they hinted at the face they belonged to, and I suspected that the countenance would match the voice.

'Child,' she began, 'in the unfortunate event that you are called upon to speak, you may address me as Madam Mournington. I am given to believe that you are called Emily, and that you have ungratefully fled the house of your Master, the Count de Rothsberg, only a day since.'

'Then, Madam, you believe wrongly,' said I. 'I have no Master.'

The woman's laugh was low and mirthless.

'We *all* have a Master, child.'

She lifted her veil, and I was accosted by two dark eyes deeply set into a face taut and tense, as though the flesh and all of its softness had eroded through years of trial, and what remained was only the thin white curtain that held the bones together. A sharp, aquiline nose imparted a decidedly haughty quality that the woman's carriage and demeanor did nothing to deny.

'What do you want of me, Madam? I suppose you are sent by the Conservatoire?'

'Then *you* believe wrongly, child. I am not from your Conservatoire—they no longer have the slightest interest in you. In fact, you have managed to make yourself quite worthless to any who have been entrusted with your care to this point.'

'It is they who are worthless to *me*. I do not covet their regard, nor do I intend to ingratiate myself back into their society.'

'*Society,*' the woman harshly interrupted, 'is no longer your concern. I am directed to remove you from society, where you would threaten to contaminate those round you with your insolence, ingratitude, violent tendencies, thievery, and, as it has now been proven by your sinful attempt upon your own life, madness.'

'Madness? *This* is madness! Whomever has directed you is mad, and I shall not suffer to be told by one more person, begging your pardon, Madam, where I am to be removed to.'

'You prefer to remain here in prison, then?'

'I do, Madam.'

'I see.'

Madam Mournington's grey-gloved fingertips traveled to her throat and lingered upon an oval cameo fastened there. The ornament was adorned with a child's silhouette, and, as she touched it, I imagined that Madam Mournington's eyes might once have been called beautiful. Abruptly, she lowered her hand and grasped it with the other, as if caught at something wicked.

'Well, that is quite impossible.'

Reaching into her handbag yet again, Madam Mournington now produced a large envelope sealed with blood-red wax.

'As you shall see, wretch, you have no say in the matter.'

She removed a document from the envelope and held it before me to inspect.

'Following your crime of attempted suicide, an act only a lunatic could contemplate without shame, the only society you are to be allowed to keep is the society of other lunatics like yourself.'

'*Lunatics like myself* . . . What *is* this?'

I lifted my eyes from the commitment form to find my mistress positively beaming with self-righteousness.

'Am I being committed to an insane asylum?'

'Not just *any* insane asylum!' she exclaimed, indignantly, as though I had gravely offended her. 'Though you certainly do *not* deserve it, you are a very lucky girl indeed, for you have been assigned a bed in the most progressively innovative, the most morally experimental, the most, ah, the most ingeniously directed medical institution for the mentally ill, governed by my own dear son, Dr. Montmorency Stockill. You, unworthy child, are now a patient of the Asylum for Wayward Victorian Girls.'

Clapping her hands, Madam Mournington quit the cell. A pair of guards stepped forwards, tearing the scarlet shawl from my shoulders before buckling a broad leather collar round my neck. I was forced into a straight-waistcoat, my arms crossed before my chest and secured tightly behind me.

THE ASYLUM FOR WAYWARD VICTORIAN GIRLS
~ ORDER FOR COMMITTMENT OF A PAUPER LUNATIC ~

Name of Patient, with Christian Name	*Emily, no last name*
Age and Sex	*17 years, female*
Married, Single, or Widowed	*Single*
If any Family	*None*
Rank, Profession, or Occupation (if any)	*None, female*
Habits of Life	*Unimportant*
Religious Persuasion	*Likely heathen*
Form of Insanity	*Melancholia, suicidal, hysterical*
Suspected Cause	*Poor character, sinful, perverse*
If Hereditary	*Likely*
If Suicidal	*Yes, has attempted*
If Dangerous to Others	*Yes, exceedingly violent*
If Destructive to Property	*Yes, has done much damage*
State of Bodily Health	*She can stand on her own*
Marks of Violence (if any)	*Self-inflicted (♡-shaped mark on chest)*
Residence at or Immediately Previous to Date Hereof	*Bainbridge*
If Previously Under Care as a Lunatic, Idiot, or Person of Unsound Mind	*No*
Name of the Person to whom Certificate of Death should be sent	*No need*
Delivered by whom	*Police Constable*

ORDER SIGNED BY   DATED

Madam Mournington, Asylum Headmistress   *the 5th of April, Eighteen hundred & forty-five*

Subjoined is a Statement of Particulars respecting said Lunatic

THE ASYLUM FOR WAYWARD VICTORIAN GIRLS
~ STATEMENT OF PARTICULARS ~

FACTS SPECIFIED IN MEDICAL CERTIFICATE
UPON WHICH OPINION OF INSANITY IS FOUNDED

1. Facts Indicating Insanity as Observed by Medical Man

Good men state she is mad, and so she is.

2. Other Facts Indicating Insanity as Communicated to Him by Others

Attempted suicide by leaping into the Thames, prior to which was physically violent towards Guardian, one Count de Rothsberg. Subsequent to rescue from drowning by fishing boat, stole valuable goods from London merchants. Intent to prostitute. Taken into police custody.

3. Witnesses of Insanity

The Unfortunate Girls' Musical Conservatoire

The Count de Rothsberg

M. Mournington-Stockill

Asylum Letter No. XIII

Ah, there seems to be a page missing . . . where could it have gone, surely it was here, I have only just written it . . . but I cannot remember how I traveled from the carriage up the steps to the Asylum's entrance, yet there I stood before the massive, moonlit structure, a monumental fortress of brick and limestone, its Gothic splendor a stark contrast to the hundreds of bar-crossed windows punctuating the vast wings that reached out on either side in a wide yet disingenuous welcome.

Gripping the leash attached to my collar was a colossal brute, hunched and mute save for the occasional grunt. He had ridden with us in the carriage, filling the confined quarters with the stench of rotting meat—I wondered that my mistress could endure it. The leviathan had hold of me with one filthy paw; his other struck a large brass bell that hung from an alcove above the doors. The rude clanging produced no response from within, and Madam Mournington stamped her boots upon the frozen porch in frustration, cracking the thin ice.

'A plague upon these blasted servants!' she fumed.

Fumbling inside of her grey wool traveling cloak, Madam Mournington produced a key attached by a long chain to a chatelaine pinned at her waist; from the chatelaine also hung a tiny pair of scissors, a needle case, a thimble, a monocle, and a little silver pencil.

A bloodcurdling scream from within the Asylum pierced the night. My heart tripled its pace and the giant at my side began to breathe heavily, sniffing the air like a hungry animal. Taking no notice, Madam Mournington fit her key into the iron lock, and had scarcely begun to turn it when the doors swung upon. Pulling them inwards were two smartly dressed butlers; they beckoned us inside with a bow and a sweep of their white-gloved hands. Madam Mournington snapped her fingers; the giant dropped my leash and ambled away.

My mistress advanced into the grand Entrance Hall whilst I remained in the doorway, the wind rushing in round me, blowing leaves and rain onto the marble floor. An enormous clock at the far end of the Hall struck four, and time seemed to stop. I commanded my feet to move me forwards, but my instruction bore far less influence over my movements than did the blazing fire before me.

Tall ivory candles ensconced in gold sparkled from their place upon the mantelpiece. The hearth itself was so large I could have walked into it upon my toes, were I so inclined. To the left of the fire, richly upholstered chairs were casually assembled round a tea table set with bone china and laden heavily with delicacies almost too beautiful to eat. Cakes stacked high and frosted with swirls of icing and lemon drops were flanked by tiered trays of strawberry tarts; a plate of biscuits glittered with coloured sugar; exquisitely sculpted marzipan fruits lay arranged in clusters; chocolates wrapped in crisp gold paper were tucked into every chink in this display, heart-breaking to the hungry captive.

To the right, a small gathering of ladies lounged upon over-stuffed settees, books and needlework upon their laps, whilst others sat round an antique harpsichord, sipping daintily from tiny teacups. All were dressed elegantly, yet with modesty; their hair was neatly plaited and coiled into becoming styles.

Upon the paneled walls hung paintings in majestic gilt frames. One canvas depicted a Persian cat sitting regally upon a yellow cushion; another was a still life of two pears and a pineapple, and there were several compulsory landscapes. Small brass plates beneath each painting bore a different female name, and I assumed that the patients themselves were the artists behind these mundane works, though why any girl, no matter how wayward, would choose to paint two pears and a pineapple was beyond my present ability to reason.

It was another painting that dominated the Hall, however—a grandiose portrait showing a young man of perhaps twenty-five with dark, loose hair framing a gaunt and sober face. He was clean-shaven, and wore a medal and two red ribbons upon the breast of his sharply tailored coat. With black eyes, brooding and deeply set, he was far from unhandsome, yet there was something in the twist of his lips I did not like. Beneath the portrait was an engraved plaque:

DR. MONTMORENCY STOCKILL:
A Saviour to the Weaker Sex

So *this* was the 'ingenious director'—the dear son of Madam Mournington.

All that I here describe my wide eyes had digested before I had taken three steps inside the Asylum. One step more and the front doors were slammed shut and bolted behind me, the resounding crash sending two housemaids scurrying forwards. The maids wore stiffly starched caps and lace aprons tied over their trim grey frocks, unnaturally broad smiles brightening their ruddy complexions. They curtseyed low as the two butlers moved to take my mistress's cloak. Upon rising, the maids recited in perfect unison:

'On behalf of our happy household, we welcome you to the Asylum for Wayward Victoria—'

'Stop!' interrupted Madam Mournington, slapping away the hand of the butler endeavoring to take her umbrella. 'Charming performance, everyone, truly charming, but it is only us—the girl has no relatives to impress; she is quite alone in the world.'

'Well now, ain't that a shame,' said a butler, eyeing me closely. 'We'll take care of the little thing like we was family, won't we, Maudsley?'

'Thank God . . . I bloody hate this bit, dress don't even fit right,' groaned one of the maids, tearing off her cap.

A woman sprawled upon a settee shouted to the maid who had just spoken.

'Mary, I get to be the 'ousemaid next time, and you can sit on yer arse with a bloomin' bible pretendin' to be mad.'

'Oh, shut up, tart,' cried Mary, tossing her cap towards the woman upon the settee; she missed. 'You're as mad as any o' them locked up, you are . . . it's not as though you've got to do any actin'.'

'Silence, slatterns!' roared Madam Mournington, pounding her umbrella upon the floor. 'One more word from any of you and you all lose cellar privileges for the month. And besides,' she added, addressing the maids, 'your speech lacked feeling, you are over-rouged, and, Mary, your cap was more crooked than your aim. See to it. Now, I shall take my tea in Dr. Stockill's Drawing Room. He must be informed of the new patient at once. As for you,' she turned to the counterfeit butlers, 'see that you are quicker to the door in future—I wait on no one. Now clear off, the lot of you . . . but not you, Maudsley. Turn in your finery and take this girl to Quarantine for the night. We shall evaluate her behaviour there before deciding where to place her permanently.'

'To the salt box? With pleasure,' replied the rogue to my right.

'We do not call it that here!' snapped my mistress as she exited the Hall, her chin pointed high, heavy skirts swishing.

'Oh, yes we do,' Maudsley muttered, too low for her to hear.

I glanced over to the ladies cavorting in the corner; they had discarded their perfectly coiffed hair, revealing their own slovenly arranged tresses. Two were locked in an obscene embrace, which was only alarming until their gowns had been torn asunder and I saw that several of the ladies had not, in fact, been ladies at all. All actors tossed their castoff costumes to the ground and bounded away, leaving us quite alone.

Maudsley had hold of my leash now, and snapped it sharply. Without the use of my arms, my balance was lost and I stumbled forwards; Maudsley did not help me up. Instead, he twisted a knob beneath one of the numerous gaslights illuminating the Hall. Instantly, the fire I had been longingly gazing into went black. The lamps dimmed, and I heard a rumbling from somewhere below us, then the turning of gears. The ground shook. The floor we stood upon began to sink.

No! We were not sinking . . . the walls round us were rising—first those to my left and right, then the panels further down the Hall, until reaching the panel behind the hearth itself—the one bearing the great clock as well as the venerable Dr. Stockill's portrait. The walls were being pulled up into the rafters. The settees and the harpsichord began to move as well, and I saw that they were fixed to a rotating section of the floor. Away went the furniture, away went the tea table, cakes and all, none of which had been real. The pieces fit together like a perfect machine . . . a clock.

What remained was a stark, cold cavern, drafty and damp, with rubble in the crooked corners and bits of flaking plaster patching the spots where the walls didn't quite meet the ceiling. The framework appeared to be falling apart round us.

Maudsley tugged at my leash, but I pulled back, genuinely frightened.

'Come on now, love,' he jeered in his rough tongue, 'is this how we want to start off in our new home?'

'This is *not* my home,' said I.

'Oh, 'course it's not. Mummy and Daddy are coming back for us—that's what they all think, poor nutters. Now, make yourself more pleasant or I *will* get rough and I *will* enjoy it.'

Maudsley was no butler; he was nothing above a common bully. Onwards was I dragged towards the hearth. Now flameless, it was a gaping hole—if the Asylum's wings were the arms of the building, then this was the mouth. Maudsley stepped inside of the hearth, and another snap of the leash told me I had no choice but to follow.

Into the catacombs I went. The cramped tunnel was lit only by the lantern Maudsley held before him. Something foul permeated the stale air that grew colder with every step. After what seemed like miles, we arrived at a gate made of crossed iron bars set into the narrow walls. Unlocking the bolt, Maudsley pulled me forwards and shoved me into the cell beyond. The gate slammed shut; the bolt was dropped.

'I can't see a thing!' I called out to him. 'Please, let me have the light. Surely you have matches to find your way back with . . .'

I tried to reach out, only then remembering that my hands were still bound behind my back. Maudsley laughed.

'Give fire to a lunatic? Not likely. Best of luck to you in gettin' through the night, love.'

I believed Maudsley had departed, but I was mistaken, for a hand was thrust through the bars. He seized my leash, pulling me hard against the cold metal.

'Then again . . . we could have some fun, you and me. I can get you things you want, you know. That's how it works in this pit, love.'

Maudsley had his groping hand about my waist now.

'At risk of being rude, Sir, I would sooner die,' I replied, wrenching my body from his grasp.

'That you probably will,' he laughed again.

Leaving me at last, Maudsley traveled back through the tunnel, the flickering lamplight growing fainter until it was gone. I turned to face the darkness, then panicked.

'Wait! My hands! How do I get out of this thing?' I shouted through the bars.

The shout came back.

'*Make friends!*'

I took a step further into the cell. Gradually, my eyes began to adjust, and I could make out several lumpy objects moving about the dirt floor. I heard mutterings . . . groans . . . The air was close, and it was difficult to breathe. I edged my body along the damp wall, hoping to locate an empty patch of ground to claim for myself.

Outside, the clouds shifted and a small, barred window high up in the wall let in a weak but welcome beam of light that passed along the opposite wall near the ceiling. There, I saw a fleeting glint, like a firefly in the night—extraordinarily present, then suddenly gone. There! There it was again! From high atop what appeared to be a tower of discarded tea crates, I saw two eyes gleaming down at me. My vision adjusting still further, I could now distinguish a creature—something crouched, like a gargoyle.

'Lay yourself down and keep quiet,' came a harsh whisper. 'We must be ready for them this time.'

The whisper was delivered with a slight accent, strangely familiar . . .

'Who's coming?'

'Go to sleep! I'm keeping watch . . .'

My hands still bound behind my back, it was all I could do to lower myself. Upon my knees, I looked up once more.

'Who *are* you?' I asked.

'I am your captain.'

All at once, the moon shone full, and I saw the creature. I saw a white shift . . . I saw striped stockings, black-and-white, black-and-white, black-and-white . . . I saw a mass of silvery hair on top of which was perched a tri-corner hat that looked as though it had been fashioned from torn scraps of paper. I saw the eyes, flashing as they stared forwards, unwavering, at our prison door . . . I saw a stream of daylight bleeding through the bars . . . an alarm was ringing loudly. The girls round me scurried about the cramped cell. I was lying upon a meager pile of dirt. A thin layer of straw had been spread over my body, my collar had been removed, and my hands had been freed.

hospital entry 14: funhouse mirrors

I have not showered since the morning I was committed. Having used up all of the moist towelettes (please tell me there is a better name for these) I was able to stash from my days in the Emergency Ward (these were the extent of the toiletries offered), I am left with a supply of rough, brown paper napkins, which I douse with soap and water, and then use to scrub down with whenever I manage to find myself in the bathroom alone.

There is a shower, of course, but it is filthy and, more importantly, cannot be used unsupervised. After our morning weigh-ins, during which I am repeatedly informed that I am far under my "ideal" weight (ideal to whom? Whose ideal must I conform to now?), all I need is for a nurse to see me naked.

Shortly after my arrival in Maximum Security, I was occupied in scrubbing my face with the brown paper napkins when I noticed that, whenever I moved, my face would change shape in the mirror. Upon examination, I saw that the mirror

is not a mirror at all, but a thin sheet of polished metal. Hell, it probably isn't even metal; it's probably plastic painted to look like metal. I tapped upon the surface. Yep. Unbreakable. The flexible sheet was badly warped, and, as I dried my face with yet *more* brown paper napkins, I considered whether it is really such a fabulous idea to offer lunatics no way to see their own faces save in what is, essentially, a funhouse mirror.

Now that I think of it though, it's perfect . . . absolutely perfect. Another joke on us, and I can take it. I can even laugh at it. But there is one thing I wonder: When, or if, we are released back into the real world, will we take this distorted image of ourselves with us?

But ah, I know what you want . . . you want to know about the letter. Shall I tell you? Shall I say? But I think you know . . . I think you know that it wasn't the last.

I have since received over a dozen more.

What I first thought was some sort of trick being played I now believe . . . I don't know what I believe.

But what frightens me is how little I care, for I have come to depend upon the Asylum letters as my only form of communication from the outside—even if it is not the outside from which I have been so uncivilly torn (which, if I'm honest, probably makes it even better).

I feel I know her . . . I feel she knows things about me . . .

And, as luck—or madness—would have it, daily have I found a fresh letter from Emily (with a 'y') tucked between the pages of my notebook. Sometimes these missives are composed of only a few sentences; sometimes they ramble on for pages; sometimes I am greeted with nothing but a simple sketch of one of the Asylum's inhabitants. But they are always the reason I open my eyes each morning.

Of course, I am hardly content with possessing my letters for the day only to give them up at night—certainly not, for these letters are the only things that truly belong to me. I have devised a system by which I retrieve my notebook at dawn, flip through the pages with pounding heart until I find the hoped for dispatch, and then, after reading it through several times, shut myself inside a bathroom stall and stow the day's Asylum letter in my right stocking before returning my notebook in the evening—

Stop.

Just stop.

Why must I sound so flippant? So hard? So fucking *proper*?

There is no one here . . . is there?

Is there?

Because I will tell you, you and only you, and only because you already know . . . the spiral wire . . . it is sharper than it looks . . . and I have lusted for it . . . but she sees me begin to unwind the coils and she writes and she writes and she says no . . . no . . . not yet . . . I am coming . . . I am growing up . . . just wait . . .

I do not know to whom Emily writes (this is not true), why she writes (this is not true), or if she is merely writing to keep herself from going mad just as I am, but, because she writes, I am never alone (this is true).

I fear for myself should she ever stop.

I fear for myself should she ever stop.

I fear for myself should she ever stop.

Asylum Letter No. XIV

Chaos and confusion. A door opposite the one I had entered the night before swung open, and my fellow prisoners fell silent. Most kept their heads down as an attendant herded us outside, down a set of stone steps, and into a fairly straight line. Determined to catch on quickly and thus remain unnoticed, I fell in behind a tall girl with open sores up and down her arms.

We were marched out to what I soon learnt was called the Bathing Court. The forest of leafless trees was a black web lit from behind by the lonely grey of early morning. It was painfully cold, and frost covered the ground, crackling under my bare feet, but it was good to be outside after a night slowly suffocating in Quarantine. I glanced at the girls round me; they varied in age and outwardly visible state of health, yet they shared the blank, hopeless stare of the long-imprisoned, and they all wore the same uniform: A thin white shift and striped stockings in black and white—a costume clearly not

designed for protection against the elements, or from anything else for that matter.

As we walked, I tried to spot my creature of the previous night amongst the girls in line. Just then, a girl marching two places ahead turned round and looked directly at me as if she knew what was in my mind. Gone was the imposing posture and the makeshift hat, yet the glint of the eye was the same, and the tangled mass of pale hair was unmistakable.

We were not the only ones being marched to the Court; from the wards at either side of the Asylum poured hundreds upon hundreds of girls. Their appearance was staggering; the inmates from one ward were bound in manacles and chains, whilst those from the other walked as freely as I did, though we were all guarded closely by attendants carrying rods and straps. By the contorted frames, bruises, and dejected countenances, it was clear that these tools of correction were employed liberally against any prisoner who stepped out of line.

But, my God! The sheer mass of us! We were a veritable army, terrifying in our numbers if not in our strength.

Now in perfect rank-and-file, we were ordered to come forwards, ten at a time, to stand against a stone wall at one side of the Court. I learnt by example that, upon our way to the wall, we were to remove our shifts and stockings and toss them into an enormous laundry bin. For myself, this meant the removal of the remaining shred of what was once a very pretty dressing gown.

What to do with the key I still held in the pocket of my gown? Lacking a superior solution, I surreptitiously hid the key in my hand, then slipped it into my mouth.

Naked, we stood before the guard with the watering hose, one end of which was attached to a mechanical pump. Three blasts and we were ordered off the Court, but not before taking a clean shift from the bin at the far end of the wall as we passed, as well as a pair of stockings from the clothesline where they had been pinned, fluttering like striped serpents in the biting wind.

We were then corralled into the Dining Hall as the next ten girls took their places before the firing squad, and thus the barbaric process continued until all were bathed.

It was in this way that I came to be just another of the convicts here in the Asylum—dressed alike, treated alike, in class, in disgrace, in uniform.

hospital entry 15: intervention

They are counting my caloric intake more strictly than an anorexic at a dinner party. In fact, they have charts that say exactly what one ought to weigh depending upon one's height, and they are viciously judging us all against these standards. And who came up with these standards anyway? The morbidly obese nurse? The half of America that's fat? Is there nothing that I am allowed control over? Is there nothing I will not be made ashamed of?

We are wandering in circles around the rooftop's perimeter, a lunatic promenade. It is gray and cold, and I wonder when they will decide that enough is enough. I can peek through the barbed-wire fence (because we'd be scaling it and throwing ourselves over willy-nilly if the barbs weren't there?) and see the busy streets far, far below, but it's a different world. I could scream and nobody down there would hear me. I'm sure I wouldn't have been the first to try.

I complete another lap and a nurse catches up with me, a clipboard in her hand. She asks me if I could do her a "little favor" as soon as I have a minute (I've got all the minutes in the world, lady). Handing me a few sheets of paper stapled together, the nurse tells me that it's just a list of questions that would really help out the staff if I would answer. Although I assume it's one of those "How Am I Driving?" sort of customer service questionnaires, I feel almost flattered, as though my opinion actually matters.

"You can go to your room now and fill it out if you like, so you have some privacy."

Privacy? Something is most definitely up. The nurse leads me back inside and down the hall; unlocking my communal room, she tells me to bring the form to the glass booth upfront as soon as I'm finished.

Seating myself on the edge of my bed, I look down at the first question:

1. How many times per day do you make yourself vomit?

Note: The question is not *do* you make yourself vomit, but an assumed *how many times*. Dear patient, your opinion is irrelevant. It's your word against ours.

Three pages of questions, not one of them asking *whether* I have an eating disorder, all of them just assuming that I *do*, and ordering me to expound upon it.

It is unbelievable.

Nobody sat down with me for a sensitively conducted chat—nobody asked me anything at all; instead, they gave me a fucking form. Not five minutes of anybody's time was spent in assessing whether or not this form would even be appropriate, whether it would offend me, whether it would freak me out, or whether it would simply be unnecessary. If I answer as they clearly expect me to and tell them how much I hate my body, and how, yes, you've caught me you brilliant sleuths, I cannot eat without making myself sick afterwards, will I then be handed another form telling me what to do about it? Are pamphlets the new psychotherapy?

Un-fucking-believable.

Of course, I am enjoying my ten minutes of authorized privacy too much to simply go handing this form back now and telling them where to put it. No, if they want answers, then answers they shall receive.

I reply to every question at prodigious length, filling up the pages until there is no more space to fill. Then, I turn the pages over and write on the backs. I am flip. I am sarcastic. But I am not unkind. I simply want them to comprehend *exactly* how asinine their questions are.

17. Why are you continuously dieting when you are already too thin?

23. How far above your ideal weight do you consider yourself?

31. Do you believe in magical beings?

*This last was a very real question.

I conclude my final answer with the declaration that unicorns are real, and that I quite enjoy my relationship with food under normal circumstances, which my current ones are most certainly not.

I have no expectation of how this will be received, but I am prepared to defend myself, not against the accusation of having an eating disorder, because, although I don't happen to have one, it isn't a crime (not like suicide or anything), but against being called a liar, because I *know* that I will not be believed.

Determined to beat the staff to the proverbial punch, I skip down the hall to the office, and, smiling, hand the papers back through the window slot to the nurse who first gave them to me. Without looking at my answers, she tells me that someone will be coming to talk with me in a moment. I can't wait.

Along comes yet another corpulent woman who introduces herself as the Hospital Nutritionist, because why the hell not? She invites me, the nurse, and some other staff members into a conference room, and we place ourselves around a large table as she flips through my answers, her face hardening as she does so. I will say nothing. I will simply wait for it . . . wait for it . . . wait for it . . .

"Well, Emilie, it looks like we've wasted your time."

There it is.

"Listen," I say, kindly, trying to lessen the shock just a bit if only because there is still this pathetic part of me that hates to see others uncomfortable no matter how much *I've* been made to feel so, "I've got a lot of problems, but an eating disorder just isn't one of them. Why were you so sure that it was?"

"Well, you *are* very thin."

"Perhaps, but that can't be all. What *specifically* did I do to make you *so sure* that we needed to have this intervention? I would sincerely like to know."

"As I said, Emilie, you *are* very thin, and we've noticed you don't eat much."

I tell the Nutritionist and all of the assemblage that there are many reasons a person could be "very thin." For example, one may be incarcerated within a mental hospital and living in a state of constant terror, leaving one with no appetite. For another, one could be incredibly depressed. Still another, and I know it's taboo to say in this current state of western society where overweight females are publicized as "real" women (which offensively implies that those of us who are healthy are "pretend" women), but one could be naturally thin. I happen to be all three of those things.

"Well . . . we'll be watching you," says the Nutritionist.

And then, the alarm screeches through the yellowing plastic speakers, for it is, oh, you guessed it, dinnertime.

Asylum Letter No. XV

It was upon my third day in the Asylum that I saw it: something sparkling from beneath the breakfast table in the Dining Hall. I peered below and recognized the little silver pencil that I had seen hanging from Madam Mournington's chatelaine upon the night I had first arrived. It must have broken from its chain, and, now, there it was, waiting for me, just begging me to snatch it up and carry it away to my cell.

The prospect of having something to write with was exhilarating . . . I felt that I simply *must* have the pencil, yet I must also act with caution. It was already reckless that I should keep Anne's key always tied just above my right knee, hidden beneath my stocking as it was; I ought not to risk anything more.

I decided to wait until breakfast was over. *Dear God*, thought I, *to be able to write . . . to have something, anything to do . . .*

Alas, when the bell rang, a girl at my table fell to the ground in a seizure. An attendant rushed forwards to drag her from the Hall, and the surrounding guards swiftly ordered us up and into line, fearing that the episode would incite hysteria amongst the rest of us. I reached my arm under the table, knowing it was not wise to do so, and was proven right as a leather strap whipped across my neck, drawing blood. Forcibly was I put in place with the other inmates.

In my cell that night, I relived the morning's events over and over in my mind, truly despising myself for having lost a thing I had never owned, but which I was yet convinced that I could not live without.

And then I heard it—a noise from the corridor—a sort of scurrying, or perhaps a clicking of fingernails, very, very quiet, yet coming closer all the time until I believed that it was *inside* the cell, then even closer until I was quite certain it was *nearing my bed.*

All fell silent.

Then came the sound of something being dropped upon the ground and rolling a short distance before coming to a halt. Whatever it was that had entered the cell left the same way it had come.

When I could no longer hear it, I extended my hand into the dark to touch the splintered floor beside my bed. Finally, my fingers found an object smooth and cold, only a few inches in length, and very narrow. I picked it up and rolled it over in my hand, but I already knew exactly what it was.

And with that, Diary, we arrive at the present. It is the following evening, and I have been using the little silver pencil to tell my story such as you have seen unfold thus far. Writing upon the scraps of black-and-white striped paper torn from my cell walls, I hope to find something more suitable on which to record my entries. No one shall read them, and I do not care—they are not for the world's blind eyes, but only for yours, Diary, whom I address as a friend, knowing well that you are merely the mirror of myself. No, it is the *act* of writing that may save me, for through my pencil the story is exorcised; left inside my head, it smothers me. May the future grant us a happier chapter . . .

Asylum Letter No. XVI

I did not come face to face with the great Dr. Stockill until I had endured five whole days in the Asylum. I had been installed in Ward A at the top of a dangerously dilapidated staircase for the last three of them, my first two being passed in the dark of Quarantine.

I had learnt that the young Doctor was most often occupied in his Laboratory, being the Asylum Chemist as well as Head Physician and Superintendent. Most institutions employed an independent chemist who was well below the physician in rank and stature, yet our medical prodigy claimed to elevate chemistry from a profession to an art, and was said to be always at his experiments, making 'new and useful discoveries' for which he was both respected and resented amongst his equally ambitious peers.

As I was led by Madam Mournington to the Doctor's chamber for the first time, an animal instinct from deep within advised me to run, but my escort gripped my arm with

a preternatural strength, sharp, skeletal talons digging into my flesh. The rings ornamenting the fingers of her other hand clicked against the large, tarnished key she held, the same that had opened the Asylum doors to me less than a week earlier. This was the closest view I had yet achieved of the Ward Key;

the object had been burnished to a dull sheen, no doubt by our Headmistress's fastidious claws.

Down the rickety staircase we went, turning left onto the stark stone landing, and finally arriving at the Medical Floor. Upon reaching the door to the chamber, Madam Mournington tapped lightly, and a silvery voice bade us to enter. I felt an icy draft rush up my legs and under my shift as I stepped across the threshold into a room decorated with such masculine refinement as to be entirely at odds with the deteriorating structure it resided in.

Dr. Stockill thanked his mother most courteously, and I was left alone with him.

From behind his desk of richly polished wood, the Doctor tapped his long, tapered fingertips together and looked at me with unmistakable disdain.

I was unknown to this man—could he dislike me already?

With studied delicacy, he lifted my commitment form from his desk. The Doctor was quite as elegant as the portrait I had seen mounted so proudly in the Entrance Hall downstairs, though it cannot be denied that he appeared crueler in person; the lines were harsher, and the mouth that I had not felt at ease with in the painting coiled into a sneer as he spoke.

'No one's head may be higher than the king's.'

He did not look up at me, but continued to peruse the document.

'I'm sorry, Sir?'

'Sit!' he barked.

I quickly installed myself in a wooden high-backed chair opposite the desk, noting the leather straps hanging loosely from the back of it.

'*Emily* . . .' he read. 'No last name. How quaint.'

The Doctor's pattern of speech was unemotional in tone, yet somehow entrancing in its strangeness. I sensed he was not waiting for an answer, and remained silent. He continued to read the document aloud.

'*Attempted suicide by leaping into the Thames* . . . Insane behaviour indeed, but not very original these days.'

'I'm afraid I had not many options at the time, Sir.'

He looked up.

'*Doctor*, if you please. *Doctor* is superior to *sir*.'

'I am sorry, Doctor, I was not aware of that.'

The Doctor glared at me.

'Once again: *Attempted suicide by leaping into the Thames, prior to which was physically violent towards Guardian, one Count de Rothsberg* . . . Tell me, Emily, do you always aim your hostility so high?'

'I consider my target rather low in this instance, Doctor.'

'Do you? *Subsequent to rescue from drowning by fishing boat, stole valuable goods from London merchants. Intent to prostitute. Taken into police custody. Declaration of Insanity signed by both present Guardian (C de R) and previous Guardian, the Unfortunate Girls' Musical Conservatoire.* There. I suppose you have something clever to add to this as well?'

'Indeed, Doctor. I assume by "valuable goods" you are referring to the bit of bread I stole from a baker's cart. Whilst I doubt that the bun was of irrecompensable value to the baker, I was starving, and so it was quite valuable to me. I had no intent to prostitute myself—that claim is false, and the rest such obvious fiction that I care not to dispute them.'

'You accuse the police of lying?'

'Would I be the first?'

'Tell me, Emily, with no last name . . . do you consider yourself mad?'

'I consider myself *considered* mad, and that is all that matters.'

'Would it surprise you terribly to know that the Count de Rothsberg is one of the Asylum's most generous benefactors?'

'Nothing would surprise me terribly, Sir.'

'*Doctor*.'

'Doctor.'

'Then I suppose you will not be surprised when I inform you that you have been committed to the Asylum for Wayward Victorian Girls for a stay of infinite length; there is not a soul who cares to petition for your release.'

'Not at all, Doctor.'

'And, as such a clever girl, you surely realize that, in the eyes of the law, you are a common criminal, and, in my eyes, you are less.'

'A common criminal receives a trial, Doctor, and, if it pleases you, send me back to prison; I would gladly have remained there, as Madam Mournington was made quite aware of at the time—'

'Do *not* speak of my mother, you filthy thing!' shouted the Doctor, having turned suddenly fierce and rising from his chair.

He was terrifically tall, and I imagined that many thought him imposing. I am not yet certain what I think him.

Turning round to a cabinet behind his desk, Dr. Stockill withdrew a small bottle of green liquid and shook precisely three drops onto his handkerchief. As he did so, I spied an object gleaming from deep within the open cabinet, elaborate designs engraved upon its oblong surface. Having wiped his bloodless hands with the handkerchief, the Doctor soon regained his calm.

'No . . . no, it would not please me to send you back to prison . . .'

He had gone to the window looking down upon the front courtyard far below; from this view he would be able to see all who came and went from the Asylum.

'It would please me . . . if you would tell me something I have always wanted to know.'

Dr. Stockill carefully folded the starched white cloth; he had a way of moving his hands that reminded me of a lace maker . . . or a spider.

'I have never understood why someone would willingly choose to die. Can you tell me that?'

'In your own estimation, Doctor, to take one's own life is madness, in which case it is impossible to explain.'

'I grant you this solitary moment in which to speak freely, and *that* is all you have to tell me?'

I chose my words carefully.

'I believe that suicide is most often committed in self-defense, Doctor.'

There was a lingering silence, and, when the Doctor again spoke, it was with civil detachment. He remained facing the window.

'Get out.'

Safe upon the other side of the door, I closed my eyes and exhaled for the first time since entering Dr. Stockill's chamber. Then, my arm was seized and I saw that Madam Mournington had been waiting just outside the door for me all the time; she marched me briskly across the Medical Floor and to the right towards the Bloodletting Wing.

hospital entry 16: what violet said

I am sitting alone upon the shabby green couch in the Day Room as the other inmates are either maundering about on their own or sitting upon the floor, rocking back and forth whilst watching random game shows on the ancient television set. I am taking advantage of this rare moment of relative solitude in which to write without having to look over my shoulder.

Violet hobbles in and comes to join me on the couch. I resent this. She doesn't look at me—she never makes eye contact with anybody, and I wonder what it feels like inside that head of hers. She is staring straight ahead. I try to ignore her, and continue writing my pointless memoirs.

"They'll read that when you're asleep," Violet mutters.

"What . . . what did you say?"

"They'll read that when you're asleep," she repeats.

"My notebook? Is that what you mean?"

Violet does not respond.

"How do you know that, Violet?"

She stands up and shuffles away.

"*Violet?*" I call.

She doesn't hear me.

Suppose the staff *does* read my notebook when I turn it in at night—the notebook containing my blackest secrets, the past year of my life . . . What happens between the moment I hand it to the nurse in the glass booth and the moment she places it in my closet compartment? Can they do that? Maybe they *have* to do it. Maybe that's why they let me have the notebook to begin with—they're setting me up.

Asylum Letter No. XVII

What luck that I should have been allowed the pleasure of an audience with both good Drs. Stockill *and* Lymer upon the same day!

Madam Mournington pulled me towards a set of doors bearing a bronze plaque engraved with this inviting title:

Dr. Francis Lymer:
BLOODLETTING

The doors crashed open from within; two medical assistants emerged carrying between them a girl paler than death. Blood soaked her white shift, and her striped legs were limp as a rag doll's. The men fumbled and the girl was nearly dropped; how fortunate she was to be unconscious.

I stood staring down at the drops of blood that had spattered onto the wooden boards, but my mistress had her pincers in my arm, and she forced me onwards.

I shall describe to you, Diary, the Bloodletting Wing: It is a vast, open room lined with row after row of metal beds set upon wheels. The beds are fitted with thick leather straps and rusty buckles. From the walls hang medical tools of a decidedly medieval appearance.

How extraordinary, I thought, *that a veritable host of diseases can be so easily cured by the draining of the patient's blood.*

In truth, Diary, it is a miracle! Headache? *Too much blood.* Melancholy? *Impure blood.* Misbehaving? *Poison in the blood.* Fainting from excessive bleeding? *Bleed some more.* Any ailment, real or imagined, is subject to the same treatment, and, in a manner of thinking, I suppose it is ingenious: Bleed a girl to within an inch of her life, and she hasn't got the strength to cause trouble. Is this how a staff of thirty manages a thousand inmates?

Dr. Lymer, a rather stout sort of man who was occupied in pounding a bladed chisel—which I have since learnt is called a *fleam*—into the arm of another inmate, commanded me to wait in a corner of the room over which hung a painted sign:

LEECHING

Every bed in the Wing was occupied save one near myself in the Leeching corner; the empty bed was spotted with fresh red stains, presumably having belonged to the girl who had been rushed from the Wing unconscious mere moments ago.

I had first learnt of leeches and their gruesome purpose upon the day that the Headmistress of the Conservatoire had fallen ill. A doctor had come bearing jars filled with the creatures, and had taken particular delight in dangling them in front of Sachiko and myself, their wriggling bodies dripping with crimson. I was more repulsed by the man than by his insects, and found the entire process highly suspect from the start.

I had asked him from whence the leeches came.

'These slippery little bloodsuckers begin their lives in your lakes, your swamps—that sort of place. Little boys and little girls, just like you, are sent bare-legged into the water, and there they wait for the leeches to bite into their flesh.'

At this, Sachiko ran screaming from the room, but I was transfixed.

Would *you* like to be a leech-catcher, little girl? You could make a penny a week, you could . . . now show Doctor your legs . . .'

I shook my head. He had been trying to frighten me, and he had succeeded.

Amused by my distress, the Doctor invited me to stay as he applied the leeches to the unconscious Headmistress's chest and throat. The very worst of it was the method by which the Doctor removed the leeches from the old woman's flesh: He poured salt over their delicate skins. I watched as they recoiled in pain, gushing forth every drop of the blood they had only just swallowed, and writhed in obvious agony as their skins dissolved. I could not sleep for days after.

Now, it was my turn.

I was lifted onto the bed by a waiting attendant, that same giant who had first led me to the Asylum by collar and leash; he wore a heavy apron of rough leather, stained with great red blotches. Nobody spoke to me; I was merely another body filled with blood that must come out. A filth-encrusted jar was opened, and the Doctor lifted out a single leech by its tail.

Naturally, I did not want the leech upon my arm—not because I was afraid of it (though it was a good deal larger than I had expected), but because of the horrific demonstration I had witnessed so long ago.

Dr. Lymer sent his brute to retrieve a cracked porcelain bowl, and I saw that it was already filled with blood—someone else's blood. Having selected a prominent blue vein within the inner part of my wrist, the Doctor dipped one of his fat fingers into the bowl and smeared the blood over the area. When I began to struggle, the giant strapped my limbs to the bed, pinning my bloody arm and tethering it beside my face.

I know what they're doing, I said to myself. *They are trying to break me by making me watch.*

The Doctor approached me with the hapless creature, and I heard myself screaming.

'No, no, no!' I cried. 'They'll kill you! They'll kill you, you idiot leech!'

Dr. Lymer nodded to his assistant, who then produced a stiff, yellowed rag and pressed it over my mouth.

'You might feel a little pinch,' said the Doctor.

Asylum Letter No. XVIII

During a girl's first week in the Asylum, she is sentenced to silent neglect by all inmates of sound mind. Her first bath, her first examination, her first leeching—all will come to her as an excruciating surprise.

With the passing days, I have begun to realise the purpose of this apparent cruelty: It is a sort of test. Would the new inmate be capable of enduring this hell with even the slightest degree of sanity after a day? Two days? A fortnight? If the poor prisoner seemed still to possess some control over her mind and had not fallen prey to babbling and hysterics, then she would be welcomed, as I have been, into the most exclusive and well-guarded organization within the Asylum: *The Striped Stocking Society*.

The S.S.S. is a small and secret consortium consisting of the inmates of intellect, and existing solely for the purpose of keeping each other alive, for we all know that once we lose our wits we will begin to die.

Asylum Letter No. XIX

I have been repeatedly awakened by a scratching emanating from somewhere inside the cell wall. I cannot guess what it is, nor can I locate the exact source, except to say that it seems to be coming from within the striped wallpaper directly behind my bed . . .

I shall report any progress I make towards enlightenment.

hospital entry 17: rat dream

After waking up at four o'clock in the morning yet again, I tried to go back to sleep, but fidgeted restlessly as I usually do.

Finally drifting off, I had the strangest dream . . . strange even for me. In it, I was lying upon a bed high up off the ground. From a dark corner of the small, confining room I was in crawled a rat. Much larger than I imagined any rat had a right to be, it moved along the floor next to my bed. A blurred female figure more familiar than I with the comings and goings of the Asylum's resident rodents entered my cell.

"What was that?" I asked the figure, whose face I could not make out, just to be certain that my eyes had not deceived me.

"A rat, of course," she replied, not at all shocked as another rat of the same size darted from one side of the room to the other, followed by several smaller rats as well as some big as dogs, all seemingly appearing out of nowhere for the solitary purpose of proving their bizarre existence.

As this extraordinary scene played out, I was hypnotized by what had become a living, bustling carpet of grays and tawny browns, and when a particularly large rat (funny how things become relative so quickly) with sleek white fur and a fawn-colored hood and stripe running down its back scurried to my bedside and raised itself to rest its hands (paws? claws?) on the edge, peering at me and sniffing like a hound, it seemed to me to be utterly natural, and I let the rat inhale me until it had learned whatever secrets I had to hide. When the fawn-colored rat had satisfied itself, away it scampered, and all of this I believed was a dream until I never woke up.

What is happening to me?

Asylum Letter No. XX

I have been an inmate of the Asylum for Wayward Victorian Girls close on three months now, and have come to know the following with the utmost certainty: If madness exists here, it does not live behind the bars.

For example, Quarantine is no such thing. Rather, it is the dungeon in which we are thrown to be punished for our misdeeds, whether we know what they are or not. The new inmate does indeed pass her first nights here just as I had, but this is hardly meant to shield the rest of us against disease from the world beyond, no indeed. It is done only to slaughter any remaining spirit in the poor girl, and to prepare her, by way of a good shock, for her life to come, if a life it can be called.

And another! Bathing. Bathing must be one of the most inhumane practices we suffer, not because it is unpleasant—everything here is unpleasant—but because of its deadly consequences. To begin with, do you remember, Diary, how we are all to come forward in groups of ten to be doused by the watering hose? Well, oftentimes, one of the more incoherent of the prisoners will not realize that she is one of the ten, and so does not step forwards with the rest. Having learnt well that all attention is dangerous here, those round her will whisper nervously, prodding her onwards. Should this not succeed, the disobedient inmate is dragged away by heavy-handed attendants to the Hydrotherapy Chamber. Here, the wretch will be submerged in icy water. If she reacts and struggles to breath, then the treatment is deemed a success, and there are congratulations all round, never mind the near certainty that the patient will die shortly afterwards from cold-induced illness. If she happens to drown and so does not react, the patient is considered to have been just another of the many 'incurables', and, as such, her death is no great loss. There is a dramatic rise in the number of fatalities resulting from pneumonia in the days immediately following our bi-monthly bath. Needless to say, the staff never seem to question this.

And now, dining. An alarm sounds at half-past six each morning, and those of us who are not chained to our cells assemble in the Dining Hall for breakfast. An enormous pot of soup is set down with a great thud at one end of each of the several dozen tables, the contents inevitably sloshing over the sides and encrusting the warped floorboards. In each pot is a rusty ladle. The inmate to reach the table first fills each of a tall stack of tin bowls, dented and scratched, and often unwashed since the last meal. She then passes them, one by one, to the other inmates as we crowd round her to receive our share before taking our places on the long benches flanking the table.

This may sound bearable enough, but prepare yourself! The soup is made of whatever scraps are left over from the staff's meals, and supplemented with whatever is left of ours from the previous day. The Asylum diet consists primarily of this soup, for, not only is it a practical choice from the point of view of the kitchen staff, requiring little effort to make as well as solving the problem of kitchen waste (that problem making the kitchen a favourite haunt for the many rats who inhabit the Asylum), but it can also be both served and eaten with a spoon—rather important criteria within an institution that does not allow the use of forks and knives.

We are given to understand that this denial of sharp objects is so that we cannot injure ourselves, but, as the staff is only too happy to use sharp objects against our persons, I have come to suspect that the withholding of proper flatware is rather so that we cannot injure the staff.

We are always kept hungry to ensure that we are too weak to cause trouble, or to fight the staff when they cause trouble for us, although many girls fight anyway, using that otherworldly strength that often accompanies madness, or desperation. Despite our hunger, some of us don't eat any breakfast on days when the soup is particularly foul. Still others don't eat at all, neither at breakfast nor at any other time, and it is a wonder to the rest of us that they are yet living.

Amendment: I have just spoken with a girl called Penny on this very subject, and am horrified to learn that those who disdain their dinners are forcibly fed with rubber tubes crammed down their throats. Not surprisingly, many girls die of choking as a result of this. I suspect I should eat everything I can manage.

The last sort of inmate is she who will ravenously devour whatever is laid before her, and will then set upon the bits leftover by those who can't stomach them. I envy these girls; no delicacy remains in them, a loss that serves them well, for, without delicacy, they can attend solely to the business of their own survival. I still have my delicacies, and so, most of the time, I starve. Thankfully, we are each given a portion of stale bread for our dinner, and without this I would surely have turned to dust already.

Once back in our wards, any hoarded goods will be used as a sort of currency, with the metal spoons we occasionally succeed in thieving from the breakfast table being a highly sought after treasure; the collections amassed by some inmates reach over two dozen, and all stashed inside their thin straw mattresses.

I suppose that, if you're not going to get a good night's sleep, you may as well have a lot of spoons.

Asylum Letter No. XXI

It was at breakfast one Sunday that a rat was found floating dead in the soup pot. It was my turn to serve, and so it was I who saw it first. I had not once wept during my incarceration, but now, the futility of our collective efforts to 'behave' or to 'get better' in the expectation of release—the complete and utter hopelessness of our condition—all descended upon me. An abject sorrow flooded my very being as I looked down at the poor creature, paws outstretched, reaching for its freedom even as it died; I could do nothing but hide my face in my hands.

In line behind me was the girl with the mass of blond hair—she who had frightened me in Quarantine upon my first night in the Asylum. She was again wearing her tri-corner hat; I believed it was meant to resemble something a pirate might sport, and I saw that it was made up of strips of our striped wallpaper—the same upon which I have been writing these entries—supplemented with druggist receipts and other rubbish no doubt found lying about the unswept floors. I had heard her referred to as Jolie Rouge, which didn't sound like a real name to me.

As I sat upon the bench, wiping away my tears, Jolie Rouge peered into the pot to see what had upset me so. She calmly lifted a bowl from the table and filled it with the rat soup. Then, she spun round and flung the bowl directly at one of the attendants—which the girls call 'Chasers' for obvious reasons—employed to keep the lunatics under control during mealtimes. The Chaser was stunned; there was a collective gasp—anyone could guess the consequence of such a rebellious act.

Knowing, as so many mad girls do, that silence is made to be broken, an inmate at the far end of the Hall erupted in hysterical shrieks of laughter. All at once, the entire Hall burst into a riot of wild shouting and flying soup bowls. As the soiled Chaser lunged at Jolie, she leaned towards me.

'Take the rat . . . we bury him in the Walking Yard today!'

As Jolie was dragged away, the other Chasers on duty made comical attempts to quell the chaos, and I saw my opportunity. I fished the rat from the pot by its tail, stripped off the stocking that was not concealing Anne's key, and stuffed the dead animal inside. Once the mayhem had been sufficiently contained, we were again locked in our cells. I had managed to sneak in my bundle unnoticed.

On Sunday afternoons, those who are able are allowed to stretch their limbs in the Walking Yard, which is really nothing more than a fenced-in patch of dirt guarded by a Chaser whose response to even the most miniscule of provocations is a strike across the face with his baton; thus, broken lips and blackened eyes are all too common to see emerging from the Yard, but, to most of us, the air is worth the injuries.

When I arrived at the gate that afternoon, one missing stocking and a dead rat held behind my back, Jolie Rouge was there to meet me. Her arms were covered in fresh purple bruises, and she walked with a limp. Before I could apologise for the punishment she had clearly taken on my behalf, she pointed to the far corner of the Yard. Eight girls, all of whom I would soon know well as members of the Striped Stocking Society, stood round a small hole dug in the dirt, concealing it from the Chaser. As Jolie and I approached, the girls moved aside to allow us into the circle, and I saw that they all clutched sad bundles of weeds against their chests.

'The deceased is now present,' announced Jolie, in her peculiar accent. 'Let the funeral commence.'

I stepped forwards and produced the rat. Kneeling in the dirt, I placed the tiny body in the ground, and ceremoniously laid the stocking over it.

'Shouldn't we say a prayer?' asked a diminutive girl with large, brown eyes.

'I think Flea's right,' said the girl next to her. 'I saw it done that way when my mother died.'

'Who should say it?' asked another inmate.

'Valentine should say it. It's her rat,' responded Jolie, turning to me.

'*Valentine*?' I asked.

'Your birthmark,' she explained, touching her soft fingertips to my cheek.

'Ah . . . well, I wasn't exactly born with it, I'm afraid . . .'

'I know.'

I asked the girls to kneel, and they did.

'Dear Lord in Heaven,' I began, unsure of what to say as I had never before attended a proper funeral service, 'please accept this poor, drowned creature into Thy Glorious Kingdom, for it was not merely another Asylum casualty—it also relieved us of the obligation to eat what was surely a bloody awful pot of soup.'

Each inmate poured a handful of dirt into the miniature grave, and the weeds were laid on top. Within only a few days of the funeral, a patch of dandelions had grown up over the spot, and, every Sunday since, we pick them and make our futile wishes as we blow the downy fluff into the air and watch it float on, past the fence and far away to where we will never go.

We may not have our freedom, our dignity, or our wits, but friendship within the Asylum is alive and well.

hospital entry 18: not exactly petite

From time to time, the asylum Nutritionist chooses to interrogate me yet again upon the topic of why I persist in denying that I have an eating disorder. The Nutritionist is convinced that I am lying, and I am convinced that she is a bitch.

Due to the whole "eating disorder" investigation, I've gotten to thinking about the only time I ever bordered on such a condition. It happened at age sixteen, during my brief affiliation with a major record label (before I got smart enough to leave and start my own), and it was brought on by the most degrading part of this experience: the Photo Shoot.

After several successive long nights recording, I was driven at dawn to a studio where a stereotypical makeup artist was waiting, brush in hand, to paint my gothic pallor stereotypically orange. The record execs told me that sun-kissed girls make better pop stars, MTV confirmed this, and we all have a job to do, right? ("Don't you want to help your family?" they said. "Don't you want to be famous?" they said. "What's wrong with you?" they said.)

The makeup guy was a perfect peach in comparison to the hag who came to direct the shoot. She pinched and poked at me, telling me how to pose—"Smile bigger! Look happy!"—and arranging me in such a way as to conceal my ass, which, apparently, was horrendously oversized (FYI, I looked exactly the same then as I do now). This woman's awful words, deadly to an adolescent girl, haunt me to this day.

"She's not exactly *petite*."

She may as well have told me I was the most disgusting, unworthy creature in existence, which, incidentally, is what I felt like at the time for even caring about such things; even then, I knew better than to concern myself with anyone's opinion of my ass. *I knew better*, and yet, I was crushed, and so I did what any teenage girl would do: I stopped eating. I didn't eat for so long that there came a day when I couldn't stand up without falling right back down again.

Even now, I am more ashamed of not eating then I ever could be for being "fat."

Asylum Letter No. XXII

Why, Diary! I've only just realised that I have not yet mentioned the walls . . .

Two days after my incarceration within the Asylum for Wayward Victorian Girls, I was removed from Quarantine and placed into Ward A in the Eastern Wing of the institution, Cell Block 2. If you recall—and you do, for what is a Diary if not an aid to memory—it was upon my first night in Ward A that I found the little silver pencil.

There are several floors lined with cells within the Asylum. The Cell Blocks are arranged by approximate age of the incarcerated, with Block 1 confining the inmates even younger than I. The cell walls are solid upon three sides, whilst iron bars stretching from floor to ceiling make up the fourth, which looks out onto a corridor that runs the length of the Ward. The walls are papered over with the broad black-and-white striped print to be found throughout much of the Asylum. This is, no doubt, an attempt to disguise the crumbling state of the boards beneath, yet I can still detect a thick film of filth, the mold multiplying in every corner, and the questionable stains left by decades of prisoners. The paper has aged badly, and the black and white are merging together into a dodgy grey.

Ward B is the ward nobody wants to be transferred to. The inmates of Ward B are subjected to the same tortures as we, and far worse besides. I have heard that the girls there are kept in chains and manacles, some being strapped down to wooden planks for years interminable, some trapped in cages that allow no movement of any kind, and all being crammed into a den not fit for an animal; the tales of terror are endless, and are a popular topic amongst the Ward A girls as, after the gaslight in the corridor has been extinguished, we lie in our beds and whisper.

I had survived in Ward A less than a week when I woke in the night to discover something peculiar, to say the least: The stripes upon the walls round me appeared to be moving. Diary, I mean this just as I say it. I swear upon what little I hold dear that the stripes were writhing slowly upon the surface, undulating like seaweed beneath ocean waves, or snakes gliding through a stream.

The cell was dimly lit by a half-concealed moon; much of the walls were hidden in shadow, and I supposed I could be dreaming (isn't it funny, the way we immediately leap to this conclusion each time we witness something unusual . . . *I could be dreaming*, we think, *I must be dreaming*, and yet we are never dreaming, and we never learn). Shivering from cold and trepidation, I sat up and tried to focus my vision.

From the bed two down from mine came a small voice.

'You see it, don't you . . .'

'What is it?' I whispered.

Though aware that what I was seeing was beyond impossible, I felt myself being pulled towards the wall by the hypnotic rippling of the stripes, and I rose from my bed.

'I'm not supposed to talk to you . . .' said the voice.

The Society's test was being enforced. A minute passed and the girl spoke again, apparently unable to contain herself.

'They say the house is alive . . . they say your eyes adjust . . . that you see it when you've been here long enough. It didn't take long for you, did it . . .'

'How is it possible?' I asked.

'Some believe that the spirits of the girls who used to sleep here are trapped inside the walls, but I don't know . . . I think it is alive . . . the Asylum I mean . . . every part of it.'

I could not look away. Lifting my arm, I extended my hand, reaching . . . reaching . . . Long tongues of wispy grey lashed and licked at my fingers as they neared the surface, the narrowing distance between my hand and the wall growing so cold it almost burned, like standing barefoot in the snow. I touched my fingertips to the wall at last; the stripes convulsed beneath them. My ears filled with deafening shrieks and wails, and the smoky tendrils shot out to grasp my arm as if to pull me into the wall itself. I wrenched myself away and fell backwards, stunned. The screams had gone silent the moment I broke contact—a door slamming shut.

I returned to my bed and watched the walls creep until light came through the bars of the tiny window.

Now, weeks later, the striped walls still move, and I, too, am convinced that this house of madness is alive, though, in truth, I rarely think on it anymore. It just . . . *is*. Just another thing one grows accustomed to. Like the talking rats.

Asylum Letter No. XXIII

It was the day after the burial of the soup rat that I heard it again: the scratching. It originated from somewhere behind my bed, I was sure of it . . . in the wall perhaps, or beneath the floor . . . from somewhere I couldn't reach. It was incessant, persistent, and it seemed to come closer with every passing minute.

Before we are locked inside our cells for the night, all of us inmates are lined up in the Ward Hall and given pills and foul-tasting liquid concoctions. These sedating draughts no longer affect me as I have gradually become insensitive to their influence, and, thus, I lay awake, listening to the scratching and going silently mad (or *madder* if my diagnosis is to be believed). I had to expose the source or I would get no rest; no rest means greater susceptibility to illness and infection, and that, of course, means death.

Stowed inside my mattress was a pitiful collection of treasures: the end of a candle from Dr. Stockill's Laboratory, a match from the floor of Dr. Lymer's torture chamber, three spoons, my silver pencil, and several scraps of paper. I lit the stub of wax and inspected my hostile surroundings. Beneath my bed, I found a small pile of debris just below a tiny hole in the wall, not more than an inch or two above the floor. As I watched, the hole grew larger, created by something drilling its way through from the other side. Alarmed, I backed away from the bed. Only a few heartbeats more, and all was still.

I held my candle near the ground; something I could not yet see crossed the flame's path, and a shadow grew large upon the opposite wall—a shadow of something awful. A profile projected in clear detail onto the striped wallpaper. I saw a pair of pointed claws outstretched, a long, snake-like tail, and there sat I with nowhere to run!

Then, from beneath the bed, a rat emerged. So *this* was my monster! It was of a respectable size, but nothing more. The rat sat up on its haunches and groomed itself thoroughly of the dust and dirt, licking its wee paws and wiping its face before straightening its whiskers. After a final shake, it looked up at me.

'Well! It's about bloody time!' said the rat.

'I beg your pardon?' said I.

'Why, it's taken me ages to get through that blasted wall. Extraordinary that such a poorly constructed building should have such a damned sturdy wall, isn't it? It's quite exhausted me. Did you know that this atrocity we dwell within was erected directly atop the city's largest rubbish heap? No doubt we'll all be buried alive someday . . .'

The rat had been sniffing the ground as he spoke, and now advanced towards me.

'I say, you wouldn't happen to have any *crumbs*, would you?' he asked, sitting upright and rubbing his paws together in a gesture tragically hopeful.

I searched my pocket—really just a bit of my shift I had tied up—for any remnants of bread I might have tucked away.

'All out, I'm afraid,' I said. 'I'm terribly sorry.'

'Of course not, of course not, no matter, my child, no matter at all. Oh, heavens above and hell below, I haven't introduced myself! Whatever would the Queen say, what *would* she say . . .'

The rat hopped up to my knee and stood tall upon his hind legs, clearing his furry little throat as though preparing to say something exceedingly important.

'I, dear Lady, am Sir Edward, formerly prized pet of, and companion to, the young Queen Victoria, now Ambassador of the League of Asylum Plague Rats, and I am entirely at your service.'

He bowed his head, and continued on.

'It is with the deepest gratitude for the kind consideration you showed to our dearly departed Percy, Head of the League's ill-fated "Operation Pantry", that I have come, on behalf of the League, to present you with a token of our appreciation and devotion.'

Sir Edward leapt down to the ground, shouting, 'Onwards, Plague Rats!'

Upon his order, a small army of rodents marched out from beneath the bed. Upon their backs they shared the burden of a large metal spoon—larger than those we use in the Dining Hall. This spoon must have been taken from the kitchen.

'And, *halt!*' commanded Sir Edward.

He waved his paw towards the spoon.

'For *me*?' I was perplexed by the gift, yet I knew that I must respond appropriately to such a venerable company as had now congregated round me. 'Well! I *am* honoured, though I do hope it won't mind living within my miserable mattress, for I haven't anywhere else . . .'

I took up the spoon and was presently overcome with a profound gratitude; tears rose to my eyes.

'I am sorry,' I said, 'I don't know what could be the matter with me.'

A small white rat with a black hood uttered a whimper in sympathy; the larger rat next to him delivered a playful slap to the back of his head.

'I will use it well, and I do thank you all very much.'

With a parting bow, Sir Edward led his League back beneath my bed and towards the opening they had entered by, their tails gliding through the wall one by one. Before disappearing himself, Sir Edward turned back to me.

'If you don't mind, my Lady, I shall leave this tunnel open. I believe we may have need of each other in the coming days.'

'Of course, Sir Edward. Oh! And I almost forgot to thank you . . . for the pencil, I mean.'

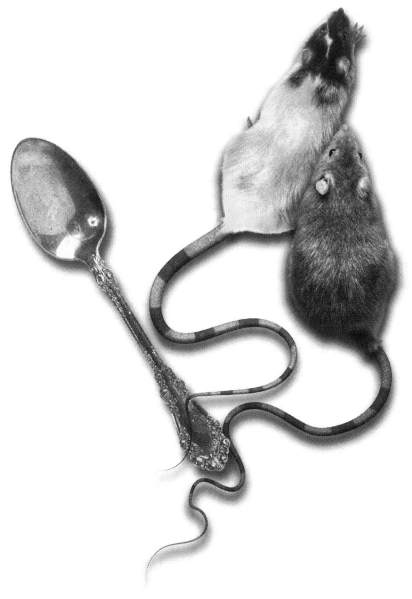

Asylum Letter No. XXIV

It is easy to be thrown into Quarantine—too easy. Refusing to take the medicine you know will make you ill; struggling against the Chasers as they drag you to the Hydrotherapy Chamber to be nearly drowned; daring to speak to Madam Mournington as she patrols the Ward before the lights go out, swinging her Ward Key upon its chain as if to taunt us with the very tool of our freedom; any disturbance in the Asylum's procrustean peace can land a girl down in the dank, dark dungeon until someone remembers to let her out, which may not happen for days, or even weeks.

Having served her sentence for the soup rat incident, Jolie Rouge has returned from Quarantine at last to join us upstairs in Ward A, Cell Block 2. I often wake in the night to see her crouched upon the bed across from mine, her slight frame turned to face the bars in frozen anticipation, just as I had seen her during my first night in Quarantine. I cannot tell when she sleeps, for surely she must, and I have begun to wonder whether it is possible to sleep with one's eyes open.

Though she has been kind to me, I must be truthful and say that Jolie Rouge frightens me a little. I do not think I am alone in this sentiment—I can see it in the eyes of the younger girls who flock round her as she stalks the Ward Hall during the day, circling the perimeter and frequently going to the small, barred window as though watching for someone. These girls admire her, for I think they do believe that she is looking out for them; everyone knows that Jolie keeps watch at night. Still, they are intimidated by her.

One morning, as we sat down to our soup in the Dining Hall, a talkative inmate of perhaps fourteen asked Jolie the reason for her commitment. The girl herself had only just arrived, and knew nothing of protocol. Jolie looked up from her bowl, her head rising proudly beneath its nest of matted hair.

'I, you may as well know, am a pirate,' said she, 'and I was captured in battle.'

'Oh! Oh my!' gasped the girl.

Muffled laughter could be heard from two older girls at the far end of the table. Jolie took no notice. I remained quiet, desirous of hearing the tale quite as much as was the new inmate.

'Did you sail in a real pirate ship?' the girl eagerly asked. 'The proper sort, with a great black flag?'

'Of course I did,' Jolie replied, clearly glad for the chance to share her story. 'My ship—for it *was* my ship and I was its Captain—my ship was the prettiest ship to ever sail the high seas.'

'But how were you captured?'

A shadow passed over Jolie's pale face, and her eyes went dark.

'We were under attack, and the enemy slew my First Mate before I could stop them. They came in the night as I was sleeping, which is not a fair way to fight, but they were not honourable pirates like I am. A pirate captain needs her First Mate . . . you know that, don't you?'

'Oh yes, yes I do!' said the girl.

At the other end of the table, the giggling continued, interrupted now and then by mocking squeals of '*Ahoi! Ahoi!*'

Again, Jolie did not respond.

'But didn't you fight them back with your sword?' asked the incredulous newcomer, who obviously believed every word.

'I certainly did!' exclaimed Jolie, in a sudden burst of indignation. 'And you may believe that the enemy did *not* sail away unscathed.'

From amongst the group rose a tall girl with her hair in long, loose braids.

'Well then, *Miss Rouge*, why don't you tell us exactly what you did? We're all dying to know.'

Jolie turned to face her antagonist with perfect calm.

'I carved a man's eye out.'

There was a collective silence; the girl looked away, sitting down again without a word.

Heaven knows the wards are full of storytellers—some mad with delusion, others merely boasters, and still others concocting fables simply for entertainment. Yet, despite her fragile build, and delicate, faerie-like features, there was something in Jolie's voice that compelled the girls to wonder whether it all might be true.

On the afternoon of that same day, I observed Jolie sitting alone before the barred window in the communal Ward Hall. She stared out onto the grounds behind the Asylum; vultures circled at our eye level, for we were considerably high up. A swarm of rats followed me as I wove my way through the sea of despondent souls—bodies and filth covering the floor. I arrived at the window. Jolie would not look at me, yet I could see that her crystal-blue eyes glistened with all the tears she was holding back. I longed to touch her . . . to comfort her in some way . . . but I did not dare.

'I believe you,' I said.

Jolie Rouge remained silent, showing no sign that she had even heard my words, and so I moved to return to my corner. I had retreated only a few steps when, without turning her head, Jolie finally spoke.

'Thank you.'

hospital entry 19: measuring the distance

There is something that I realized about society long before I was committed, and it is this: People are rabidly fascinated by tales of life inside of a mental institution. This interest is a phenomenon that stretches back hundreds of years, as evidenced by the numerous observer reports of lunatic asylums throughout the seventeenth, eighteenth, and nineteenth centuries all the way up to the plethora (what a word) of books written about these institutions and the lives led inside of them even now, not to mention the movies depicting it all.

Why is this?

I believe it is because an asylum is a parallel universe with its own rules and social structure, and is therefore different and interesting, but also because people want to know if they could ever end up here as well. It is the same reason why people are so disturbingly obsessed with celebrities—their relationships, their ups and downs, their eating disorders . . . *Am I like them?* people wonder, half revolted by the idea that they could be, half wishing that they were.

People aren't just reading—they're measuring the distance.

141

If I ever get out of here, I wonder if I will write about it. And, if I do, will I disclose all? Am I brave enough?

Oh, who am I bloody kidding? I'll tell people more than they *ever* wanted to know. I'll never shut up. Perhaps the doctors know this. Perhaps *that* is why I am still here.

Asylum Letter No. XXV

Whilst Madam Mournington is essential to the maintenance of the Asylum's façade, our mistress's most vital role is that of guardian and sole operator of the Asylum's Ward Key. She has the key about her always, swinging it upon the silver chain dangling from the chatelaine pinned ever at her waist. The Ward Key fits every lock within the institution, but is most jealously guarded for its access to the prison-barred landing of the Lunatic Wards.

Past the bars, the Ward Hall shoots off in opposite directions, one door leading East to Ward A, the other West to Ward B. The separate wards are locked as well, and open by the turn of this same key. Madame Mournington permits no copies to be made, not even for the Chasers entrusted to guard us during the day, and so she is required to appear early every morning so that we may be led to the Dining Hall, and late every night as we are locked away again.

I can see that Madam Mournington takes great pride in this duty; she is necessary to the institution, and I believe that this awareness of being needed is the only thing that fulfills her, for, as far as I can tell, she is a lonely old woman who has but little else.

As for our Superintendent, he displays the strangest behaviour I have ever seen in a man of his age. Whilst he appears utterly inhuman to all, when he is with his mother, he is a different man. He grovels for her praise and attention like a child, or a dog. He is eager that she should be in attendance at the institution as consistently as possible, almost as though he is afraid that, should she leave, she might not return.

Asylum Letter No. XXVI

With each new addition to the Asylum, our knowledge of what is happening in the outside world grows.

It is most fascinating, Diary, to see what sort of creatures are committed to our care. Girls in the flower of youth, young brides, mothers, ladies with formidable educations, writers, poets, artists, accomplished musicians, even girls from the so-called 'lower professions'—music hall performers, dancers, and an exorbitant number of prostitutes—grace our decaying institution, and I am not surprised to find captivating characters and worthy friends amongst all of our ranks.

There is a voluptuous beauty called Veronica who occupies the bed next to mine in Ward A. Veronica had begun her career as a dance hall girl, but had later developed her own act, or so she says. A gifted raconteur, Veronica delights in telling us of her life upon the stage, her tales faithfully peppered with racy anecdotes entirely unsuitable for younger ears.

Whilst perhaps eccentric, Veronica possesses only two legitimate oddities that I can perceive, the first being her absolute belief that she has been pardoned and will be sent home the following day. It is tragic indeed to see her delude herself so, yet, when the following day finally arrives, she seems to have no recollection of having said the very same thing the day before, and goes on to say it again.

I have come to realize that it is precisely this delusion that enables Veronica to exist from one day to the next with her ebullient disposition intact. Notoriously calling out to the Chasers as they patrol the corridor outside of our cells, she taunts them into giving her things she wants—usually a bit of food, or a newspaper in which she follows the playbills—in exchange for particular 'favours'. Her shouts of, '*Who wants to kiss me?*' echo throughout Ward A thrice daily, at the very least.

And this leads us to Veronica's second oddity: She seems always to be in the act of taking off her clothes, and makes quite a show of it, as though she were still upon the stage before the limelight and a voracious audience. I do in fact believe that she is most at ease in a state of nudity, for, even with knotted hair, and covered in bruises and cuts, she never stops the show, and I hope she never will.

Whilst each inmate has her own reason for being here, and her own exceptional story to tell, there are common elements that bind us all together.

Some are born mad, some achieve madness, and some have madness thrust upon 'em.

Had Shakespeare paid us a visit, he might forgive me my bastardization of his brilliant line, but greatness and madness are bedfellows in the brains of so many excellent souls that my version may be more apt than my humility will allow me to own.

It is true that many of the girls here have loosened the reins upon their wits, some having been born disturbed, yet most having become so through years of suffering, caught in that vain struggle to survive a harsh and unjust society that grants them few of the rights given to men, and even less of the respect. Despite our differences in class, station, and relative degree of sanity, most of us are united by the fact that we do not belong here.

Asylum Letter No. XXVII

'How, then,' faithful Diary, 'does a girl come to be imprisoned with no trial and no cause?' you surely ask. It is tragically simple really—all that is in fact required is the word of a man who wants her out of the way.

In short, any male figure in a female's life has the God-given right to have her committed and forever branded as a lunatic, with no proof save his own good word. What's more, the unfortunate female can legally be released only into the hands of the man who first had her committed. Naturally, it follows that not a single one of us who pass through the Asylum gates will ever stand upon the other side of them again.

If a visitor to our institution were allowed to see its inmates rather than its actors, he would no doubt be shocked by our conditions and the torture we suffer daily, and would also be surprised by our general youth; most girls who are admitted when they are young will not live to become old, and the few who do are locked up with the deformed in a dark corner of Ward B where they are forgotten until they simply rot away. This is the dismal destiny of we who are strong enough to endure the torture, and we all know it. And yet we breathe.

Besides falsehood and treachery, there are reasons enough why any female may be thought insane by the medical community, her family, and society in general. Opposing an arranged marriage, for example; expressing ambivalence towards the non-negotiable prospect of motherhood; being melancholy after giving birth (or being melancholy at all); lacking enthusiasm for religion; evidencing a particular fondness for her fellow females; being too high-spirited, too low-spirited, mildly disagreeable or simply 'moody'—any behaviour thought aberrant by the impossibly narrow standards of our day is attributed to the inherent weakness and waywardness of the female gender.

But, sisters, never fear! There are many methods by which female 'insanity' can be treated: A girl who engages in intimate relations before she is married, even if such relations are entirely against her will, is branded 'promiscuous', and is thus insane (insanity being the direct cause of promiscuity in women). And yet, a common treatment administered to our girls suffering from fits of what our good doctors have termed 'hysterics' is, in fact, forced intercourse. Is there not some irony in this? It is thought that the supposed hysteria emanates from the young lady's reproductive organs having nothing useful to do, and, by putting these idle organs to good use, the problem shall be solved and the lady restored to sanity, which would seem perfectly rational if it were not so utterly absurd.

Dr. Stockill will have nothing to do with this practice as he seems to loathe our very flesh, but Dr. Lymer is all too eager to perform his duties in such cases, as are his assistants whom he allows to aid him in every capacity, all foul-mouthed brutes who smell of filth. Even advances upon our persons by the Chasers are hardly frowned upon. It should thus come as no surprise to you that no condition is better represented in the Asylum than that of hysteria. The number of us diagnosed with the disease is truly staggering—it is an epidemic, they say, sweeping the country like the plague, and every female is at risk, for her hysterical condition could easily lead her to 'unclean' actions.

But, hark! There is something that can be done to cure the mental invalid whilst making society a safer, better, more wholesome place for everyone: As a means of eliminating even the remote possibility of female physical pleasure, which hysteria would invariably increase the appetite for, and the existence of which threatens the entire order of civilization, clitoridectomies are routinely performed upon girls who are thought particularly disturbed, girls labeled as 'immoral' (though, most often, they have done nothing to earn this title), or who have, for lack of other means by which to earn their bread, turned to, or were forced into, prostitution (I myself had been forced into it, had I not?).

To anyone who should ever chance to find this diary once I am gone: If you do not know what a clitoridectomy is, enjoy your ignorance, for I shall not be the one to enlighten you.

hospital entry 20: if leeches ate peaches

Since my incarceration, I have drawn more pictures of more leeches than could possibly be healthy. Not that I am aware of the statistically agreed upon number of leeches that *would* be considered healthy, but anyway, my notebook is filled with them, and rats too, and I fear it has become an obsession—before, it was merely a fetish.

Turning through the pages, it is pathetically clear what I'm doing: I am creating characters—personalities—just to have someone to talk to.

Every few days, an inmate's parents or even an embarrassed husband will come to visit, tears and shame in their downcast eyes, not wanting to look at our surroundings, not wanting to see how horrible they are. The visitors sit quietly in a corner of the Day Room, trying hard to ignore the rest of us.

But I? I have never been so utterly alone as I am now—completely isolated and entirely forgotten. No one has come to visit me. No one has even called. It's not their fault—nobody knows where to find me, and there is nobody to tell them.

I am forgotten even by the staff, which is what happens when you've been here longer than a week; you become a fixture—something that exists here, like the stained green sofa or the buzzing fluorescent lights. As long as you're not screaming, you don't need to be attended to. And, even if you are, well, good luck.

Though I was positively drowning in disturbing doctor visits downstairs in the Emergency Ward, I have not seen a proper doctor since my arrival in Maximum Security—counselors and nutritionists, yes, but no doctor; I have not been scheduled a single hour with a psychiatrist—nothing. Which is not to say that a doctor has not been seeing me.

Two days into my residency in Maximum Security, who was there waiting for me in my prison-barred bedroom? Dr. Sharp. From behind the Day Room door where he thinks I can't see him, who lurks, just staring at me? Dr. Sharp. In the makeshift classroom where we lunatics are forced to sit together in circles and draw pictures in finger paint, I hear a voice from the table behind me, and who's there, just waiting for me to turn around? Let's all say it together now: DR. FUCKING SHARP.

I am officially creeped out now—I am being stalked within a mental hospital by the chief resident psychiatrist, whilst being held here against my will. Does it get any crazier than this? Dr. Sharp doesn't work up here in Maximum Security. He has absolutely no reason to be here, for he directs his attentions toward no one but me, and, *by* being here, he is neglecting his duties elsewhere. I wonder what the staff thinks about this? Surely they must notice.

I've had enough. I turn to face the Doctor; he is smiling flirtatiously; he's been waiting for me to notice him . . . surprise! I will say nothing. I will not acknowledge him. If he believes I welcome his impromptu appearances, he will never stop. I turn back to my table with a sudden renewed interest in the work of art a manic kid called Brian is painting for me as a gift. I return to my own painting—it is a portrait of yet another leech, gasping for blood, starving. Above the leech are the words:

"That's very good!" says Dr. Sharp, from over my shoulder. And, finally, I snap.

Rising from my orange plastic chair, I advance toward the Doctor, meeting him eye to eye.

"If leeches ate peaches instead of my blood, then I would be free to drink tea in the mud!"

Did I just say that out loud? What the hell am I doing?

The Doctor is flustered.

"Uh, what was that? You've lost me," he says, still smiling.

I am angry and it feels so good to free it, even in my own peculiar way.

"How could you *possibly* think," I begin, my voice rising involuntarily with each word, "that this . . . *this* was the place to put a suicidally depressed girl? Have you no idea what goes on up here?"

I'm chastising the head shrink in front of everybody, and I don't care. Besides, I'm the only one here who hasn't yet had a screaming fit, and maybe it's about time I try to fit in.

"What do you mean?" asks Dr. Sharp, now looking shocked—wounded even. "What happened?"

"What *happened*? Where shall I begin? Let's start with poor Lucy over here."

I point to a shy older woman in the corner who, like me, does not belong here.

"She's lucky to be alive, and why? Because she nearly got her head bashed in by a schizophrenic wielding a goddamned guitar. Why doesn't somebody ask *her* what happened?"

Lucy looks embarrassed, but it gives me strength to have somebody to fight for. I can never fight for myself, but, for others, I can kill.

"I swear, Emilie," says Dr. Sharp, "things like that almost *never* happen up here."

"Really, Doctor? *Really*? Because, how would you know that? When was the last time you were up here with the crazies? The *real* crazies—not the people who have had a bad day, or who have popped a few too many pills. How much time do you spend up here in Maximum Security?"

I'm in his face now.

"Permit me to enlighten you: 'Things like that' happen here *every fucking day.*"

"What . . . what do you mean?" stammers Dr. Sharp; I guess our "date" isn't going quite as he had planned.

I tell him how terrorizing it is for me to be in the constant vicinity of loud and aggressive males—how I am more depressed, more emaciated, more afraid, and more ill in every way than I have ever been in the entirety of my life.

"Look, I'm shaking! I can't stop shaking!" I say. "Oh, yes, I'm feeling *really* safe here—I am *so* much less suicidal now. In fact, I'm fucking cured, so get me the *hell* out of here!"

Hmm. Maybe I can fight for myself after all.

Dr. Sharp mumbles some weak apology as the counselor who is supervising art hour announces that time is up and we all have to return to the Day Room for afternoon drugs. The inmates shuffle out of the room, leaving their sticky messes behind.

"Emilie, time to go," the counselor tells me.

"I'm coming!" I shout.

Can't she see I'm having a conversation?

"*You* put me here," I tell Dr. Sharp. "*You* are responsible for this. Did you really think that *this* is where I belonged?"

"Emilie," calls the counselor again, "we have to go."

"I'm *coming*!" I shout again.

"Dr. Sharp . . . I tried to kill myself. I am a sad, *sad* girl. This is *not* where you put a sad girl to make her get happy."

"*Emilie!*" shouts the counselor, her patience having reached its natural end.

I turn to collect my leech painting as Dr. Sharp stands in front of me looking bewildered; when I turn back, he is slinking away without a word.

It's time for drugs.

I take my place in the med-line and receive my pills in their paper cup as the nurse watches me with her hawk eye to make sure I'm not tonguing them. Patients tongue their drugs (holding the pills temporarily inside of their mouths when they're being watched, removing them when they're not) for any of three reasons: They could spit them out, they could stockpile the pills and use them as currency within the nuttery, or they could stockpile the pills and take them all at once, overdosing being one of the very few ways in which a patient can exercise any control over herself and her body.

I haven't yet learned the fine art of tonguing, so I swallow the drugs. Afterwards, I shut myself in the bathroom and cry.

Asylum Letter No. XXVIII

I often forget why I am here—what it is that has branded me 'mad', and then I remember my crime: I attempted to take my own life.

By all logic, I had every reason to do so, if not the right. Even now, I have no motivation whatever to continue on in this world, such as it is, were it not for the promise I made to Anne in the churchyard.

But no, I am not honest, Diary, there is something more: An undeniable bond has developed between many of us. We give each other a reason to keep fighting, to keep waiting, though for what we do not know. For Madam Mournington to leave her Ward Key in the lock? For the visiting inspectors to look beyond the pretty veneers? For mercy? Perhaps, but also we fear leaving each other alone in this place.

Whilst it is positively shocking how many girls are here for wishing to die and failing at it, it is even more incredible how many in the world outside are succeeding. News from beyond the gates is bursting with suicides—bodies found poisoned, washed up on the shore, smashed upon the rocks, or fished from the river, just as I had been. The press is not kind to our memories. In exercising the one option remaining after all others had deserted us, we are weak and wicked; we have committed an offense against God himself, and we are thus condemned to burn for it. Anne was denied a proper burial because she had sinned against God and nature and was thus unclean, unprincipled, and destined for Hell or something like it. She had defied the religious belief in the sanctity of life. But whose life? Was her life sacred? Who protected her? Who is protecting us?

You must not think, Diary, that I recommend suicide under any circumstance—I do not! I merely question the sanity of those who would criminalize, and, worse, brand as insane, the poor, the wretched, the oppressed, the persecuted, the abused, who find a death of their own choosing preferable to a life of someone else's. I was one of those girls.

The only thing more alarming to me than the growing rate of female suicide in London is the phenomenon of the artist intent on glamourising the act. The papers are full of them—images of ladies in mid-air, hair flowing, their lovely forms falling to lovelier deaths driven by beautiful despair, and even the forbidden peek of an occasional ankle beneath a diaphanous nightgown, framed by the proscenium arch of a perfect, moonlit sky . . . all serve to idolize—perhaps even, dare I breathe it, to sexualize—this image of the fallen and falling female.

Undoubtedly, many of these images are marvelous in their execution and even touching in their sentiment, but they are not honouring us; they are glorifying our perceived (perhaps assigned?) weakness, belittling our suffering, and cheapening our deaths, thereby encouraging all.

hospital entry 21: four o'clock

It's happening again.

There is a phenomenon that occurs in the minds of many manic depressives when entering into either a manic or a depressive state that nobody claims to understand, but that bipolars from the far corners of the world can attest to: the consistent waking up at four o'clock in the morning. And when I say *four o'clock*, I mean *four o'clock on the fucking dot*.

How many times have I given myself chills, waking up yet again after only two hours of sleep and looking over at the blinking red of a digital alarm clock only to see that number staring back at me? I've lost count. And the thing is, you don't just wake up. You wake up with your mind racing, music churning over and over inside your head, the internal noise, words, pictures, absolutely unbearable, and it is absolutely impossible to go back to sleep.

I used to lie in bed for as long as I could stand the torture before giving up and rising to go and work at something or other, but, in recent months, I'd stopped bothering. When the clock strikes four, I'm up and out of bed, making the tea (it is four o'clock after all) and sitting down to scribble things. It is enough to drive one mad if one wasn't already, which I suppose is impossible since madness is the only reason this happens.

Here in the Psych Ward, I do not have the luxury of getting up to write a symphony or make a pot of Lady Grey, and so I lie in the dark, my cellmates creeping silently about the room, counting the minutes until the alarm buzzes, the fluorescent lights flicker on, and the nurse's voice pipes in announcing that it is morning, as though it were not morning until she said so.

I am no longer responding to the sleeping pills as I should be and I know that I am on the verge of a manic state. Their drugs are doing nothing but making me sick.

Seeing metaphors in everything again.

One of the defining characteristics of my thought process when entering into a manic state is my uncontrollable compulsion (redundant?) to make everything related in some way to everything else. This involuntary association game spins swiftly out of control, and so rapidly, so relentlessly, that ordinary words cannot keep up, and so, automatically, my brain switches gear from words to pictures, then continues on the same bend, though now entirely in metaphor.

A person with a mental illness becomes a child with a parasitic twin, becomes a flea upon a Plague Rat, becomes a sniper with a gun shooting at JFK, becomes the shadow that stalks you throughout your entire existence, and all this only in pictures, because words are too slow. If I manage to pause, the words are there, waiting, all lined up in the right order, and sometimes with witty (or so I like to delude myself) captions corresponding to the pictures . . . but words are not necessary. The whole world exists without them.

There must be a name for this kind of brain that must make metaphors of everything, that sees pictures in every word, words in every picture, words in every word, hears numbers, sees letters, tastes music, and has a corresponding color for every note of the scale, letter of the alphabet, day of the year

. . . or perhaps it is not important or special enough to have a name. Perhaps it is simply called "being awake."

Sometimes, these sensory phantoms correspond with each other, but I cannot discern what the association between the differing symbols means. In one particular case, the note "A" is brown, and so is the number "5", and the letter "F". The following makes a bit more sense: The note "B" is blue, dark blue, as is the letter "B" and the number "2". The note "C" is a warm, creamy white and has a light glowing from the inside. The letter "C" is also cream, but without the light, as is the number "1". Then, we connect the number "1" as corresponding to the note "C", being the first note of the most basic diatonic scale.

Now, here is where things begin to get a little fuzzy, because many symbols are not solid, ordinary colors. Some are oddly changeable combinations of colors like green and yellow, but with lights showing through and a shadow over one side. These colors have no names, so I categorize them as simply "greenish" or "reddish black," knowing that these descriptions do no justice to what I am seeing in my mind, or in the air before me.

A peculiarity: The numbers "10", "100", "1000", "10,000", and all variants of ones and zeroes, are always a combination of all the other colors, with the resulting color "pixels", as it were, vibrating so quickly that the number becomes almost transparent.

It is precisely because the notes and corresponding colors trigger an emotional reaction that a piece by Bach in the key of b minor is not only the color blue, but potentially suicide-inducing.

NOTES:
A = Brown
B = Dark Blue
C = Cream
D = Golden
E = Yellow

F = Brown
G = Rust

LETTERS:
A = Dark Red
B = Dark Blue
C = Cream
D = Golden
E = Yellow
F = Brown
G = Rust
H = Brown
I = Gray
J = Yellowish Brown
K = Brownish Yellow
L = Grayish
M = Green
N = Brownish Gold
O = Cream
P = Dark Purply Blue
Q = Brownish Orange
R = Reddish Black
S = Greenish Bluish Black
T = Brownish Black
U = Beige
V = Yellowish Green
W = Light Greenish
X = Black
Y = Yellow
Z = Black

NUMBERS:
1 = Cream
2 = Dark Blue
3 = Green

4 = Salmon
5 = Dark Brown
6 = Pale Yellow
7 = Golden Orange
8 = Green
9 = Gray
10 = Combination
11 = Silver
12 = Blue
13 = Green
14 = Salmon
15 = Brown
16 = Green
17 = Golden Orange
18 = Green
19 = Gray
20 = Blue
30 = Green
40 = Salmon
50 = Brown
60 = Light Yellow
70 = Golden Orange
80 = Green
90 = Gray
100 = Combination

Asylum Letter No. XXIX

Every Spring, the Asylum opens its false doors to society's elite for the purpose of fundraising, as well as for Dr. Stockill getting his name in the papers, fame being a thing he covets. Madam Mournington thrives upon her role as Mistress of Ceremonies, and orders everyone about in her strident tongue like a commanding general.

Veronica has described to me last year's event: the Asylum's 'Mad Tea Party'.

Befeathered ladies and their gentlemen had been served an extravagant tea inside an enormous tent erected upon our front lawn. The inmates who were not wholly unappetizing to look at had been directed to 'frolic' within viewing distance in their shifts and stockings, with a chain whipping promised if they misbehaved or made a run for the gate.

This year, there is to be an entirely new production. Ever the shrewd proprietor, Dr. Stockill has recognized that there is big business in our patron saint of bridge hopping: the Fair Ophelia.

Somehow, Shakespeare's darling has risen from her watery, three-hundred-year-old grave to set the public's imagination afire. The morbidly romantic suicide paintings were only part of the trend—now, people want to see her in the flesh. They can no longer distinguish between fictional personality and true sufferer, and so a third character is born: Ophelia the Icon. It is she whom the aristocrats will pay, and pay well, to see played out before them, and, during every afternoon for a month, a rude public will hand over their shillings to see the show as well.

As I write this, I am preparing to take the stage, and the following, Diary, is how I arrived at the present point:

Early this morning, Madam Mournington strode through our Ward as she does upon every other. But, today, she commanded all of us to stand against the bars and display our hair. Having no choice but to obey this strange request, we did so, though we had no idea what fresh torment lay before us. To her squinting eye, our Headmistress raised the silver monocle attached to her chatelaine, and, peering down her pointed nose, studied us closely as she passed, swinging her Ward Key all the while.

As Madam Mournington pointed the key at a select few of us, Maudsley pulled the chosen from our cells and lined us up in the corridor. I tried to determine what it was that distinguished the selected from those left behind, but all I could tell was that the girls at whom the key pointed were either exceptionally pretty or showed at least some sort of physical grace. They also had the longest and most splendid hair, which is why I was not surprised when the key was pointed my way; I have never considered myself a beauty, yet I will take my pride in my red hair to the grave, for it is all I have that hints at any particular ancestry.

After pointing at Veronica, Madam Mournington stood contemplating Jolie Rouge, who met her eagle's gaze.

Since the day of the rat burial, Jolie had addressed me as 'Valentine' because of my heart-shaped scar; in turn, I had come to call the self-proclaimed pirate 'the Captain', and, soon, so did everybody else. Jolie was wearing her paper hat, and, even through the stench of unwashed bodies, I smelled trouble.

'Remove that rubbish from your head, wretch!' shouted Madam Mournington.

The Captain hesitated, then complied, holding the hat securely behind her back.

'Hmmm . . .' pondered our Headmistress, 'the face is pleasant enough, but the hair is revolting. However, I suppose it can be combed out . . .'

At last, the Ward Key was pointed towards the Captain.

Outside and into the raw wind we were marched, arriving at the Bathing Court where we were sprayed down with more than the usual attention. We were each given a bar of lavender soap with which to wash our hair—an incredible luxury even in the freezing cold, and nearly enough to bring tears to our eyes, so starved were we of pleasant sensory experiences. The locks of many of the girls had not been properly groomed in months, or even years, and they were roughly handled as a pair of kitchen maids tore through the tangled masses, snipping away the snarled strands with a pair of sewing shears.

I hurried to rinse my hair clean and free of knots, but the Captain was struggling with hers. I moved to help her, and was forced back. As the maids approached the Captain, she twisted her arms round her head, covering her hair as best she could. Though she had tried slapping them away, the two maids were now raking their fingers through the Captain's hair; she was screaming as if in excruciating pain. The maids stepped back in horror—piles of hair had come away in their hands.

'Her hair's comin' out! Her hair's comin' out!' the duller of the maids began to shriek as she fled the Bathing Court for the safety of the building. Now restrained by Maudsley, the Captain continued to scream.

'Give it back! It's mine!'

Finally, Madam Mournington entered the Court, her heels clicking sharply upon the wet stone. Seeing the loosened hair, she ordered the remaining maid to crop the Captain's locks as closely as she could with the shears, adding to Maudsley that Jolie's scalp must then be shaven clean, following which she should be placed into Quarantine until further notice. Helpless and heartbroken by her cries, we watched until every last strand of the Captain's hair had fallen in soggy clumps at her bare feet.

Once bathed, our small band was led upstairs to one of the many chambers in the Upper Staff apartments; there, we were each given a cup of tea, and I felt almost guilty at the ecstasy I experienced as the bitter liquid touched my lips. We wandered about the room, passing our emaciated fingers over the gold trim of the mantelpiece, the silken curtains, the finely woven carpets—such things as we had not seen in . . . well, longer than we could remember.

When Madam Mournington arrived, all of my anger flooded back. What violent enmity I felt towards this woman; she had ordered the Captain's lovely head shaved without an ounce of feeling, and I hated her for it.

Each day for the following month, our mistress informed us, we were to be the 'Ophelias' in a new Asylum fundraising attraction: the Ophelia Gallery.

As we were being instructed in our duties, the door was flung wide, revealing an odd little man in purple trousers. Bounding with comical liveliness, he was certainly the most flamboyant personage I had ever encountered. Introduced to us as a stage actor, he had been brought in from the city for the express purpose of teaching us to convey the Icon as the Asylum wished to portray her, for, though we would not profit by it in any way, a great deal of money rested upon the quality of our performance.

Having been directed to languish, to sigh, our hands to our foreheads as though we would faint, it was time to don our costumes. We were dressed in long, sheer gowns that moved like air against our skins. A man of many talents, our tutor helped us to weave jasmine flowers through our freshly clean locks, their delicious scent a potent drug. Finally, he rouged our lips, and our eyes were theatrically blackened.

We stood together before the glass. I scarcely knew myself; my heart-shaped scar had darkened, and I was painfully thin, my ribs protruding. Yet, with our drooping flowers and long, shimmering hair, we were somehow . . . magnificent.

Asylum Letter No. XXX

I have survived my first day as a showgirl—an entertainer of the masses—and this is what I have to report:

My sisters and I were led to the tents that had been raised upon the front lawn. They were very grand in black and white, a stunning contrast to the soft colours and fabrics, petals and flowing fountains that waited inside. Our cages, painted in gold, sparkled in the lamplight; flowering vines twined up and round the bars, evoking an enchanted prison. Some of the cages were tall enough to stand upright inside; mine even had a little hanging swing from which I had been instructed to appear in a constant state of falling—a suicide pantomime.

A string quartet tuned up as we were fashioned into living paintings by our acting master, who skipped about the tents, nearly hysterical with excitement. I inspected the lead violinist—a stodgy old man with a sour expression—and I longed to wrench the instrument from his hands; I knew I could still play it, and play it better. It was horrible to think that I would never make music again.

Still, I reminded myself of how desperately I had wanted to be upon the stage—of how arduously I had worked for the opportunity to speak and be heard, even if it were only through my hands. What if this was it—all I get? My only chance? And so, I determined to fall from a swing better than anyone had ever fallen from a bloody swing in the entire bloody history of swinging.

The tents were opened, and there was a collective gasp from the incoming crowd. No one had expected anything so lovely.

Asylum Letter No. XXXI

We are now a week into our performance as the Opheliacs. Dr. Stockill had protested the name, with the complaint that it was nonsensical and ugly besides, but Dr. Lymer, who had coined the term, put forth the following argument and won:

'If you were to host an Insomnia Gallery, or a Hypochondria Gallery, or Pneumonia, say, or a gallery of some other such disease, would you not call your subjects the *Insomniacs*? The *Hypochondriacs*? The *Pneumoniacs*?'

'Firstly, my dear Lymer, a Hypochondria Gallery is a ridiculous thing to imagine, even for the sake of argument. Secondly, I am not entirely convinced that Pneumoniac is a word. And, thirdly, what is the disease of *Ophelia*?'

'Why, the disease of Ophelia is the disease of the melancholy, mad, and female, and we, my dear Stockill, own a great deal of *stock* in it!'

Asylum Letter No. XXXII

The greatest luxury of being an Opheliac is that we are not made to return to our wards at night, but are instead housed temporarily in the servants' quarters below the kitchen. This is a palace after what we have endured within our cells upstairs, and we only feel the sorrier for those who are not here with us.

I think of the Captain often, and have a sneaking suspicion that I do not yet wish to share . . .

Asylum Letter No. XXXIII

Something ghastly has occurred today, something I do not expect to quickly recover from, though the events of which I shall speak resulted in the solidification of my suspicion regarding the Captain—not through fact, but through feeling.

Having grown weary of the pointing and staring, I could bring myself to do nothing more than sit upon the floor of my cage, facing the wall, with my head resting upon the swing, and, in retrospect, I suppose I looked melancholy enough to *be* Ophelia herself.

Abruptly, my stomach seized, and I could not breathe. I turned to see a man making his way through the line. Spotting the crimson patch over his left eye, my heart ceased to beat, and I hid my face in the fabric of my gown. When I felt brave enough to look out, the man was gone.

A wave of illness passed over me and I doubled over in pain, unable to raise myself. Lacking sufficient air, I called to our livery-clad Chasers for help, but they were occupied in helping themselves to the champagne intended for the guests.

The pain in my abdomen soon became unbearable. The callous crowd was entertained by my suffering and howled with merciless glee, but, when I began to bleed, the taunts turned to screams of horror.

When I awoke, I was lying upon a cold, hard surface. I was still in my costume but it was soiled with blood, and a pile of rags had been stuffed between my legs. I opened my eyes and found myself alone in a cell I did not recognize. Upon the ground by my side lay a crumpled shift and the familiar stockings of the lowly prisoner; my privileges had run out. In a daze, I tried vainly to recollect what had transpired during my last moments of consciousness, yet my head pounded terribly and I could not think.

Then, I remembered the man passing my cage. I dare not mention this sighting to the Captain. My desire to know if I am right is not nearly as important to me as her relative peace, and her time in Quarantine can not have been good for her nerves. Has she even been released yet?

I sat up and strained to focus my vision in the deepening darkness. Gradually, I became aware of the inmates inhabiting the cells surrounding mine; their eyes burned in their skulls, their postures crouched like animals, and many simply stood facing the striped, writhing walls. It was clear from their appearance that they had not seen daylight in a very long time.

And then, I realised where I was.

Asylum Letter No. XXXIV

There are no beds in Ward B; we sleep upon piles of straw like beasts. Just as it was in Ward A, the cells at either side of the long corridor are visible through a wall of prison bars extending from floor to ceiling, leaving them open to the drafts, the stench, and the probing eyes of the Chasers.

I have been assigned to cell number W14, this being located upon the fourteenth tier of the Western Wing enclosures. I am alone in this barren chamber, and my view is limited to that offered through the typical small, barred window looking out onto the front courtyard far below. Denied windowpanes, it is unbearably cold, and I wonder how we should live through winter.

Through the tenebrous haze, I can see that some of the other cells contain narrow cages within which prisoners lie trapped, unable to move. What could a girl possibly have done to warrant such treatment?

All of the stories were true, and worse. In the cell directly opposite mine, there is a device made up of iron bands that clamp round the victim's neck, chest, and arms, keeping her pinned to the wall, trapped within what can only be described as an iron skeleton.

Most of Ward B's inhabitants are indeed quite frightening to look upon, for they are not bathed regularly here, and pass the years lying in their straw and slowly dying. I do pity them, but I hope to keep this cell to myself.

I have the cell to myself no longer, but have been invaded by a welcome guest.

Earlier this afternoon, I heard a fuss in the corridor. Through the bars, I saw Veronica being led by a chain attached to a collar round her neck. Her hands were bound behind her back, yet, despite her degrading circumstance, Veronica proudly pranced, sauntering almost, and taunting the young Chaser who walked before her. It came as no surprise to me that she was also completely naked, save her striped stockings.

'Oh, come on now, Charlie, you strappin' steed, turn round! What are you afraid of?'

The Chaser snapped the chain and Veronica stumbled forwards.

'Oh, Charlie! *Yes!* Pull me 'arder!'

They continued down the corridor, Veronica kicking out her long legs and calling playfully to the prisoners on either side.

Reaching my cell, the Chaser unlocked the door and shoved the still shouting Veronica inside. He attached her chain to a ring set into the wall before producing a dirty shift from his pocket and flinging it at her. Veronica laughed uproariously at his frustration.

'Unlock my 'ands,' she cooed, detaining the guard with her saucy eyes as he turned to exit the cell.

The Chaser looked back at her.

'Unlock my 'ands, Charlie boy. Come on, who wants to kiss me?'

The Chaser sighed heavily. Then, with the same key he had used to unlock the cell, he released Veronica from the iron band clamped tight about her wrists. The moment she was free, out thrashed her arms, clawing at the young man's face. He leapt back before any real damage could be done, and, cursing, stormed from the cell, locking us inside.

'Works every time,' said Veronica, seemingly quite satisfied with herself, as she stepped into the shift and pulled it up. 'He never learns, poor thing.'

'Oh, V!' I went to embrace her but was defied by her bulky collar and chain. 'What's all this, then?' I asked. 'You've been advancing through the ranks, I see.'

'Em! It's perfectly marvelous what's 'appened!' Veronica gripped my shoulders. 'I must always be chained now as I am "a danger to myself and others". I feel terribly important.'

'What do you mean, V? What's wrong with you?'

I began to think that this place was finally getting to her.

'I am a *nymphomaniac*,' she announced with pride.

'What's a nymphomaniac?'

'Well, now, I don't know *exactly*, but it sounds delicious, don't you think?'

I studied Veronica closely as she busied herself with braiding her lustrous black hair into numerous thin plaits. Plucking bits of straw from the floor, she wove them into the plaits. I went to sit upon the ground behind her and did my best to smooth the hair she was quickly tangling.

'They're lettin' me go tomorrow, Emmy . . . you can come an' visit me at the music hall. I'll see you get into the show without payin' a penny . . . truly love, you won't pay a bloomin' cent.'

I wrapped my arms round Veronica from behind.

'Thank you, darling,' I said.

Asylum Letter No. XXXV

During what was left of the day and much of the night, I have fallen in and out of a feverish slumber filled with shapeless phantoms and watery visions, and I fear that my miscarriage has left me unwell. Though I had not known it was coming, I am hardly surprised. It happened to one or the other of us far too often; we are not fit to sustain life within us—we have barely enough for ourselves. I am glad to have it ended by nature rather than the ministrations of a visiting surgeon with rusty tools and careless hands.

As I lie in the black, scribbling these words without the aid of sight, I hear a sort of creaking—quiet, and very far away. It grows louder, closer, and, finally, I recognize the turning of wheels grinding upon the cobblestone drive outside. I rise from my straw to look out, and see an open cart being pulled by a hackneyed old horse. Even from far above, I can detect a dark figure perched at the front of the cart, the heavy contents of which are covered with a cloth.

The clock in the Entrance Hall downstairs strikes four. Morning, but still dark, the moon glares down upon the courtyard, casting a garish glow upon the scene. I watch the cart until it turns the corner of the building and I can see it no more.

As the creak of the wheels grows ever more distant, my awareness turns to the frantic muttering emanating from the cells round me. Someone begins to shriek, high-pitched and panicked. Veronica raises herself slightly.

'Ladies, please!' she shouts.

'It's four o'clock in the morning, V . . . where was that cart going at this hour?' I ask her.

'There's a ditch, Em . . .' she says, sleepily, 'somewhere in the field . . . it goes there . . .'

'A ditch? Why? What for?'

But, even now, I know.

'The . . . the Death Cart, they calls it . . .'

Yawning, Veronica lay back.

'Takes the bodies to be buried in the ditch each night. No, not the ditch, that's wrong . . . what'd she say it was . . . the Pits! Yes, the Death Pits. 'Eard it for the first time last night when you was out like a stone. After you left, they shut down the Gallery . . . bad press, they said, which addled me as I was always taught there weren't no such thing as bad press.'

'It comes every night?'

'We dies every day.'

I had hoped, against all reason, that our bodies were hidden away in a forgotten churchyard, buried with some version of dignity . . . and all this time, the Death Cart had been making its ghoulish rounds. It did not pass by the Eastern Wing of the Asylum housing Ward A, and so I had never heard it until this night.

From the cell next to Veronica's and mine, a girl is sniffling. She is repeating a name.

'Jenny . . . Jenny . . . Jenny . . .'

'Oh bother, Penny, it weren't bleedin' Jenny,' says Veronica, without raising her head. 'I saw 'er myself bein' led to 'er royal bedchamber.'

'She could have died in her cell,' whimpers Penny.

'For the last time, it weren't Jenny. I'm goin' 'ome tomorrow and I needs my beauty rest.'

'You're always going home tomorrow, V,' comes another voice—one I recognize from Ward A. 'You're not going anywhere. None of us are.'

Veronica says nothing; she is still, then turns to face the wall. The ward is silent again, and I can hear Veronica whispering to herself as though half asleep.

'I'm goin' 'ome . . . I'm goin' 'ome . . . I'm goin' 'ome . . .'

Asylum Letter No. XXXVI

The days are grey and gloomy, the sun having forfeited its place in the sky to the vultures that can be seen swooping in and out of the brume rolling in from the city below. Often, the great birds disappear in the direction that the Death Cart travels each night, round the side of the building to where I cannot see. I know that there is a field, bordered by the forest of barren black trees, and it is in this field that I suppose the vultures must find sustenance of some sort, for I hear them hissing and screeching, their signature steam engine growl reaching all the way up to my ears through the barred window. I refuse to consider the possibility of what they could be fighting over . . .

Whilst I fight to keep my wits, my heart breaks for those who have lost them. A Chaser is prodding a girl with his baton. She huddles further into the corner, and, despite the torment, makes no sound.

'What's wrong with her?' I ask the inmate across from me.

'Don't know . . . she never speaks. "Silent Sarah" we calls her, don't know her real name. Deaf mute. Don't try and touch her, she goes wild at that. Best stay clear altogether. She's a thief too. Protect your valuables.'

I laugh at her last words, but not at the inmate in the corner, for, when at last she rises, I see that she is the tallest woman I have ever beheld.

Day after day, Silent Sarah sits in her corner, ignoring all, her towering frame hunched to the size of a child, long, unruly hair pulled over her face. But when the inmates round her surrender themselves to their drugged slumber, she goes to them, one by one, and searches the straw beneath them for their stolen spoons. Thieving any she finds, she then retreats, hiding the utensils under her own bedding. If a girl should wake to catch her in the act, Silent Sarah will lunge forwards, hissing ferociously, then rush back to her corner, the spoon still in her possession. Most are resigned to the loss of the occasional treasure rather than incite her to violence, for her height alone intimidates.

Sleep is a luxury I do not often indulge in, for Silent Sarah scrapes at the ground to no purpose, making rasping noises into the wee hours. I wish she may find peace so that I may find it as well.

I have begun to hear the grinding of the wheels even during the day, when the Cart is nowhere near. I also find myself counting heads at breakfast each morning. It could be any one of us, at any time, and there are so many ways to die . . .

Asylum Letter No. XXXVII

The shaving of the Captain's head has made a profound impact upon the inmates of both wards as word spread of the shocking scene. Every girl wonders if it could happen to her, for our hair is all we have left.

I had suggested that we ought to arrange some sort of gesture for the Captain to welcome her back to us once she was released from Quarantine. Perhaps, I thought, we might all donate a bit of our own hair, since she no longer had any.

I have not shared this with the girls, but a strange theory has taken root in my mind, Diary, and it's twisted branches grow stronger with each drop of attention I turn to it. I wonder if the fallen hair that convinced the maids, as well as Madam Mournington, that the Captain had contracted some disease of the scalp and must be shaved, was not, in fact, the Captain's hair at all. Indeed, it was of a similar texture, and the colour was the same, but I suspect that the locks had been added to her own by artifice. I base this belief upon my observation that, when the hair came loose, it seemed simply to fall away as though it had never been attached. Perhaps it was indeed a form of madness that compelled her to collect stray strands and conceal them amongst her own, but, as it was clearly of such great importance to her, the cause did not matter to me.

The girls were willing, and so we settled upon the following plan: Each inmate was to part with a bit of hair, which we could then weave together into a single braid. Offering to assist, the Plague Rats used their blade-edged incisors to sever the small amount required from each.

I began with my own; once I had a thin braid measuring the length of my arm, Veronica wove her long, dark strands into my red ones and continued it. We kept hold of one end of the rope as Sir Edward took the other in his teeth and carried it to our neighbors. It was in this way that the braid grew in length, lacing in and out of the bars from cell to cell, a silken cord of many colours. When the last inmate had added her bit from the far end of the corridor, I reeled the completed cord back into my cell, coiled it, and hid it inside the little rat hole in the corner that was already inhabited by my precious spoon, which the league had carried back to me after I had been forced to leave it inside my mattress in Ward A. Thankfully, the rats had been good enough to bring my silver pencil as well, for, had they not, this narrative would have ended abruptly.

Less than a fortnight had passed when we were herded through the Ward Hall after breakfast and found our Captain sitting at her usual spot before the window. She was almost unrecognizable; her hair was still closely cropped, having only begun to grow back, and her scalp showed open sores where it had been rubbed raw by a dull razor. She was thinner than ever, and her protruding spine was bent as though she had not the strength to hold herself upright. The Captain's eyes were bandaged to protect them from the light after weeks in the pitch black of Quarantine, and I supposed that the rats had shown her this kindness, as surely no one else would have.

Upon seeing her, the girls squealed in elated surprise, but the Captain clapped her hands over her ears; she had not heard voices in such a long time that her senses were stunned by the sudden presence of them. I hushed my sisters and went to retrieve the braid; approaching the Captain, I gently took her hand so as not to frighten her. I ran the braid over her open palm, and she closed her fingers round it.

hospital entry 22:
electroconvulsive therapy

I have spent my life trying to stay out of Electroconvulsive Therapy, a.k.a. Electric Shock Treatment, a.k.a. ECT.

It's not pretty, they say.

It's not even humane.

But they also say that it, occasionally, works.

Much like Lithium, however, the doctors have no idea why it, occasionally, works. And it really doesn't matter because, by the time you go in for ECT, you have nothing left to lose. It is the last chance of the suicidally depressed—one step before the end—and you'll only get that chance if you happen to be institutionalized at the time, which is not likely to be the case for many suicidally depressed people, most of whom can't even get out of bed.

Besides, the majority of those prescribed the treatment refuse to undergo the process. Think of it like chemotherapy: Many cancer patients feel that the treatment is worse than the death they will inevitably face if they don't get the treatment, and thus choose to discontinue the treatment—my own father felt this way, and made this choice, and, having watched the treatment administered and the torture behind his eyes as it was, I could not possibly blame him.

I have never undergone ECT. I have only smelled the terror rising in those who are led down that path.

Shortly after my imprisonment, I had entered my communal bedroom to find a new inmate huddled upon the bed next to mine. She was clearly anorexic (she, unlike myself, admitted this to the staff, which automatically put her on their good side whilst I remained a dishonest child), but still pretty, with short black hair in a somewhat androgynous cut, which I particularly liked. The girl was reading a book about ECT, one of many on the subject she had stacked upon her bed. She did not look up when I came in.

I understood this perfectly; when coexisting with the clinically depressed, one must become accustomed to being ignored—it is all part of the isolation process, and I am no exception. There are some days when I simply cannot speak. There are a lot of days like that, actually. And, despite my social criticisms of the general approach toward the mentally ill, I do pity the friends of the severely depressed. Despite faking it for the comfort of others most of the time, there are months out of the year when I cannot help but isolate myself, and so I am aware that I will be apologizing constantly for the rest of my life; it is a horrible feeling.

Later that afternoon, I plied a nurse for details about my new roommate. She told me that the girl's name was Chloe, and that Chloe was scheduled to undergo ECT the following morning. The nurse warned me that Chloe didn't talk to anyone, and that I shouldn't be offended when Chloe didn't talk to me.

Back in my room that night, drugged yet no longer reacting to the drugs, I lay awake in the hazy black, waiting for the morning alarm to sound just as I always did. Then, Chloe spoke to me. I was not surprised—I knew that she would.

"You're Emilie, right?"

"Yeah."

"I'm Chloe. I just wanted to tell you that, at four o'clock this morning, the nurses are going to come in and take me to ECT. I wanted to say I'm sorry, 'cause you'll probably wake up with all the noise."

"Oh lord, don't even worry about that. It's more than likely I'll be awake anyway. Four o'clock is the witching hour for manic depressives."

"Oh, OK . . . thanks."

Silence. And then it came.

"I'm really, really scared."

I told Chloe about the session I'd once had with my psychiatrist during which he'd told me all about ECT. He had said that the process (I didn't mention the word "occasionally") worked wonders on people who simply hadn't responded to medication of any sort. I told her that he had also said it didn't hurt at all, and that it really wasn't so bad, which was a lie—the shrink had never said anything of the kind. In fact, he had described how brutal, how painful, and how ineffective the treatment often was, but I didn't see the point in relaying that bit of information. What she needed now was hope.

I asked Chloe why the doctors felt she needed ECT in the first place.

"I'm just really depressed, and I can't function anymore. I can't do anything, and I can't make this depression go away."

"Did anything happen to trigger your depression?"

"No, nothing. I just . . . got sad. I can't go back home because I'll just lie in bed all day and cry. Nothing has helped, and the doctors don't know what else to do. I want to get the treatment—people say I don't want to get better, but I really do. I wasn't always like this, you know. I actually used to be a really happy person. I don't want to be this way, but I'm still really scared. I've read all these books about ETC, but they haven't made me feel any better. Oh god, I am so scared . . ."

Chloe began to cry.

"Listen to me, sister," I said. "You are going to be OK. In fact, you are going to be better than OK. You are going to go into that ECT room tomorrow, and you are going to kick ECT's ass. You are going to be so tough, and so strong, and so OK, and I will tell you why: because *I* need you to be OK. I need you to come back and tell me that it was fine, and easy, and that you feel better, because someday *I* will need to get ECT, and *I'm* going to be scared, and so I need *you* to be OK so that you can tell *me* that it's OK. Can you do that for me?"

"Yes."

Chloe calmed down and began to talk more freely, just as any normal person would who wasn't about to get her brain violently shocked into oblivion. She asked me why I had been committed, and, this time, I could tell the story like it really happened. Chloe had never attempted suicide and couldn't imagine doing so, even as depressed as she was. She thought it was sad that I had to go through this alone, a fact that seemed as though no one else had even noticed. At least her family supported her, she said, and was waiting for her to come home as soon as she possibly could. They hadn't given up on her.

I was beyond being jealous—I have no real feelings anymore. I am growing more anesthetized with every passing day, and it terrifies me. Will the numbness go away once I get out of here? And what if it doesn't? Will I ever be able to *create* again?

"Do you feel like being here is helping you?" Chloe asked.

"God, no. If anything, it's making me worse. I have to fake that I'm all right all the time just to get through the day. Everyone is flipping out around me, and I refuse to give in to that. Observing the freak show only forces me to stay collected."

"But have you tried just being open? Letting yourself 'flip out' if you need to? That's what we're all here for—to let it out, to be completely natural in a safe place. It might actually help you."

"That's the problem though. This isn't a safe place."

Had Chloe remained in Ward B for more than a single night, she would have known that. But I didn't want to defend myself, and I didn't want to argue. And besides, she was right. We *are* here to give it all up—to be naked (sometimes literally), open, free of social constraints, and even free of the laws that demand that we contain ourselves, not hit people, not throw things, which is ironic because, for many of us, it was the law that demanded that we be here in the first place.

But I can never put down my shield as the other inmates do, and, no wonder—I never feel safe; most of the others are either too witless to feel the danger, or else they are the cause of it. And maybe it all makes more sense than I had thought: Take a suicidal girl and put her in a war zone—some place where she can think of nothing but survival just to get through breakfast. Maybe there's method in this madness after all.

Chloe and I didn't sleep that night. We talked about everything from what kind of music I made to the Hollywood goth clubs that she used to frequent when she had been happy. I told her that I always ended up dancing on a table, and she told me that she always ended up taking off her shirt.

At four o'clock, the nurses came. Chloe got out of bed, and so did I. She was shaking. I held her tightly and told her that I loved her. She told me she loved me too. Then, Chloe switched off; she put her head down, went limp, and let the nurses fold her into the wheelchair they had brought to take her away.

Once Chloe was gone, I tore the corner of the previous day's Asylum letter into the shape of a heart. Upon the heart, I wrote Chloe a note. I told her that, soon, when she got out of here, she was to go directly to the club we had talked about. There, I wrote, she would find me dancing on a table, and she'd better be prepared to take her shirt off.

I never saw Chloe again.

Asylum Letter No. XXXVIII

Much of what Dr. Stockill does in his Laboratory remains an utter mystery to me. I know that he is mixing his chemicals and composing our medicines, our sleeping pills, our purges, our injections, our strangely coloured—and even more strangely smelling—tonics, yet I also know that there is something more than this.

The Superintendent is always watching us. When we are out at the Bathing Court, I never fail to spot him looking down at us from his Laboratory window high above the wards.

Since my incarceration, Dr. Stockill has rarely visited our wards, instead ordering the Chasers to deliver us to him for 'treatments'. But there has been a change. When we are locked up for the night, Dr. Stockill is now heard stalking the corridors, his step slow and deliberate as his speech, shining his torch into our cells with all the covertness of a grave robber. There, he searches for, and snatches away, any girl who suits his unknown purpose.

The inmates that the Doctor selects never return to the wards, though it took us some time to determine this with absolute certitude, such is the vastness of our establishment. During our peregrination to the Bathing Court one morning, we witnessed the bodies of several recently disappeared inmates being hastily removed from Dr. Stockill's Laboratory by a bevy of Chasers. The dead girls were covered in bloody lesions, their faces twisted in anguish almost beyond recognition; they had not died peacefully. No, there is no doubt of it—being selected by Dr. Stockill is a girl's last stop.

What does he want?

I have studied his interactions with the other doctors—not only with Dr. Lymer, but also with our visiting surgeons who perform the necessary removal of things that are not . . . wanted. Dr. Stockill feels superior to them—I can see that. He is disgusted by their vulgar methods—I can see that too. And yet, he cares not what the others do with us so long as it does not interfere with his experiments, nor does he care what is done with us once these experiments are carried out and we are no longer of use to him.

We supply the Doctor with a ready store of bodies—that is all. He may select one of his desired age, desired race, eye colour, build, and so forth, and then test whatever it is he is testing, a fact I desperately wish I knew.

Or do I?

Asylum Letter No. XXXIX

Do you remember, Diary, the day I was first introduced to the Superintendent? I had spotted a coruscating object within his cabinet, behind the bottle of green liquid. Whilst I could not then identify the object, I have since learnt, and learnt well: The thing is a sort of fleam, but not at all like the rude varieties that Dr. Lymer is so very fond of. No indeed, this elegant weapon is designed to rest gently in the palm of the hand, the silver shaft engraved with intricate motifs encircling the Doctor's monogram: 'M.S.'.

Now for the interesting bit: When a hidden latch upon the end of the handle is triggered, a series of spring-loaded blades shoot out from the side, spreading open like a lady's fan, and all in half a second. The Doctor may then select a blade from the assortment and tuck the others away. Numbering seven in total, each blade is different from the next. One is thin and double-edged, with a blunted tip like a shaving razor; another resembles the fleams I have known before, with a pointed chisel protruding from the blade. Still another twists into a winding screw at the tip, whilst another is curved like a hook at the end. This exquisite instrument appears to combine, in miniature, all of the necessaries for ordinary operations in a form that Dr. Stockill finds palatable, such is its vicious yet feminine delicacy (traits that we women combine so well).

This device has been applied to my flesh a dozen times now, for, though he seems sickened to do it, it is, apparently, necessary for the Doctor to cleave our flesh in order to deposit his chemical concoctions directly into our bloodstreams.

In flagrant contrast, Dr. Lymer delights in watching our blood flow—he makes no secret of it. In the demeanor of the visiting doctors, there is always a relish with which they perform their operations that is monstrous, yes, but there is something right in that: A mad man does a mad thing and he madly enjoys it. But not our celebrated Superintendent; I have never seen him show a speck of sorrow, nor of joy. I cannot read him, and this is what frightens me.

Asylum Letter No. XL

I have been called into Dr. Stockill's private chamber yet again. It is peculiar . . . though we are all subjected to the chemical experiments he administers in his Laboratory upstairs, he seems to call me, and me alone, into his chamber downstairs—the very same in which I was first accosted by those darkling eyes nearly seven years past—only to inject me with a multitude of serums and speak to me in his impenetrably phlegmatic manner, as though my thoughts were worth anything, for, after all, I am a lunatic.

'Tell me, Emily, with no last name, are you suffering here in the Asylum?'

'I'm sorry, Doctor?'

'It is a simple question which demands a simple answer: Are you suffering?'

'Only as much as the rest, Doctor.'

'And do you still think of death? Of taking your own life, I mean?'

'I have not the luxury to think of it. We are well guarded, Doctor.'

'Others have managed it.'

'I am afraid to leave those that would remain.'

I wished I had not said that last.

'Why should you care for them? They are the filth that paved the streets.'

'Why should they care for me? I am no better. And yet they do.'

'You would endure this suffering for the company of whores?'

'I would, Doctor.'

Dr. Stockill is clearly seeking some information from me, and I am too daft to know what it is.

hospital entry 23: credibility

It is impossibly easy to get committed—getting out is the hard part.

Most of the inmates here either see Jesus or think they are Jesus.

And me?

Well, I only find letters from a parallel universe waiting for me in my notebook every morning—a universe that is becoming ever more indiscernible from my own. I am even beginning to forget whether my name is spelled with an "ie" or a "y."

Worse, I feel a manic state rising within me, and each day I feel an ever greater desire to cut myself.

But isn't cutting something that attention-starved teenagers do—an act that lies within that fuzzy gray area between a cry for help and a desperate attempt to look dangerous, and, therefore, cool? Yes, that's what I thought too, until I found myself locked in the bathroom several times a day and most of the night, razorblade in hand. Which bathroom it was didn't seem to matter to me—home, coffee shops, friend's houses, they were all more than sufficient.

I have never taken a drug that wasn't prescribed; I have never smoked a cigarette; I have never been addicted to anything except the sight of my own blood and the pain that comes with it.

What nobody seems to understand is that this behavior is not the *cause* of the illness—it is the *result* of it.

Now, I know that it is extremely commonplace to confuse the symptom with the disease. Perhaps it is the desire in people to look for the easiest, cleanest, least scary answer. Scotland Yard would call this lazy detective work, and I would agree, because I AM TELLING YOU ALL WHAT IS WRONG, AND YOU REFUSE TO ACCEPT IT!

I am more self-aware than it is healthy for anyone to be—the internal dialogue is deafening. I know *precisely* what is wrong with me, and I can explain it in brutal, unvarnished clarity if anyone cares to listen, but the fact is that, once you've been prescribed a psychiatric drug, you have lost all credibility, and this is *before* you've been committed, after which it's all over for you. You no longer know what is wrong with yourself, what is good for yourself, or, rather, you do, but civilized society does not think so, and where is the power?

In numbers.

I am only *one*, and I am *crazy*.

Oh, and I'm also a girl, which is never a plus in any situation. Children are children; lunatics are children; women are children. This is, after all, why markets and pharmacies stock the feminine products right next to the baby products. Think I'm reading too much into this? Well, fuck you. We know nothing about anything, least of all ourselves and our bodies.

I am beginning to understand what might make a mental patient smash a guitar against a nurse's booth.

Asylum Letter No. XLI

It is now three weeks since we were honoured by the presence of one Dr. Ramage, whose defining characteristics include a crossed eye, a weak chin, and a religious fanaticism bordering on mania.

At the start of Dr. Ramage's visit, he had been allowed to inspect each inmate's commitment form, and had determined to do the Lord's work by removing the uterus of every girl who had attempted suicide—an ambitious undertaking that he was fortunately unable to carry out in full before his stay was up.

However! I should like to request a parade in my honour, for I have now the sole distinction of being the first inmate of the Asylum for Wayward Victorian Girls to live longer than ten days after the surgical removal of her uterus. It was stolen from my body via abdominal incision, and was as painful as you may imagine it would be, yet I regret to say that I've endured worse.

Sir Edward has collected for me an assortment of lovely papers to write upon as a *get well* gift, and, if I am to suffer from the fatal infection that my predecessors have, I am committed to my writing until the end, and I have decided that my last written word shall be *degringolade*, for no other reason than that I have always thought it quite a silly one, and have been saving it up for a very special occasion.

Will I miss it, my little uterus? I suppose I shall, as, once I realised what I was in for, I christened her Victoria, in tribute to our fair institution's namesake, and promised to remember her always.

I should add that I have been warned of Dr. Ramage's intention to return next month, and that, should he find me still melancholy (as though I could exist in any other state), he will be forced to conclude that the cause of my insanity was *not* in fact my uterus (too late), but is instead a demon that, due to my inherent female weakness, has taken up residence in my bloodstream. In that scenario, the cure could only be arrived at by thrice daily bleedings and a religious ceremony performed for the purpose of exorcising the devil.

Before I quit this theme, Diary, and fall face down into my bit of hay, permit me to write a brief discourse upon the subject of Dr. Ramage's bedside manner, or the distinct lack thereof:

The Doctor felt quite passionately about inflicting as much pain as possible during the operation. As I begged for gentleness in the name of all that was merciful, he explained to me quite calmly that childbirth is painful only because God intended it should be so as a punishment to all women (the falling of Eve and such), and so, obviously, pain connected with *any* female part related to the process of childbirth, which would include all of them, should be endured to its fullest, with no attempt made towards its alleviation in any way.

Wholly convinced by such a watertight argument, I lay back and listened as Dr. Ramage fumed over the theories published recently by a fellow called Darwin. It seems they are to do with *evolution*, and, besides the idea that all species advance and develop through a sort of 'weeding out' of the inferior specimens so that the strong may survive and reproduce, this Darwin's theories propose, to the great vexation of all good Christians, that we are not in fact descended from Adam and Eve, but from monkeys instead.

It was all I could do to stop myself telling the good Doctor that, whilst women may indeed have evolved from monkeys, men have not evolved at all.

Asylum Letter No. XLII

There has been talk amongst the Chasers that we are to welcome a new addition to the Asylum staff. He is rumoured to be a surgeon, news that is welcomed by none of us.

The new doctor has come. We are all dreadfully curious to learn more of our latest caregiver. He arrived in a hansom cab this morning, causing quite a clatter as an inordinate number of trunks and cases were carried into the Asylum and up the stairs to the old Operating Theatre—a great, circular hall in the center of the institution, which has long lay in disuse.

Under a former superintendent, the Theatre had been the silent witness of countless dissections performed by the Asylum surgeons of yesteryear for both the education of visiting students and the entertainment of inquisitive aristocrats. Dr. Stockill had no desire to teach, and we had not a legitimate surgeon of our own (though Dr. Lymer does his very best to cut us open at every opportunity), and, thus, the Theatre had been shut up. Now, our new arrival's possessions are being carried in, and I wonder what the next act will be . . .

MADAM MOURNINGTON
LETTER NO. 1

To: Augusta Mournington
The Mourning Room Tea House
Coventry
From: Prudence Mournington-Stockill
The Asylum F.W.V.G.
London

My Dear Augusta,

I fear I am not well, and, at my age, one never fears, but knows.

There are things here to trouble my poor mind . . . dark, dirty things.

I have begun to have trouble sleeping again, such as I have not suffered since my Violet died all these years ago.

The Asylum has newly appointed a surgeon called Greavesly, and I have newly appointed a strong dislike for him, though I dare not oppose Monty upon such matters, and keep silent, attending to my duties as mistress of these wicked girls as I always do.

I need quiet—more quiet—and perhaps a rest.

But Monty . . . could I leave him alone?

Surely not, the funny lamb . . . he cannot seem to go a day without me.

Is it not a wonderful thing to be needed?

Your affectionate sister,

Prudence

Asylum Letter No. XLIII

The Asylum's latest addition is indeed a surgeon, and his name is Dr. Gower Greavesly, which is a perfectly hideous name if you ask me, fit only for a gravedigger or an undertaker. Or a surgeon.

I have just now returned from my first examination by this Dr. Greavesly, and am none the better for it.

A Chaser had escorted me to the Theatre, in the center of which stands a large wooden slab. This is the operating table. Lining the circumference of the Theatre are tiers of balconies providing a disgracefully clear view of the performance taking place upon the floor below to all spectators.

Grey and ghastly figures watched me from the balconies, but I have become accustomed to the ghosts. No, what frightened me was the thought of those very real people who used to fill these galleries, and who may soon do so again, waiting with gruesome delight for the victim below to be dissected—the best show in town. The vision sent chills through me, and I chided myself for being susceptible to chills at this point.

On smaller tables scattered about the room lie rows of surgical instruments, set out seemingly for the sole purpose of display. The tools are far more threatening than Dr. Lymer's blades and bleeding machines, for these new blades are not crafted to cut through mere flesh, but to sever bone as well.

There are saws with jagged teeth, long knives that seem to belong more to a slaughterhouse than a hospital, pincers, pliers, and metal drills with bloodstained handles.

Along the shelves lining the Theatre walls are specimen jars in sundry sizes containing organs submerged in a pale pink fluid; at first glance I identified a brain, a heart, something that I believed to be a kidney, a human fœtus, and an entire arm. There are several empty jars as well—whom are they waiting for, I wonder?

Nails jutting from the wall hold three aprons, stiff with gore. Gazing upwards, I spotted several rusty hooks attached to heavy chains hanging from the vaulted ceiling. The surgeon has made quick work of decorating, hasn't he? But *three* aprons . . . that means he has brought assistants. Not good.

Dr. Greavesly was waiting for me, and I will give you, Diary, my first impression of him:

The surgeon is neither young nor old. He is of a sinuous build, lean of limb, but with surprising strength, a stealthy gait, and a feline spirit coiled like a spring. Of a twitching temperament, he turns often to sedative substances—both opium and spirits during my first appointment alone—in order to steady his hands which display long fingernails trapping filth beneath as though he had been digging in the dirt. He sports a prodigious quantity of red, wild hair, though not as red as mine. With an animalistic nature more feral than tame, I suppose he is what a clever one might call 'mercurial', and I imagine that his heart beats rapidly all the time.

My examination had been brief, but thorough. My shift was torn away, and I stood in my stockings before the surgeon as he passed his nervous hands over me, showing particular attention to my abdomen. I knew what he was looking for, and what he will never find again.

MADAM MOURNINGTON
LETTER NO. 2

To: Augusta Mournington
The Mourning Room Tea House
Coventry
From: Prudence Mournington-Stockill
The Asylum F.W.V.G.
London

My Dear Augusta,

I fear a dark day ahead.

I dream that my infant daughter is alive before me. She is wearing the wretched costume of our ungrateful lunatics—the tiny stockings fit perfectly to her bonny toes. She plays with a peach and laughs, her darling smile just as I remember it, but then she shows me the fruit and I see that it is rotten, the pit crawling with worms.

I wake in a panic, my head swimming in that unmistakable scent that surrounded my Violet when the angels took her, yet before that precious ability to detect all odor was burned from me entirely. It was a sweet perfume, this last I ever experienced—like almonds or cherries—and I believe it to have been the scent of the angels, but in my dreams it is choking me.

I wonder if you would let me come and visit for a little while? Perhaps I simply need a rest, and some quiet.

Your affectionate sister,

Prudence

Asylum Letter No. XLIV

We are told that Dr. Greavesly has been brought to the Asylum to enact reforms, and he appears to be wasting no time.

The surgeon has spent the past fortnight examining inmates and cataloguing us into a red leather-bound book of considerable proportions. I have not seen what he writes, but I do know that he does not document our names, instead referring to us only by our cell numbers (I've become accustomed to having no last name, but this is ridiculous). Those of us who share a cell are differentiated by the addition of a letter following our cell number. Thus, my home address is:

The Asylum for Wayward Victorian Girls
Ward B, Cell Block W14
Patient A

My name is simply W14A.

Veronica is W14B, and the Captain, who has been housed in our cell since returning from Quarantine, is W14C.

And, lest we should ever forget, the surgeon's assistants have permanently branded our upper right arms with these classifying codes by means of a simple needle and black ink.

With hundreds of inmates now tattooed like criminals, we are easy to identify, and no one need bother us with a proper name ever again.

People have names, and we are not people.

We are bodies.

Numbered parts.

Nothing more.

Asylum Letter No. XLV

Thrice now have I been summoned back to Dr. Greavesly's Operating Theatre. The first I have already spoken of; the second was much the same, though I was obliged to endure an invasive physical examination as well, and was introduced to an array of tools designed specifically for this purpose, though one would never guess it by the injuries they cause. *Bloody hell*, I thought, as I lay upon the operating table, *would it have killed someone to warm these things up first?*

I should have felt pain, but everything has become pain to me, and thus little is worthy of note. I should also have felt shame, or at least indignity, but dignity is dead, and shame implies the loss of a thing I have not had for some time.

My third examination took place this morning. As usual was I led by a Chaser into the Theatre and shoved inside, the door locked behind me, but, this time, Dr. Greavesly was nowhere to be seen. I looked about, wandering amongst the tables, my inquisitive fingers grazing the tools of the surgeon's abattoir. Each device I touched filled my head with the screams of its previous victims; they were deafening, and I put my hands to my ears.

Violently was I roused by a loud crashing close behind me. I turned to see a young man hastening to pick up the shattered bits of a glass pane. He had, evidently, emerged from behind one of the heavy moleskin curtains that shielded the storage areas from the greater part of the room.

I inspected the young man with a thorough eye. He could be a new surgical assistant in training with Dr. Greavesly, which would make him my natural enemy. Yet he looked nothing like the others; where their features were monstrous and mean, his were refined, even inviting. *This is what a gentleman ought to look like*, thought I, and I felt sure, quite sure, that, whatever he was, he did not intend to harm me.

'I'm awfully sorry,' he said, his fair face flushed. 'You startled me . . . I did not hear you come in.'

'And how could you?' said I, looking down at my stocking feet, noting with dismay the threadbare knees and tattered toes where my flesh peeked through. 'We're not allowed any shoes.'

The stranger appeared somewhat taken aback by my words, but then he smiled.

'Well, then,' he said, 'I ought to clear this blasted glass off the floor at once, or you're sure to cut yourself.'

Having collected the larger pieces, he rose and went in search of a broom. Seeing an unchained being, someone who did not belong here—who was not part of the institution or at least did not appear to be—made me all the more aware of my imprisonment.

'How lovely it would be . . .' I said, haltingly, feeling suddenly awkward. I wished I were not so dirty. I wished I were not so thin.

'I beg your pardon, Miss?'

'How lovely it would be,' I began again, 'if all that cuts me could be swept away by your broom.'

Goodness, what a fool I sounded. The young man stopped his sweeping.

'I'm afraid I don't understand you,' he said, an apology in his voice.

Just then, a door slammed, and Dr. Greavesly stormed in from the other side of the Theatre, the thud of his heavy boots reverberating off the lofty ceiling. His arms were loaded with willow branches and sundry forage, and I concluded that, already, this had been the most peculiar examination yet.

I had prepared myself for that sickening moment wherein Dr. Greavesly would lift me onto the operating table, but he did not. Instead, he ordered the young man to arrange what he called an *apparatus* in front of a large screen that had been draped with swaths of sheer muslin.

I watched as my new acquaintance positioned a wooden box with a sort of bellows attached atop a tall, three-legged stand. He had beside him the remainder of his glass panes, and was fitting one of them into the back of the box. After looking closely into one end, he adjusted the bellows, which tilted the front of the box away from the back. A black cloth was then laid over the entire contraption.

Meanwhile, the Doctor had piled his mass of flora onto the operating table, seemingly oblivious to my presence as he laid out the foliage like so many surgical instruments.

At last, both men had finished their mysterious preparations. Calling me by my cell name of W14A, which embarrassed me somewhat though ordinarily I scarcely notice, Dr. Greavesly demanded I follow him. When I hesitated, he took hold of my arm and pushed me down onto a low chaise placed before the screen, leaving the marks from his dirty fingernails behind.

'Stay perfectly still.'

'Yes, Doctor.'

'I am going to place these flowers upon your head, and you are not to touch them.'

'Yes, Doctor.'

Am I to revise my role as the mad Ophelia so soon? I wondered.

The surgeon had selected a handful of poppies and attempted to weave them through my tangled hair, but his twitching hands were ill equipped for a task of such delicacy, and I dreaded to think what they would do with a surgeon's knife. At last, he succeeded in piling an assortment of greenery atop my head, but, upon standing back to review his work, was displeased, and angrily swept the entire arrangement away before stalking back to his chair beside the young man, who was busy peering into the box and making adjustments.

'I haven't got the eye for this sort of thing at all, Thomas.'

'The name is Thomson, Dr. Greavesly.'

'Details. By any name, you're a delicate sort of chap I daresay; perhaps *you've* got the touch.'

Seemingly unsure of whether he ought to thank the Doctor for the insult or curse him for the compliment, Thomson— whether that was his first name or his last I did not know— hesitated.

'Well, go on, I don't *think* she bites,' prodded the Doctor. 'Or perhaps you'd care for an opium cigarette first. I find they help me in my work. Steadies the hands.'

Declining the opium, Thomson moved from behind his contraption and stepped towards me. He bent to retrieve the poppies strewn about by the frustrated surgeon.

'I seem destined to reside upon the floor today,' he said, as one wishing to lighten a grave situation.

Then, Thomson was standing beside me, so close that I could hear his heart beating against his chest. *He really is quite young*, I thought. We have seen very few young men at the Asylum—they have not the heart for it, or perhaps they have too much.

'Do forgive me,' said Thomson.

He took a very deep breath, then twined a poppy through the knotted hair above my right ear. His fingers trembled slightly; I pretended not to notice. Thomson seemed pleased with the blossom's placement, for he continued on, and soon had every stem of vegetation back upon my head, yet, apparently, in a far more becoming manner, for, after some moments in the company of his opium, the surgeon leapt forwards.

'Why, Thomas,' he exclaimed, 'you're an absolute artist, just as your old Bryson said you were. It's no wonder the Queen has her royal eye upon you, the old bird . . .'

'It's Thomson, Dr. Greavesly.'

'So you claim. But don't you think we ought to disguise that unsightly mark somehow? Turn the slut to the other side, perhaps?'

I flinched at his ugly word, and so did Thomson.

'That heart-shaped scar, you mean? I must confess I disagree with you, Dr. Greavesly. To my eye, the scar is the very soul of the portrait. It shows a history.'

He met my eyes, just the hint of a smile flickering behind his own.

'A past is nothing to be ashamed of, is it?'

Sensing an argument ahead, Thomson added, 'And besides, the light is better on this side.'

'Hmpf! You young romantics find your "soul" in the strangest of places. But you're quite right—I daresay our clientele might have a particular appreciation for battle scars. Carry on, Thomas.'

Dr. Greavesly had been advancing towards me as he spoke in order to better inspect my ancient wound. Now that Thomson had turned his attention back to his wooden contraption, the Doctor dragged his bloodstained hand along my bruised arm and up to my chest; I thought how very different was his touch from the young man's. His long, loose mane was falling over my face; his fingers curled round the back of my neck, pointed thumbnail slowly scraping my scar. I closed my eyes to shut him out, but my ears were under no such government, and I heard too well the rumbling in his throat, like the purring of a great cat. He slid his fingers down to my mouth, pulling my bottom lip painfully, his thumb forcing its way between my teeth, and I turned my head in disgust. His vulgar action sent my thoughts to the Count de Rothsberg, and I wondered why it was that men seemed so desirous of putting their fingers into my mouth.

Dr. Greavesly sneered at me through his long teeth, and, with a low and growling laugh, returned to his chair where he lit another opium cigarette.

He is just like the Count, I thought. *They are of the same breed—our disdain is wasted upon men such as these. They thrive upon it, and our disgust is the sauce they savour it with. I will show him nothing, do what he will.*

Having completed his adjustments, Thomson explained to me that he was going to take my photograph, and that, after the sparks appeared, I must remain completely still until he said it was all right to move again. I knew then that Thomson's wooden box was a *camera*. I had heard of such a device, yet had never seen one, and had certainly never imagined that I should be photographed, especially in an unfortunate setting. I would have loved to have a picture of myself performing upon the stage as I had always dreamt. But I should not be immortalized like *this*. I wanted to run.

My anxiety must have suited me, for, Thomson, pulling the black cloth over the camera as well as himself, said, 'You're posed quite perfectly as you are, Miss. Though, perhaps . . . yes, perhaps you could lift your chin just a bit, and turn your lovely face to the light for me.'

I did so. I wondered if he were satisfied with the result, for he stood gazing at me in silence for a peculiarly long time.

'Yes, I think that's all right,' he spoke at last. 'Please, don't move.'

With one hand, Thomson slid open the camera's shutter. With the other, he lifted a lit taper from the small table beside him and touched the flame to a metal dish laden with a fine powder. Without warning, a bright flash quite blinded me;

this was followed by much smoke and falling ash. I felt an age had passed before Thomson allowed me to move again.

'Thank you,' he said, softly, strangely bashful now that his work was done.

The brilliant burst of light had ignited something deep within me. I felt . . . unsettled.

'I've done nothing,' I said, abruptly.

Unaccustomed to kindness from any man, I almost bristled at it, and was quicker with my reply than I had intended. Dr. Greavesly snubbed out his cigarette and rose from his chair.

'Quite so, you haven't,' he spat. 'I'm afraid I was hasty in my compliments. This poetic pageant of melancholy may delight the pretentious idealists, but the cynics will be bored to tears, and if there is anything Whitechapel has taught me it is that the cynics are our primary patrons, and idealists are always poor. You know Whitechapel, don't you, Thomas?'

'No, I don't. Should I, Dr. Greavesly?'

'Ah, well . . . I suppose you don't go in for that sort of thing, not yet anyway. Now, look here, boy.'

The surgeon was again at my side and tearing at my shift now, pulling it down over one shoulder, revealing enough to make Thomson blush.

I was sick inside, yet I kept my vow not to show it.

Dr. Greavesly had forced me to one side of the chaise until I was leaning clear off the edge; my flowers began to fall.

I must have had something of my dignity left after all, for it had been offended. I glared directly at my antagonist.

'Yes!' shouted the surgeon, taken of a sudden passion. '*That* has a touch of madness in it. Thomas, my boy! Capture *that!*'

Thomson had been watching Dr. Greavesly handle me, and I believe I saw upon the young man's countenance the uneasy look of someone torn between two courses of action.

The surgeon stepped away from me to allow the camera full view. Thomson could see my face, and, no doubt, my fury. Something had inflamed him as well, for he quickly slid a fresh pane of glass into the camera, and added more powder to the plate.

'Stay as you are!' Thomson said. 'It's real. It's perfect. *This* is how I've always imagined Ophelia! No woman would have drowned without a fight . . .'

Dr. Greavesly paced the room in agitated excitement. The second photograph taken, he fell back into his chair and lit still another cigarette.

'Dear, young, naive Thomas . . . today we have begun a new chapter in a very old book, and *that*,' he gestured towards me, 'is the image that will sell it.'

Asylum Letter No. XLVI

Dr. Stockill has relocated our colloquies from his chamber downstairs to his Laboratory above, for he seems mystified by my reactions to the injections he has been administering and now requires me to lie upon his table and undergo more invasive treatments.

A change in questioning has taken place as well.

'Let's play a game,' he said.

'What sort of game?'

'It is quite simple. I will ask you a question and you will answer it quickly, and without thinking. This is a test of your cognitive skills under medication. Shall we begin?'

'Have I a choice?'

'That was my first question and your first answer, so it rather seems you have the idea. Let us continue.'

As Dr. Stockill cut my flesh and poisoned my body, he went on to ask the most peculiar questions, all seemingly related to my existence within the Asylum, why I cared for my fellow inmates, how I would attempt escape, and what I would do if I succeeded.

To speak this plainly regarding my dissatisfaction with my treatment was at first strange to me, but the Doctor is well aware of our misery—it is not as though he could be offended, for he knows what he does, and does not wish us any happier, feeling quite strongly that we do not deserve to be. Instead, he seems genuinely curious, and, such is the frequency of these interviews, I find myself conversing more with the man I hate most than to nearly any other person.

MADAM MOURNINGTON
LETTER NO. 3

To: Augusta Mournington
The Mourning Room Tea House
Coventry
From: Prudence Mournington-Stockill
The Asylum F.W.V.G.
London

My Dear Augusta,

I fear I have not the heart for this work.
Yet, have I the heart for other work?
I am well kept here. I am needed. I will harden my heart.

Your affectionate sister,

Prudence

Asylum Letter No. XLVII

From the Asylum stock of approximately two thousand, less than one hundred girls have been selected to be photographed, and I have the peculiar honour of being the only inmate called back to be photographed more than once.

Several portraits have now been taken, and, though being in the presence of the surgeon's leering eyes turns my stomach, I endure it almost willingly, for it allows me temporal freedom from my cell, and also because . . . well, because I have, Diary, grown rather fond of Thomson's company.

The budding photographer has been granted a room of his own in which to carry out his work, as it is necessary for Dr. Greavesly to resume his surgical duties, for which he requires the unobstructed usage of his Theatre.

And yet, I feel unbearably guilty at not being the body upon the operating table—at being loosed from my cage whilst my sisters suffer in its cramped, cold corners. Nevertheless, the fact remains that I am ordered to sit for these photographs—I do not request it, and, should I ask to be relieved of this duty, I would not be allowed, for it is, in fact, arranged by the surgeon himself, though for what purpose I cannot begin to guess. Should I say one word in protest, I would be tossed into Quarantine for my rebelliousness. Wouldn't I?

Now, as I recline comfortably before the camera, warm, with fragrant flowers in my hair and a cup of tea at my side, my shame at being preferred threatens to consume me, and I wonder if it is truly guilt alone that presses this heaviness upon my heart, or, perhaps, fear of any small happiness that I know cannot last. I have lost what little I ever owned, and my sole consolation in this world is that I can lose no more. Yet, by gaining a thing I am afraid to be deprived of, have I not lost this consolation? Perhaps, then, there is *always* more to lose, no matter how little one has to begin with.

Thomson seems ever to be searching in his work—for truth, he says, or reality. He believes that the soul of a person can be photographed if only the subject is willing to share it, provided that the photographer knows how to draw it out. It is not that he despises physical beauty for its own sake—on the contrary, he has the greatest respect for it; I had known this from the moment he twined that first poppy into my hair. It is simply that his is a higher aspiration, and I am glad to assist him in his quest.

'I hope someday to capture people as they are,' Thomson said to me, as I sat before him for the fifth time.

The gloaming was swiftly swallowing up what little sunlight the clouds had allowed us, and there was no longer any chance of a properly illuminated portrait.

'I believe that photography could be used to inspire change. It could tell the truth, and force people to pay attention. I cannot pursue that now, Em, for people want portraits, and portraits alone, but I think that a portrait is a terribly false thing, for what shows in a portrait is little more than a mask made of all that the subject would like the viewer to believe he is.'

'And am I a terribly false thing?' I asked Thomson.

'You,' he said, 'are a terribly real thing in a terribly false world, and that, I believe, is why you are in so much pain.'

Thomson had spoken the single, solitary sentiment I knew to be true, but it seemed a cruel turn to show one her own image when she could not change it.

Tears rolled down my cheeks—great, heavy, hot tears. These were the hopeless tears that Ophelia cried before she leapt into the brook—the tears of every girl who has been pushed too far and cannot find her way back again. I could have filled the Thames with my tears, yet not express half of what was inside me.

My too-honest friend left his post behind the camera and knelt down beside the chaise I sat upon. He wiped away my tears with his pale, intelligent hands, and, for one moment, a moment that would likely never come again, I thought not of survival, but only of my heart.

Asylum Letter No. XLVIII

A horrible day . . .

It began with such cacophony as only Dr. Greavesly can inspire, for all inmates strike their stolen spoons upon the iron bars at the appearance of the surgeon.

The spoons proving quite as ineffectual as one might expect, Dr. Greavesly separated me from my fellow inmates. Clutching his red leather book under one arm, he forced me down the corridor and, to my considerable relief, up the stairs leading from Ward B to the Upper Staff apartments where Thomson's temporary studio was located.

Once inside, the Doctor shouted to Thomson, but received no reply. Shrugging, he released his grip, then recognised that he could not very well leave the door unlocked lest I should escape. Tossing his book upon the desk at which Thomson developed photographs, he searched his pockets for the key. At last, Dr. Greavesly left me, locking the door behind him.

I knew it would not be long before Dr. Greavesly saw what he was missing and came back for it. I bounded to the desk. I touched the buttery leather. I had done this before, but where? The spindly fingers of memory reached out to me from another realm, another lifetime, and I was there, hiding in the attic with Sachiko, drunk on sherry, and opening the volume containing the painted portraits of the girls who had left the school.

The girls who had left the school . . .

Instantly, I knew everything—I had only to lift the cover to confirm it. I did so—oh, despair that I did so—and there they were: page after page of photographs . . . strange photographs . . . followed by records of age, physical characteristics (the deformities of particular girls were actually listed as selling points), assurances of virginity (ha!), and, of course, price. Price per hour.

All of the pretty girls from the Ophelia Gallery were there, and dozens more. Worst of all, the lurid filth commenced with a large card printed with *my* picture, the same that Thomson had taken of me upon that first day—the day that he had shattered glass and I had thought him beautiful. I removed the card from the book and turned it over; upon the back was a notice for a brothel, a house of prostitution—call it what you like—but it was our house. The card was advertising the Asylum.

Through my image, I was helping to sell these girls, my cellmates, my sisters, and myself into the hands of criminals who desire nothing more than the novelty of molesting a mad girl, which is (who knew?) quite a delicacy. I was helping to line the pockets of the doctors, for God knows not a penny of the proceeds would go towards the upkeep of our crumbling institution.

My photographs were featured as the very archetype of what was for sale. The prices were impossibly high, yet also impossibly low. *This is how much we are worth?* I thought. *And how little?* This, the fruit of my hours with Thomson and his camera . . . oh! What had my fair friend done to me? To all of us?

I wrenched the hideous volume from the desk and threw it to the ground; there, I tore through the pages, ripping out any that bore my likeness.

The door crashed open, and in rushed Thomson, out of breath. He bolted to where I knelt and pulled me from the floor.

'I've got to get you away from here! Oh, Em, I've been so stupid . . . God forgive me, I've been so stupid . . . I've been to the city . . . I saw, oh, Em, we haven't time now—you've got to run away from this place!'

I wrested myself from his arms and pushed him away, overcome with rage; the sting of betrayal was a piercing bullet, burning into my chest.

'Emily, please!' cried Thomson.

'Please?' I spat the word. 'Run away? I've got to run away, have I? Well, that's just bloody brilliant! Why in Heaven's name didn't I think of that? And which locked door shall I walk through to my waiting freedom? Which armed guard shall I trot past with a wink and a smile? *Where do you think we are?* Oh, Thomson . . . why did you come here . . .'

I was choking upon a torrent of tears and anger, and could not form the words to express it all.

'Emily, please listen to me—I didn't know!'

'You didn't know? You didn't *know*? How could you *not know*? How much were they paying you to *not know*?'

'They said it was all a study, a sort of experiment, an attempt to prove the humanity of the mentally . . . whatever! I thought it was all for good, I truly did, but I am so sorry, so very sorry . . . I never meant for this to happen, please . . . please believe me . . . I will fix this somehow, Emily, dearest . . .'

Again he tried to hold me close, and, this time, I did not fight him, for I knew it was the last time we would ever touch.

'Please, come with me . . . just come with me . . . I couldn't bear for it to go forwards . . . it simply cannot happen . . . not to you.'

'And what of the rest of us? No, my foolish friend, you cannot fix this, for there is nothing to fix—everything has happened just as it was always meant to.'

I heard myself laughing as I held Thomson's face in my hands, but the sincerity in his clear blue eyes only cut me more deeply, and again I pushed him away.

'And yet, I am to believe you knew nothing? What of this *clientele*? Their *preferences*? You knew nothing? I am a prisoner here. I *am* nothing. I can ask no questions. But you could. And you didn't. Did you think nothing of *that*?'

Thomson sank to the floor, kneeling at my feet, wrapping his arms round me like a child.

'I thought of nothing but you,' he wept.

'Do not say that to me. You have killed me—if not through betrayal, then through your wretched ignorance. One is little better than the other.'

Dr. Stockill entered the room, accompanied by two Chasers, and followed by his mother.

'What is *this*?' cried my Headmistress, clearly astonished to see both the photography equipment and an inmate inside an Upper Staff apartment. Had she not known?

'It's nothing, Mother dearest,' said the Doctor. 'Leave us, please.'

'Monty . . .'

'*Leave us!*'

Indignantly, Madam Mournington swept from the room as the Superintendent turned to the Chasers.

'Quarantine. *Now!*' he ordered.

The Chasers came at me prepared for a fight, but they got none. I held out my hands to be bound, yet I never took my eyes from Thomson. It was he who protested and thrust himself between me and my captors.

'I love you!'

His tortured screams shook the windows, and my stomach lurched, silent sobs stopping my breath.

'*I love you! I love you! I love y—*'

Dr. Stockill stepped forwards and covered Thomson's mouth with a handkerchief; my former friend quickly collapsed. It tore my heart to see this, yet I knew that Thomson was far from dead; I had seen the Doctor subdue many a rebellious inmate in this way. The victim would awaken a day later with a pounding headache, but none the worse. Thomson would be far away by then—it would be too indiscreet to murder him, and also unnecessary, for there were other ways to keep him silent.

I do believe, Diary, that Thomson had not set out to betray me—to betray all of us—yet I could not conceal my resentment at the part he had played, and it was best to say goodbye.

I hope that, someday, he *will* take that picture that will change things . . . that will force people to pay attention. I wish it could have been mine.

MADAM MOURNINGTON
LETTER NO. 4

To: Augusta Mournington
The Mourning Room Tea House
Coventry
From: Prudence Mournington-Stockill
The Asylum F.W.V.G.
London

My Dear Augusta,

I fear sleep.

My dream of my baby daughter comes to me every night, without mercy.

I also see the husband dead only days before my little girl was gone. His face is the cruel one he had in life. He stands before me . . . he does not advance to strike me, yet his stillness is worse, and I wake gasping for air, the odor that exists only in my fevered dreams stifling me.

I wish to tell my son—to seek his counsel and comfort, and perhaps ask him to give me something to calm my nerves, but I can speak to him less than ever now . . .

Oh! My son . . .

I confess to you alone, dear Sister, that I have begun to feel a little afraid of him. You alone know how I have struggled to be affectionate with him always, and perhaps I go too far in this, if only, I suspect of myself, to disguise the strangeness that I have always felt towards him. I have tried, Lord knows I have, and I believe that I have come to love him, though whether it be for lack of anything else to love, I do not know.

Monty dotes upon me like the devoted boy he has always been. But he seems also to have become quite suspicious, and believes that either the servants or I have been in his Laboratory almost daily. His primary concern is that his chambers should not be entered, and he guards himself and his work with a dreadful passion.

Augusta, have I ever told you how, when Monty was a child, I caught him stepping upon snails in the garden just to make Violet scream? I took her up in my arms and ran into our little cottage, the one you were so ashamed to visit. I will never forget how he looked at me when I found him . . . without remorse, without apology . . . he was taking *pleasure* in frightening her. I never saw him do anything so vile again, but then Violet was gone soon after . . . so soon . . . and when I would often find dead rats lined up in perfect rows beneath his bed, or teacups filled with crickets floating in some strange fluid, I always wondered . . . I am surely a horrible mother . . . how could I think such things?

These dreams awaken fragments of myself that I should much prefer to let sleep, and so I keep to my bed and leave the daily running of the Asylum to my son and his staff, appearing only to unlock the Lunatic Wards for the attendants in the morning and to lock them up again at night, for I dare not trust anyone of them with the Ward Key . . . they are vagrant rogues, all.

I desire to be useful again, but I must have a rest first . . . I am not myself.

I should very much like to come and visit you whilst your granddaughter is abroad, for I am afraid it still pains me to be in the company of female children, and I hope you will take pity on me and forgive me my rude request, for I do not think that I shall ever mend.

Your affectionate sister,

Prudence

Asylum Letter No. XLIX

We, the members of the Striped Stocking Society, intend to hold a meeting in the Ward Hall this very evening. We mean to discuss the potential purposes of, and possible strategies to avoid, Dr. Stockill's increasingly lethal chemical experiments. Sir Edward has promised to introduce to us someone who may shed a toothful of light onto the situation, and we are eager to see who it is.

'My dearest Children,' began Sir Edward, 'we, the League, feel that there are truths of which it is time you were aware regarding the wicked plot with which we are all inadvertently connected. We ourselves have been endeavoring to understand the purpose of these deadly experiments that lady and rat alike have been subjected to for a very long time now, but it was not until recently that we were gifted with the very insight we require if we are to formulate any plan of defense. It is, thus, with prodigious pride that I now introduce to you the rat who has made the greatest advances in this quest for knowledge, and at immense peril to his own person. May I present, dear Children, Basil.'

Sir Edward gestured towards a smaller rat, who bashfully shrugged off the attention.

'Oh, Sir Edward, you flatter me, you do,' said Basil, in a brisk Bow-bell Cockney.

Then, he sneezed.

'Oh! Do pardon me, Ladies!'

Another sneeze.

'Ahem! It's quite as 'e says, Ladies. I have passed many a moon within the Laboratory of Superintendent Stockill, an exploit that was said to be impossible—or inadvisable, at the very least—due to the cleanliness and order in which the Doctor maintains 'is surroundings, that order leavin' us "vermin" little chance of obscurity. Nonetheless, due to my native genius for espionage, Basil Basil 'as managed to remain entirely 'idden from view; I've observed the Doctor as he tortured an' killed countless of *both* our kindred species in the name of "discovery", all the while bein' powerless to stop 'im, wee as I am. And make no mistake, Ladies, I *am* strong, but I'm wee, I know I am . . . I would've saved 'em if I weren't so bloomin' wee . . .'

Sneeze.

'Good Ladies, sweet Ladies, all I've witnessed 'as left a stain upon my 'eart that I will bear to the end of my days . . .'

Sneeze. Sneeze again.

"owever! I, your 'umble Basil Basil, am in possession of a medical instrument of my own, and one more powerful than any in Dr. Stockill's Laboratory . . .'

Here, Basil paused, ostensibly for dramatic effect.

'What was your instrument, Mr. Basil?' asked the Captain, suspecting that our honoured speaker was unlikely to continue until *someone* did so.

'I'd 'oped you would ask, Basil Basil did. The instrument, good Ladies . . . is *this!*'

Basil tapped his snout, then sneezed.

'You see, dear Ladies, young Stockill may spend weeks, months, even years testin' 'is formulas, yet what 'e wouldn't give for the decipherin' capabilities of a lowly rodent, for our sense of smell is nearly one million times stronger than that belongin' to an 'uman, meanin' no disrespect to you, Ladies.'

'None taken, Sir—pray go on,' I said, struggling to conceal my impatience.

'What I mean to say', Basil continued, 'is that I 'ave identified the precise ingredients makin' up Dr. Stockill's formulas and matched 'em to diseases rampant within both our institution and society outside. Basil Basil now believes, the *League* now believes, that we 'ave all been mere whetstones upon which the Superintendent 'as been sharpenin' 'is ultimate weapon.'

Allowing Basil to bask in the splendor of his analogy, Sir Edward intercepted his speech.

'And yet, dear Children, like the *whetstone*,' he gestured to Basil, who beamed with satisfaction, 'we are, united, intrinsically stronger than the weapon we are being used to create.'

'YES!' screamed Basil.

A series of sneezes followed this outburst, and Sir Edward explained that prolonged exposure to the Doctor's chemicals had irreversibly compromised Basil's delicate respiratory system.

Having recovered somewhat, Basil continued on to tell us, between sneezes, how, through communication with ship rats arriving in England's ports from more exotic locals, the League had already learnt that the dreaded Plague had hit Asia, and that pockets of Europe had already been infected; millions were dead with more sure to follow. There was growing terror in England that the fatal virus would demolish our own country as well, just as it had during the devastating era of the infamous Black Death; every chemist of note had been experimenting day and night to concoct a cure, though none had yet been successful.

Dr. Stockill had instantly recognized that there lay far more power in the hands of one who could *cause* the Plague than in those of one who could merely cure it, and that to accomplish both would be to control society completely, rendering one a veritable god amongst the entire human race—worshipped and obeyed by all.

Of course, there could be but one way in which Dr. Stockill may insure himself to be the only man with the cure, and this was to create the disease himself.

To that end, he had been systematically infecting the Asylum rats with mutated strains of the bubonic virus in order to measure the effect of the altered illness—first upon the hosts (the rats), and then upon the surrounding population (in this case, the inmates). The Doctor had also been successfully infecting the girls directly for some time, as our Death Pits tragically corroborate, and had sacrificed thousands of us in doing so as he struggled to create an 'improved' form of the virus—a form upon which he could depend to be utterly resistant to any remedy *but his own.*

Quite aware of the dangers his experiments expose himself to, the Doctor wears a heavy black robe as he wanders down our corridor at midnight, his face shielded from pestilence by a mask chillingly similar to those employed five hundred years past, its long, pointed beak packed with protective herbs and oils, the round, screen-covered cavities, ghastly and hollow, lending him the vacant stare of the soulless executioner.

Feeling himself upon the very verge of a cure, he eats little, sleeps less, and paces our darkened halls like a man possessed. But, what is a cure if the disease cannot spread? How to infect the public? How to ensure certain death to all who shun his solution? This is what haunts the Doctor.

Yet, for all of his knowledge, there is but one excruciatingly important detail of which our enemy remains entirely unaware: Dr. Stockill has not yet deduced that it had never been the *rats* spreading the Plague in the first place—the *fleas* stowing away upon the backs of the rats were the responsible party. Therefore, to infect the rats themselves with the aim of achieving an outbreak amongst the human population is a shameful exercise in futility.

'We must use Dr. Stockill's ignorance upon this point to our benefit,' said Sir Edward, 'and we must also do our parts to hinder the successful creation of this "cure", for, once a cure exists, the Doctor *will* find a way to distribute the disease, rats or no rats.'

"ow can we stop 'im?' asked Veronica.

'Disturb his formulas. Tip his vials. And instruct your fellows to do the same. Use your perceived madness to your own advantage, and to the advantage of the entire world.'

Though I longed to be as inspired by Sir Edward's speech as appeared the girls round me, I could not be.

'The world is a wretched place, Sir Edward,' I said, before I could stop myself. 'It was this world that sent us here, after all. Forgive me, but why should we care what happens outside?'

Sir Edward answered me without reproach, yet sternly.

'It matters not *why* you should care, my Lady, for care you do, whether you choose to admit it or not.'

Asylum Letter No. L

Having attempted several times now to disrupt our Superintendent's work as Sir Edward commanded—break his bottles, rearrange his notes—I am now strapped to the table as the Doctor sharpens his chemical weapons upon my body, testing and refining, preparing them for release into their ultimate destination: the world outside.

'Let's play our game.'

'Yes, Doctor.'

'Where would you go?'

'I'd try to run.'

'Who do you know?'

'I . . .'

'Faster.'

'I don't know. I'd tell someone. Anyone.'

'Come now, you're cleverer than that. How would you escape in the first place?'

'I'd use the key.'

'How would you get it?'

'Someday you'll see . . .'

'Is that a threat?'

These are the last words that I remember, for the Doctor has been pushing my body to the limits of consciousness.

How much longer do I have? How many days with the Captain? How many nights with Veronica?

Asylum Letter No. LI

A suite of rooms upstairs has been decorated in gaudy fashion for the pleasure of the 'clientele' Dr. Greavesly had spoken of— the men who visit the Asylum in order to partake of only our finest lunatics; the men who received our adverts and responded as our depraved surgeon had known they would. They want us at our best: wild, in tatters, in tears, and, of course, bound.

I cannot say that being used thus does not affect my mind in gruesome ways, but, rather than breaking me beyond what has already been done, I feel myself hardening—outwardly becoming more resilient whilst, inside, my ability to escape into my own world grows ever stronger.

In my dreams I see another version of myself, or I think it is myself, for I cannot see her face, but I sense the likeness—even her cheek is marked like mine. She is imprisoned too, and she writes as I do, to keep herself from becoming as mad as she is told that she is. Sometimes I can feel her watching me, even when I am awake.

The ghosts have been quiet of late, yet they speak to me now, and I sit with my hands pressed against the weeping walls of Ward B, Cell W14, and feel the stripes stir beneath my palms. I have undergone such a transformation during my nine years within this prison that my demeanor as a victim of this latest offence is one of defiance—I do as I am bid, and I dare them to do their worst.

hospital entry 24: coming down

My surrounding inmates are either shuffling around the Day Room in a sedated stupor or violently attacking both property and people in frightening fits of psychotic rage. There is no one in between besides me, and so I end up standing in a corner by myself, waiting for someone to notice that I don't belong here. Nobody notices.

I am coming down now . . . down from the bouncing, chattering mania of the past week.

Soon I will be so low that they will not be able to pull me out of bed. I look forward to this . . . I want to close my eyes.

I am calm.

I behave myself.

But I have within me that which could tear this place apart . . .

There is a Quiet Room just off the hallway—a padded cell, soundproof, with a tiny, letterbox window, like in the movies. When it is empty, I slip inside and shut the door behind me. I sit, facing the wall, and I know that I don't belong here yet.

But, in a week, I will.

For we do not go to the asylum to be cured. We go to the asylum to die.

This is not the bitter voice of one solitary crazy girl.

This is the truth.

MADAM MOURNINGTON
LETTER NO. 5

To: Augusta Mournington
The Mourning Room Tea House
Coventry
From: Prudence Mournington-Stockill
The Asylum F.W.V.G.
London

My Dear Augusta,

I fear something has gone terribly wrong, and I know not how to right it.

I serve my son, and I exist to promote his genius and all the good that he does for these wayward girls and the whole of society, yet I am not at ease with this new development in commerce within the Asylum.

I realize that those we admit are defective, most often criminal, and, in every single case, a plague upon society itself, and I do believe we treat them better than they deserve, and as well as they could expect. But I had never intended to become the mistress of a house of human traffic. I am quite sure I have this beastly Greavesly fellow to thank, for I know my son could never have authored such a scheme. Surely he is not aware of what is taking place, or he would never support it. I am right to think this, am I not?

I should speak to Monty and tell him what a devil he has hired in Dr. Greavesly, but, in truth, I have come to be afraid of the surgeon, and I dread to think what might happen if I were to cross him, for I know he is a violent man.

Whilst it is my duty to society and to my country to rid the civilized of the feral, to clean the streets of those unclean of mind and body, I cannot stay to watch countless girls, however defective, be abused physically for the institution's profit. And I know . . . I know now that their inevitable and unwanted offspring will be torn from inside them, a week after which they will be up for market again.

None of these girls could possibly deserve this. Not one.

I feel I should be away from the Asylum for a time, until all of this rights itself. I shall arrive in Coventry by the first train next Tuesday.

Your affectionate sister,

Prudence

Asylum Letter No. LII

Daybreak found me peering through the bars as a coach wheeled into the courtyard below. Madam Mournington emerged from the Asylum, and my old friend Maudsley followed her with a traveling trunk. I wonder who will be in command of the Ward Key during her absence . . .

I am disappointed to find that it is Dr. Stockill himself who will be fulfilling our Headmistress's duties and seizing control of the Ward Key. It is no surprise, of course—none of the staff are particularly reliable, not even our other doctors, who frequently disappear to drink or engage in some debauchery or other. Dr. Stockill is the only one who never leaves.

'Let's play our game,' he says . . .

Asylum Letter No. LIII

Whilst we inmates have gained a tormentor in Dr. Greavesly, Dr. Lymer has gained a mentor. He has even been trying his hand at the smaller surgeries, and I fear where this path will lead.

Upon my most recent visit to the Bloodletting Wing, I observed Dr. Lymer as he produced, from a velvet-lined case, a silver spike pointed at one end to the breadth of a needle. He had buckled a screaming inmate to one of the metal bleeding beds, and I watched in disbelief as, with the aid of a heavy mallet, Dr. Lymer drove the tip of the spike directly into the poor girl's forehead. I heard the crack of her skull as it was pierced, and she fell suddenly silent. Though internally frantic, I did my best to pretend calm, recognizing that the more 'hysterical' I appeared, the greater my likelihood of undergoing the same procedure.

As the Doctor revealed to his assistants, he believes that many of the more severe cases of madness are caused by excess pressure being applied to the skull by the swollen brain within. Comparable to the philosophy behind our bloodletting, this being that madness courses through the blood and must be forced out by any means, Dr. Lymer's new theory is that, by puncturing the skull, the internal pressure shall be lessened, and the subject returned to 'normal'.

And God bless Dr. Lymer's eternal optimism, for he has christened the procedure a *lobotomy* and continues to practice the operation upon inmate after inmate, despite the best success the procedure has yet been met with being the ability of one solitary girl to remain alive for a whole week afterwards. During this time, she was perfectly calm and did nothing but lie upon her back and stare at the ceiling, nary a flicker remaining of the complex, sentient, and utterly sane being she had once been.

Of course, this was viewed amongst the medical staff as a great achievement—the patient had indeed been quieted, and, thus, caused no more trouble to anyone. The eventual death of the girl only proved that the operation had not come soon enough.

Asylum Letter No. LIV

Having been dubbed 'The Cell', the Asylum's fledgling flesh-trade has proved a smashing success from its commencement, our photographs having worked their mad charm upon our madder clientele who had already experienced every other diversion the world had to offer.

I have come to the realisation that this undoubtedly illegal operation is inextricably linked with that which governed the Conservatoire, as well as the other factions of which Anne had told me. The reliance upon visual solicitation—first paintings, now photographs—suggests this, and Dr. Stockill's close financial affiliation with the Count de Rothsberg and others of his set confirms it. How much of the world might be connected thus? What secret alliances might be made right under the noses of an unsuspecting public?

By midnight, a light rain was falling outside the barred window of Cell W14, delivering the scent of horses and wet leather from the courtyard below. Several of our fair Ophelias had been 'entertaining' in the dedicated suite, and the temporarily sated gentlemen were just then departing. The Captain and I watched as Maudsley and two more of our Chasers performed their masquerade, escorting our customers from the Asylum, lighting the way to their waiting carriages.

A tall man walked down the front steps under the protection of Maudsley's umbrella. The umbrella was lowered, and the man helped into his carriage. He leant from the window, tossing a disdainful coin to the mock servant, and the Captain's hand gripped my arm; I had seen him too.

The carriages departed, I remained standing at the window beside the Captain, staring out at a cold red moon, for I was afraid to look at her directly. She did not speak, and so I knew that I must.

'You will not believe me, Captain, but that man was an enemy I once knew well.'

The Captain said nothing for a long while.

'It was he you were running from when you leapt from the bridge . . .'

'That is true. But I am not alone in loathing that man, am I?'

The Captain was again silent.

'Despite your admirable self-control, my friend, you seized my arm a moment ago—here is the mark to prove it. And I think I know why.'

'Nobody knows why.'

'I know that you had a sister once, and that she looked just like you.'

The Captain turned to face me, and I saw that her hands were trembling.

'How can you know that? I have never spoken of it.'

'I also know that she was killed, and that, at the time of her discovery, she had upon her head more hair than she was buried with. That day, in the Bathing Court . . . it wasn't *your* hair that came away in the maid's hands . . . was it? And when the servants at Bainbridge gossiped . . . they weren't wrong . . . were they?'

'Please, Valentine . . . don't.'

'Jolie, sweet friend . . . I am not speaking of such things to give you pain. But this man has followed us from that world into this, and, if we are to have any chance of escaping his cruelty once more, we must be honest with one another. We may perish here yet, but it must not be by *his* hand.'

Slowly, the Captain nodded her head.

'I am so awfully sorry for what he did to your sister . . . for what he did to you. If the Count returns, I will do everything I can to keep him from you. You have kept watch for us all these years. Let me keep watch for you now.'

'But he hurt you too.'

'What a man does to an orphaned girl is a terrible thing. What a father does to his own daughters is infinitely worse.'

'I fell asleep . . .'

'I know.'

I settled upon my straw and held up my hand to her. The Captain lowered herself, and, after a brief hesitation, lay her head upon my lap. Within moments, I knew, from her deep and steady breathing, that she was sleeping at last.

Asylum Letter No. LV

Insanity is on the rise, or so they say, and a witch-hunt for the mad is spreading its poisoned shadow over the country.

Obsessively devoted to their cause, the medical community had first convinced the county heads, and their church officials, that they must increase their vigilance in the watch for any lunatics lying hidden in their boroughs; in turn, the counties and churches instructed their flocks, commoners and gentry alike, to observe their fellow citizens for any sign of madness—any small deviance from the social norm. Ripe for a panic, the public has complied.

Upon receiving word, the local police swiftly dispatch a madhouse representative to sequester the accused for the well-being of all, and thus the people are always on their guard, fearful of being watched as they are watching others.

The acquaintances of these supposed lunatics are not accurately told what will become of the abducted, and those who point their self-righteous fingers at their neighbors never regret their hasty act, for they never learn the true consequence of what they have done.

It is frighteningly commonplace for families to accuse their own, for they have been assured that any hope of rehabilitation lay entirely in early detection, and removal from the home.

The important thing is that the mentally unwell are going to receive treatment. What sort of treatment, and what exactly is in need of treating, is of little significance, for is it not always safer to err upon the side of caution?

The country's insane asylums have eagerly taken advantage of the public's predilection towards fear, and are only too glad to accept the nominal sum they have been offered by our government for each new patient accepted into their care. Naturally, this financial incentive encourages many less-than-upstanding superintendents to commit a greater number of patients than they can reasonably house, and many more than they can even pretend to care for.

As for the Asylum for Wayward Victorian Girls, we too are crowded with the influx of new inmates, and this only increases the neglect, the violence, and the unsanitary conditions for all.

Collectively, we know that it is impossible to maintain even the semblance of a proper hospital under these circumstances. There must be a public outcry against it; somehow, the people must know. Something must change.

Asylum Letter No. LVI

The Asylum is in something of a tumult, for the Royal Lunacy Board will soon be visiting the institution to perform an inspection of our building, our grounds, and our methods of caring for the mad.

Annual inspections are usually no great cause for alarm to the staff. Our honoured guests whip their horses up the steep incline towards our monument to misdirected funds, and are then led into the Entrance Hall where the subterfuge of artificial architecture and servants play-acting as patients will impress them with the civility of our establishment. Look how much care has been taken to beautify the institution! Look how gentle and subdued are its inmates! A good lunch in Dr. Stockill's quarters, and several bottles of the Asylum's best port later, and the Board is generally delighted to affix their seal of approval and trot along home, spreading the good word, and leaving the Superintendent to run his enterprise as he wishes, until the next visit.

This time will be different.

This is no routine review of the facilities and the relative health of its patients; people in the city below have spotted the vultures circling above our grounds, and have begun to inquire.

I pray that this is our chance—that someone will come and look closer at last. All they need do is open their eyes, and we will be free.

Asylum Letter No. LVII

Earlier this afternoon, a cart drawn by all of six great Shire horses drove through the Asylum gates, conveying an enormous wooden crate. It took ten of our Chasers to get the thing inside, and, once done, we endured several hours of the clanging and hammering that echoed up to us from the basement before quiet finally came.

It is now four o'clock the following morning, and I am waiting, as I always do, but the creaking of the Death Cart has not yet come. I know I should be relieved . . . but I'm not.

hospital entry 25: the jury

I stand before the jury—ten people with clipboards, pens raised and ready. I banter on at top speed, attempting witticisms, apt observations, and generally being what I imagine is charming.

I don't know why I do this.

The visiting staff smile and laugh.

They ask me if I'm famous (wouldn't they know it if I were?).

They ask me what sort of music I play (ask Dr. Sharp).

They do all this.

But they don't let me go.

Why do I get the feeling that they are only keeping me here to find out what happens next?

Dr. Sharp accused me of being here for the sake of research. But maybe *I'm* not the one writing a book.

Asylum Letter No. LVIII

As the doctors immerse themselves ever more into their 'work', the Chasers are becoming ever more vicious. The brutes are frustrated by the greater number of inmates they are now charged to monitor and control, and they are wielding their annoyance upon the only ones who can't fight back.

We have developed hand signals used to warn each other of approaching staff, and we strike our stolen spoons against the bars of our cells in an attempt to distract them once they arrive. We do not always succeed, but we do our best to minimize the damage.

Silent Sarah has become more bold in her thievery, lifting the spoons from the Dining Hall just as the inmates have finished with them. The occasional skirmish does occur, for a spoon should rightly be stolen only by the inmate who had been using it, but Silent Sarah always wins.

And our Superintendent? Dr. Stockill's experiments continue day and night.

In his presence have I passed nearly a decade now, listening to his voice as he listens to mine. I have watched his obsession consume him entirely, and he has watched me grow thinner and more unruly. I wonder that he does not kill me. I have seen too many led to the Doctor's Laboratory never to return to imagine I could be spared much longer. Why he has let me live to this day, I do not know.

But, where my will to survive should have decreased in correspondence to the misery in which I have existed, it has done quite the opposite. When I think of myself, I am without hope, or faith, or any such thing as one is accustomed to living for. Yet, when I think of my fellow inmates, my sisters, those I love and would indeed die for, I feel my heart beating with a strength it should not, by all medical reasoning, be capable of.

Meanwhile, our numbers are dwindling, for Dr. Greavesly has now embarked upon the illegal sale of our corpses, either whole or limb by limb, whichever the anatomy colleges require. Thus, those of us who have not been sliced to death are nearly dead in our minds or deathly ill, suffering from infection, paralysis, and a hundred ailments that have no name.

Those who do not mend quietly disappear, and still no Death Cart. The wards have gone silent. Terror reigns.

Asylum Letter No. LIX

Through our solitary view of the world outside of Ward B, we have observed that nearly all of the vultures have flown away. We cannot fathom what might have been done to accomplish this, but the Londoners are satisfied, and the inspection of the Asylum has been called off—there will be no visitors this year.

The wind howls as it blasts great torrents of snow into our cells, rotting our beds of straw. Yet, strangely, the Wards are warmer, despite the bitter weather. The entire institution is warmer in fact, and, thus, our collective health has bettered, if only slightly. It is hoped that improvements are finally being made for our benefit.

Still, things are not as they should be. Inmates have been disappearing at an even more alarming rate, and entire cells are empty for the first time. When the Death Cart had been making its nightly rounds, there were only as many missing from the breakfast table as the cart could hold. Now, there are twenty, thirty, forty girls simply vanishing each day, and no one knows to where.

I must learn what becomes of the lost. Might there be significance to the recent delivery and subsequent construction? This has been the only alteration to our establishment, has it not? Whatever was in that box is now installed within the basement, which, if my assumptions are correct, also houses the motorized workings for the Asylum's theatrical scenery. I am determined to find my way down by whatever means possible, and soon.

Somehow, I feel certain that we are facing the final chapter of our horrific history; things have gone too far—become too monstrous—to continue on as they are. We are being exterminated. We are the laboratory rats, and we have multiplied. The public had sent in their multitudes, and the Asylum had welcomed them, along with the income they brought. But now, the facilities are overrun, the staff are overwhelmed, and we are being cut down to size.

I suspect this means that Dr. Stockill is nearing the success of his grand experiment, and that, soon, we will no longer be needed at all.

As if all of this was not dismal enough, my spoon, the large one given to me by Sir Edward and the League, has gone missing.

Asylum Letter No. LX

I return to you, Diary, after an eventful absence, during which time my raw and ragged hands were needed elsewhere. I will now endeavor to faithfully recount the three days that followed my entry above, and which blasted our world wide apart:

It was in the eventide that Veronica began to worry me. Her spirits seemed to be falling, and, as I depended upon her to bolster my own, I must do something.

'What can be the matter, darling?' I asked her.

'I'm not goin' anywhere', she said to me, somewhat absently, and very quiet.

'But of course you are! What a thing to say! Why, surely tomorrow . . .'

'I won't be 'ere tomorrow.'

'Quite right, my sweet love. You won't be here at all. You'll be on the stage again, and better than ever you were.'

'I won't be on the stage neither.'

I kissed her lips, and they were cold. I began to feel frightened.

'Perhaps you could sing for us? You know how happy it makes me when you sing.'

If she could not slip back into her delusions, I thought I should die. Too much of reality. Too much of truth. I wanted none of it. To my boundless relief, Veronica smiled, and I knew that she had returned to me.

'You'd be such a star, Em, such a dazzler, those pretty eyes, those pretty legs . . . why not come with me tomorrow? We could make a new act of it, the two of us.'

'Me? And what would *I* do?' I laughed, grateful to be part of her game again.

'I'll teach you. Now, you've got to stand up, to begin with. Always stand up, because you've got to show your legs. Yes, like that, Emmy, lovely. See, the trick of it is, when you 'old your fans,' and here Veronica bent down to grasp a fistful of straw in each hand, 'you've got to think of 'em as an extension of your arms. Graceful-like.'

She waved her straw, and I did so as well. Bits fell from our hands, but she did not notice. As I studied Veronica's movements, I saw that several of the girls in the nearby cells were doing the same, mimicking her as best they could, even those whose chains restricted them.

'Then, you cover the parts you want 'em lookin' at.'

'And what parts do we want them looking at?'

She stared at me, shocked at my stupidity.

'The parts as makes 'em pay, girl!'

Laughter rang out round me, and I was so glad of it I could have wept.

'Now, I'm not much for boys, but it's boys who pays, an' they like it when you start off nice and quiet-like . . . makes 'em wait for it. In my act, the one as made my name, we start it off just so.'

Slowly and sweetly, Veronica began to sing.

Verse I:
There was an English lass
As pretty as a rose
But chaste she was and never would she play
From her pretty little a - - (hands)

To her pretty little toes
A waste it was to keep them hid away
The gentlemen who called her she denied
And, like a proper lady would, she cried:

Presently, I swear I saw her fistfuls of straw transform into great fans of jeweled ostrich.

Chorus:
You may paint my portrait and buy me champagne
But don't kiss me!
You may pet me over and over again
But don't kiss me!
You may call me 'darling' and ask me to dance
For dancing is my cup of tea
No, these lips are not for the taking
But if you'll only agree
That we never should part, you'll be breaking my heart
If you don't kiss me!

Veronica's tattered shift had become a satin corset; strands of sparkling beads splashed against her gartered thighs; her lips were red and she had feathers in her hair.

Verse II:
No lovers would she claim
All sweethearts would she scorn
But one day when a suitor came to call
She saw that, to her shame
Her stockings she had torn
And at her feet the gentleman did fall
She swished her fan to keep the hound at bay
And, like the bless'd Madonna, did she say:

And as Veronica went on to sing and dance the second chorus, the girls who were strong enough to join in (and even many of those who were not) attempted the few words they knew, which were, primarily, three.

Chorus:
You may paint my portrait and buy me champagne
But don't kiss me!
You may pet me over and over again
But don't kiss me!
You may call me 'darling' and ask me to dance
For dancing is my cup of tea
No, these lips are not for the taking
But if you'll only agree
That we never should part, you'll be breaking my heart
If you don't kiss me!

Veronica then demanded that we all sing along with her one last round, and so, to as much as our talents allowed, we did. Two lines in and she was shouting for only the lads to sing, which was comical indeed as we looked round at one another, unsure of who should respond. Faster and faster went the piano—the piano I could now hear as clearly as my own laughter. Nearing the end of the chorus, I looked about the Ward and saw the faces now joyous, heard the voices now shrieking in merriment instead of pain, all of us transported to another place entirely by one solitary creature who, in her own mind, still lived there. If Veronica was mad, her madness was a gift to us that made us less so.

She riled us to our jubilant close:

That we never should part, you'll be breaking my heart
If we ever should part, you'll be breaking my heart
That we never should part, you'll be breaking my heart
If you don't kiss—

As Veronica drew the breath she intended to spend in the shouting of her triumphant last word, a hand clapped over her mouth from behind. Dr. Stockill pressed a chemical-soaked handkerchief to her face, and she soon collapsed against him, her long legs going slack beneath her.

I screamed and clawed at the Doctor, but to no avail; a Chaser close behind pulled me away and held my hands behind my back until Veronica was dragged down the corridor and out of my sight. This the Chaser cruelly allowed me to watch before he took me by the hair and threw me headlong against the bars, striking me unconscious.

I awoke in Quarantine.

Asylum Letter No. LXI

Sir Edward and Basil had stowed away in my pocket, and I was glad of it, for even Quarantine was empty. Crouched upon the damp earth and settling into the blackness, I heard a sound from directly beneath us—something like the gunning of a freight train . . . a great puff of steam followed by a low rumble. My eyes adjusting, I watched in bewilderment as Sir Edward leapt from my shoulder and flattened his furry body against the ground. Basil followed and did the same. The two rats scurried about the cell, pausing after every few steps to press their heads to the floor, their whiskers twitching. At last, Sir Edward raised himself.

'If you wish to see into the basement, my Lady, I believe we can be of some assistance, for we are directly above it.'

Sir Edward led me to the far corner of the cell where the boards below the soil were thin and weakest. I cleared a layer of dirt from the area quickly enough, and the rats set to work, shredding the wooden beams with their astonishingly power-ful jaws. Not an hour later, an opening had been made, and a shaft of light infiltrated our cell from below. I brought my face to the ground.

The hollow beneath us was cavernous and unfurnished, as though it had only recently been occupied. Hanging gaslights encircled a wooden slab in the center of the room, coarse and stained. Deep within the surrounding shadows, I could faintly distinguish the outlines of machinery—enormous gears and wheels, levers, cogs, and chains surrounded an iron vault.

A curtain hung round the shoddy operating table, drawn open and tied off to one side. I saw Dr. Stockill and another man bending over the slab, engaged in the inspection of something a third had just deposited there. When the men raised themselves, I could see the body of a girl I recognized from Ward B. She was clearly dead—her limbs limp, her face blue and bloodless. The third man, whose identity I could not yet decipher, divested the dead girl of her striped stockings, then tossed them into a copper coal scuttle already overflowing with such garments.

'I don't mind touchin' the live ones,' he said, 'but I'm not too keen on strippin' the dead. 'Course, that's just me.'

'Your delicacy is admirable, young Charles,' remarked Dr. Stockill in his vacuous intonation, 'but there's no need to burn the stockings. We pride ourselves on wasting nothing here, don't we, Greavesly?'

The second man stepped into the light, and I saw that it was indeed our own butcher, as I had suspected.

And then, horror . . . horror such as I can never describe . . . several more bodies were piled nearby, naked, one on top of the other. Stockings removed, the girl upon the table was tossed onto this pile like nothing more than a piece of discarded meat thrown out by the kitchen staff. I felt faint, but I could not look away. The bodies were fresh, as though they had been alive only an hour before; their eyes were open, their blank stares like dead fish at market.

'Stockill,' objected Dr. Greavesly, 'I don't know why you insist upon killing the sluts *before* tossing them into the furnace, especially since you refuse to have any fun with it. It's a waste of time, I say, not to mention a waste of those precious chemicals you spend every penny on. We'd be stinking rich if you didn't squander so.'

So that's *where the Asylum's profits go*, I thought.

'Your vulgar methods, Greavesly, disgust me immensely. You would no doubt have me slit the things open and roll about in their innards if you could.'

'I'd respect you for it! You're too delicate to be a proper doctor, I say.'

The butcher slurred his speech as though he had been drinking, which did not surprise me.

'I am *not* delicate,' shot Dr. Stockill with a sudden intensity that startled even his opponent, 'and you would be wise to curb your tongue whilst you continue to work under my protection.'

Protection? What did that mean? Was Dr. Greavesly hiding?

'Oh foxpiss, Stockill, calm down . . . you'll spill your cyanide.'

'Furthermore,' the Superintendent returned his attention to his subject, 'I have not the slightest interest in the bodies of these . . . *abominations*.'

He snapped his fingers. Charlie, the very Chaser who had led a chained Veronica to my cell upon that first day in Ward B, brought forth yet another inmate, this one still living. Her hands were bound across her chest; a gag was tied over her mouth. Tangled hair fell forwards over her bowed head.

'On the table!' Dr. Stockill directed, stepping backwards.

Charlie forced the struggling girl onto the wooden slab, then retrieved a set of straps from a nearby shelf.

'No, no, that won't be necessary. Leave us.'

The Doctor bent over his patient.

'She won't be going anywhere, will you, my dear?'

The inmate shook her head, her dark hair still concealing her features.

Charlie moved to step away from the scene, then paused to look over his shoulder at the girl, seemingly concerned. The moment over, he obeyed, turned his back, and left the basement.

Producing the elegant weapon from his breast pocket, Dr. Stockill stroked the trigger; the blades sprung open, and he selected the glinting razor attachment, deftly employing it to sever the prisoner's bonds.

'I can kill them . . . I can cure them . . . but I cannot understand them.'

His voice grew distant as he spoke, as though he were slipping away into some other world—a world that he alone inhabited.

'A scientific mind does not do well deprived of comprehension. Not well at all.'

Leaning over the girl, he brushed the black strands away from her face, now shielded from my view by the Doctor's long shadow.

'Look closely into her eyes when she is afraid. Her pupils dilate . . . it is quite beyond her control. See her tremble . . . contractions of the *musculus mentalis* . . . an involuntary reaction to a single emotion: fear.'

Dr. Stockill lifted his blade to the inmate's cheek and passed it before her view.

'What causes the eyes to glisten? What causes the heart to race?'

He raised himself and his shadow retreated with him.

'*Veronica!*' I gasped.

Dr. Stockill glanced furtively towards my present location.

'Did you hear something just now, Greavesly?'

'Hmm? What's that?'

The surgeon had lit an opium cigarette and was blowing smoke rings towards his colleague.

'Put that out immediately!' shouted Dr. Stockill.

'What the devil?'

'Bloody imbecile! Don't you know never to bring an open flame near these chemicals? No, of course you wouldn't know that. You butchers never do.'

In his agitation, Dr. Stockill had forgotten all about the noise.

'What is he doing?'

My voice quivered, for I already knew the answer.

'I am sorry, my dear Lady, but you cannot help her now,' whispered Sir Edward into my ear.

'I have to try. Help me break through to the basement.'

'If you join her now, you may join her in death.'

'I would join her anywhere.'

I dug deeper into the dirt and pounded upon the boards beneath. Basil and Sir Edward seemed unsure of what to do next.

'Help me!' I screamed at them.

Seeing that I could not be dissuaded, the rats determined to assist me instead. We clawed at the ground. We tore at the slats. But we were not fast enough.

Dr. Stockill had returned his attention to his victim, seeming not to hear us after all. His spider's fingers were round Veronica's throat now; her eyes open wide, she shook violently, attempting to speak. The Doctor gently pressed a long forefinger to her lips.

'We will have no noise,' he said, his voice taking on that silvery, persuasive quality I knew so well.

Veronica nodded.

'If only obedience would save her,' I sobbed to the rats.

'I am not a cruel man, you see,' said the Doctor. 'I am going to give you something that will make all of this go away. But first, there is something I need you to do for me.'

Veronica nodded again.

'What a good girl you are! Now, I need you to listen closely to what I am about to tell you. There is, behind you, a door made of iron. That door opens into a chamber fitted with heating elements—elements that can reach a temperature hot enough to turn a horse to a pile of ash in less time than it takes to brew a cup of tea.'

Dr. Stockill's hand still grasped Veronica's soft white neck.

'In one, brief moment, I am going to put you into that chamber.'

Veronica's eyes flooded; she made a small, desperate sound, like a dying animal, and tried to shake her head, but the Doctor only tightened his grip.

'Are you suffering?' hissed Dr. Stockill.

Veronica was now suspended in shock. Her lack of response frustrated the Doctor. He leapt onto the operating table and climbed on top of her, one hand twisting its way through her hair and seizing it firmly by the roots. Dr. Greavesly moved closer, viewing the scene with rabid fascination. It was agony to behold.

'*Are you suffering?*'

Dr. Stockill was snarling in Veronica's face now, baring his teeth like a beast.

'You will suffer as you made me suffer! You came to take her away from me! Why? Why? *Why?*'

With each of these last three incomprehensible words, the Doctor pounded Veronica's head against the slab. Blood pooled beneath her.

'Good God, man!' exclaimed Dr. Greavesly, bounding forwards to push Dr. Stockill from the table. 'Have you gone entirely mad, Stockill?'

'Don't you touch me!' spat the Superintendent.

Straightening his waistcoat, he took up a bottle of amber glass and dampened a rag with its contents. My friend was dying . . . I was watching her die . . . the scraping of her breath was the creaking of a thousand Death Carts.

'How very fortunate you are,' he said, returning to Veronica and adopting his deliberate tone once more, the feral passion of a moment ago having drained from his being. 'You shall never feel the pain of your flesh melting away from your bones.'

The beautiful eyes I loved so well pleaded for mercy, and I continued to strike at the boards as the rats gnawed as fast as they were able. Then, my breath stopped as these same eyes shot directly to where I hid, meeting mine in the dark as if she knew I was there—as though she could feel my presence, hear my pounding heart. The blood gushing from the back of her head had already soaked the wood beneath, and now spilled over the table's edge, soiling the floor. I could hear the steady trickle with deafening clarity.

'You shall not feel it, my dear, because you'll already be dead.'

The good Doctor pressed the soaked rag over Veronica's mouth. Her face transformed from terror to despair, then, finally, to nothingness; her eyelids fluttered to a close at last.

Dr. Stockill studied Veronica's face closely as she expired, as though he were recording it in his memory to recall and write down at some later hour. Moving swiftly, mechanically, he again produced his bloodletting device, cutting a deep, wide slit in Veronica's wrist. He held an empty bottle beneath the gash, filling it with her essence. Once done, he wiped his razor, snapped the blades shut, and tucked the corked bottle inside his coat.

Turning away from the body in apparent disgust, Dr. Stockill left the basement.

'Take the parts you want, Greavesly, and burn what's left. Just get rid of her.'

I didn't know I was screaming until my throat seared from the strain.

Dr. Greavesly had gone, presumably to obtain his tools of dismemberment, and I knew what he would do to Veronica's body. Tearing at the boards with bleeding fingertips, I heard a cracking beneath me and the slats upon which I knelt gave way. Amidst splintering wood and a deluge of dirt and straw, I crashed through the shattered floor of Quarantine and into the basement at last.

Asylum Letter No. LXII

In an instant, I was up and on the table with Veronica's head in my hands, shaking her body, pressing my mouth to her own, forcing my breath inside her, but she did not keep it. I pressed my hand to her chest, willing my pulse to waken hers, but no heartbeat met my palm.

Just as I despaired, her head turned to the side and she coughed, lightly. Her eyes opened, and her breath came, but faintly, faintly . . . She may have survived the poison, a blessed miscalculation on the Doctor's part, but too much blood had been lost. I pressed my fingers to the back of her skull and felt the fracture. I took her in my arms and cradled her sweet face, bringing my own close enough that I could hear her fading breath, the scent of bitter almonds still strong upon her lips.

'Please, V . . . please don't leave me here alone . . . please don't go . . .'

'Don't cry, Em . . .' she whispered, raising her hand to touch my face before it fell again, her strength now gone.

'Please . . . let me come with you . . .'

'No . . .' she smiled, weakly. 'Not yet. But I'll be waiting . . .'

I knew I had but seconds left with her.

'*There was an English lass, as pretty as a rose* . . .' I faltered, through sobs.

Veronica's body seized and shuddered in my arms as though her spirit struggled to leave it, and I knew she was holding on to life only for my sake. I must let her go.

I kissed her.

'You're going home.'

I was roused from an exhausted daze by the sound of footsteps in the dark of the basement.

Click . . . click . . . click . . .

My bloody arms still entwined with Veronica's lifeless ones behind the curtain of the operating table. I listened, and did not breathe. These were not the footsteps of Dr. Stockill . . . nor of Dr. Greavesly. No, I *knew* these steps. A gaslight was ignited, and a musty yellow bled over the walls, casting the distorted shadow of a figure across the floor. Through the narrow parting in the cloth, I saw her.

Madam Mournington moved slowly amongst the shelves stacked with glass tubes, bottles, and piles of blood-soaked rags. She paused to lift a stocking from the coal scuttle, then let it drop from her fingertips.

Still wearing her gloves and traveling hat, she appeared to have only just returned to us. Clearly unfamiliar with the basement and its contents, she passed her hand over the door of the metal furnace and turned the heavy iron wheel that opened the incinerator. I could not see inside, but I could smell the ashes. Her footsteps grew closer, and I knew it would be but a moment before she drew aside the curtain that concealed the operating table—the table upon which I lay with my fallen friend.

The curtain was torn away just as I slid down to the ground and crouched beneath the slab. I heard a gasp, and peered upwards. Stepping back, Madam Mournington appeared startled at the sight of Veronica's body. Then, she did something I thought very strange: Approaching the operating table once more, she placed her grey gloved hands upon the edge, and breathed deeply—a long, drawn breath, eyes closed and chin raised as though she were inhaling the essence of something foreign and trying to discern its origin. She brought her face close to Veronica's and breathed again. Rising, the gaslight reflected in the wet streak upon her withered cheek, and she bowed her head.

From beyond my view, I heard the creak of a door, and Dr. Stockill emerged. Hurriedly he walked, carrying a crate of chemicals. Upon seeing his mother, the Doctor froze. Slowly, he set down the crate. He had gone shock white.

'Mother . . .' he said, his voice thin and tremulous, 'I did not realize you had returned. What are you doing down here? Why don't you come upstairs and let me bring you some tea? The journey has surely exhausted you.'

Madam Mournington had her back to her son; hidden beneath the table, I had view of them both.

'Mother, please . . . come upstairs. Come and tell me of your time in Coventry. I trust Aunt Augusta is well? Please, Mother dearest, come . . . this is no place for you . . .'

For the first time since I had known the man, Dr. Stockill sounded frightened. After a dreadful silence, Madam Mournington spoke. She did not turn round.

'There was a part of me that always knew . . .' she said, her voice no more than a whisper.

'Mother . . .'

'I always knew, and yet I did not believe it. How could I? How could a mother think such a thing of her own child?'

'Mother, please . . . you don't know what you're saying . . . you're tired—'

Madam Mournington turned to face the Doctor at last, a piece of cloth quivering in her outstretched hand—the cloth that Dr. Stockill had used just hours before to end Veronica's life.

'My son . . . my son, you know well that I . . . I cannot smell a thing in this world . . . cannot detect odor of any kind . . . and yet, I can smell *this*. How can that be?' she begged him, fluttering her fingers against the cameo brooch at her throat. 'You are a doctor . . . a good, learned doctor . . . can you tell me this? I can smell the body of this girl . . . it is on her breath still . . . Tell me, Monty, my son, my own boy, my only . . . was she awake when you put this cloth over her mouth? Did she cry? Did my daughter cry?'

Madam Mournington's voice had become strained and tight—a thread threatening to snap. The cloth fell from her hand. Her son advanced towards her, but she backed away, retreating to the other side of the table as though truly afraid of him. If she only lowered her eyes, she would see me, crouched at her feet.

'Almonds . . . cherries . . . peach pits . . .' she said, sniffing the air once again.

It was then that I saw the bottle. Upon the ground, just out of my reach, the vessel of amber glass had toppled from the table when I had leapt upon it. My mistress had seen it too, for she bent to retrieve it, nearly touching my hand in the process.

Rising, Madam Mournington studied the label.

'*Cyanide*. Poison . . . even an ignorant old woman knows that much. How would you have obtained such a chemical at that age?'

'Mother—'

'You took from me the only thing that ever gave me the slightest happiness . . . that ever gave me a single shred of joy. You robbed me of my child. You robbed me of my life. I could have been human—I could have been *alive*, but you took my heart and you murdered it. You made me into *this*! A hard, bitter, cruel old woman who can feel nothing . . . and now it is too late . . . my God, what have I done . . . what have I done . . .'

Nervously fingering the Ward Key suspended from her corseted waist, Madam Mournington turned away, still clutching the bottle. She walked a distance from the table and, when she turned back, her eyes found mine. We stared at one another, my pulse pounding in my ears. Surely my mistress would alert the Doctor to my presence, and I would be the next inmate burnt alive. She had only to point her finger in my direction. But she did not.

'*I* am your child, Mother,' said the Doctor, but slowly, treading carefully.

'You are not my child. You are a monster. And *why*?'

She was pleading now.

'Why did you do it? She was your sister! Your own blood!'

The Doctor cringed at this last word.

'But I had to, Mother,' he answered, with terrifying calm. 'I couldn't let her steal you from me, could I? I couldn't share you. You can understand that, can't you? I did it for you, Mother—for us. You didn't really want her, did you? One was enough. You didn't really want her, and I saved you . . .'

'You're mad . . . you're truly mad . . .' gasped Madam Mournington in disbelief.

The Doctor began to walk towards her; she backed away.

'Don't come near me!'

'Mother, I had to . . .'

Dr. Stockill halted mid-step as his mother lifted the bottle of cyanide.

'Because of you, I have wasted my life in misery,' said she, an unnerving tranquility having possessed her. 'Because of you, I have nothing. Because of my own pain, I have hurt others without a thought. But you will never understand this, because you are dead inside. And now, so am I.'

Madam Mournington raised the bottle to her lips and drank its contents in a single swallow. From Dr. Stockill arose a high-pitched shriek; he started towards his mother as the bottle slipped from her hand, crashing to the floor, releasing the suffocating scent of almonds into the stale air. The poison had not yet overtaken her, and she rushed across the room to where I hid, stumbling as her limbs tensed and spasmed. Dr. Stockill strove to reach her, but Madam Mournington threw her body against a series of shelves laden with glass, toppling the structures and trapping her son beneath.

My tormentor of ten long years approached me; I crouched before her in utter astonishment. She was breathing hard, and could not speak. She clutched at her stomach, her face twisted in anguish. Her skin was flushed, her lips flecked with foam and blood. Groaning, she lurched forwards. The sight was awful; I inched away from her. This was the woman who had robbed me of my freedom upon that wet London night what seemed a lifetime ago; she had fulfilled the request of a murderer, charged me with the crime of madness for wanting to escape such a life, and then locked me inside a house of horrors to die by torture instead. She may not have held the knife, but she was part of this just the same. What could she want with me now?

Her body contorted violently, yet she managed to locate the Ward Key from within the folds of her heavy skirt. Snapping the chain that attached the key to her waist, she held it out to me. Stunned, I could not move to take it. I stared into the old woman's face and saw that the eyes I still believed had once been beautiful were wild with grief and desperation. Clenching the key that had taunted me for so long, her trembling hand still reached towards me, as though begging me to take it from her—to relieve her of her burden at last.

Rising, I took a single step towards my enemy; I held out my hand and cautiously accepted the key from Madam Mournington's quavering fingertips. Having accomplished this one, solitary act of decency, she collapsed to the ground, and with her dying breath came the hoarse whisper: '*Run away . . .*'

Her body writhed upon the broken glass, and, with one final convulsion, and a harsh rasp sounding from deep within her throat, I knew that Madam Mournington was dead.

But the Ward Key . . . it was in my hand. It was actually *in my hand.*

Stirred to action by the Doctor's screams as he struggled to free himself of the wreckage, I looked to the open door of the basement, and I did as Madam Mournington bade me. I did as Anne bade me. I did as Sachiko bade me. I *ran.*

Upon his feet again, the Doctor sprinted after me, barring the door before I could reach it. Where a rational creature may have seen nothing but defeat, I saw one remaining chance, and I was mad enough to attempt it. Darting back towards the operating table, I leapt upon the slab and threw myself against a tall shelf nearby. As it gave way beneath me, I clambered to the top and, with strength I am quite certain I had never before possessed, launched myself upwards, clawing my way back into the cell I had only just fought to escape.

Now in Quarantine, the Ward Key unlocked the bolt as though it knew its task. Past the gate I tore, through the tunnel, and finally emerging from the hearth, my stocking feet sliding into the Entrance Hall. A swarm of our hideous grey ghosts flew close in front of my face, cavernous eyes wide, the gaping black holes of their mouths forming the word '*RUN*' as a piercing shriek from all corners of the Asylum echoed the same, rising in volume as I raced onwards.

Grasping the Ward Key ever tighter in my hand, I bolted up the several flights of decaying stairs, only just avoiding my own demise as the rotting wood snapped beneath me and the railings crumbled away, smashing upon the ground far below. I heard the grinding of the gears, the rattle of unseen machinery, and I knew that Dr. Stockill was securing the Asylum.

Surviving the ascent, I reached the barred landing of the Lunatic Wards. I fit the key into the lock and turned it; that too familiar click, and I was in! Once through the bars, I unlocked the doors of both Wards and, from a nail in the wall outside of each, took up the two rings of smaller keys used by the Chasers to lock us in our individual cells and fetters. I began with Ward B, for I knew that it would take more time to free the chained and caged than it would to loose the girls in the less confining Ward.

With the Ward Key between my teeth, I unlocked Cell W14 and tossed one of the rings to the Captain, giving her instructions to free every last prisoner, and quickly. I repeated the procedure in Ward A; within seconds, a flood of inmates and the rats who had been guarding them came pouring forth from the Wards, and onto the landing.

'Wait!' came a shout.

I turned to see Silent Sarah standing behind me, a heavy bundle in her hands. She set her burden upon the ground.

'Take.'

Stunned to hear her speak, I watched as she pulled back the cloth to reveal the consequence of her labour: hundreds of spoons, their handles sharpened to points more menacing than any dagger. Whilst the rest of us suffered and hoped in ignorance, Silent Sarah had known this day would come, and she had prepared us. She drew from amongst the weapons my own large spoon, that which I had thought lost forever. Holding it out to me, Silent Sarah smiled, for the first time since I had known her. With haste, I took the spoon from her hand and kissed her cheek.

"Arm yourselves, Ladies!' I called out.

The inmates raided this blessed arsenal, and we were off. Towards the gate we fled, an army of girls and the entire League of Plague Rats behind me.

In the midst of this chaotic muddle of stockings, claws, and tails, I stumbled and fell forwards, releasing my hard-won possessions. Helplessly I stared as the key launched itself from my hand. I was back in the gilded foyer of Bainbridge, and Anne was sliding the Master Key across the floor of polished marble. But then it had been coming closer, and now it was moving further away, speeding like a bullet across the filthy floor towards the open gate and out of my reach.

A black-shod foot came down, stopping the key and concealing it from my view. I raised my head to see Dr. Stockill towering above me, a seething fury in his scarlet-rimmed eyes. Without a word, the Doctor snatched up the key and turned back towards the gate. Before I knew my own mind, I lunged at the Doctor, leaping upon his back, sinking my teeth into his neck in an attempt to gain the freedom I was determined not to lose.

Blessed be their loyalty, for every girl and rodent alike rushed forwards to my aid, sharpened spoons brandished, but my emaciated limbs were no match for my opponent; he had pocketed the Ward Key and now shook me off, pulling me close in front of him. My back was pressed against his chest; his fingers clenched mercilessly round my throat just as he had done to my poor Veronica. With his free hand, he reached into his breast pocket and withdrew his weapon, snapping it open and pressing the razor to my neck.

'What is she worth to you?' he growled, his blade already carving a shallow line across my throat.

Seeing the blood, my army stood down. With violent force, the Doctor shoved me back into the crowd, then ran out and down the stairs, locking the gate behind him.

It was unbearable. We had come so close, and now we were further away than ever, for, within moments, the staff would be alerted to our attempted escape and we would be done with. It was over. All this time had we clung to life through impossible odds, and it was over; we would never have this chance again. Never. I sank to the ground, knowing that we were all dead. I believe that most of the girls were too astounded to completely fathom what had just occurred; they only knew that we were free, and then we were not.

I cannot comprehend what happened next, Diary . . . I can only tell my story and pray that someday I will understand:

As I knelt upon the cold, stone floor, I became aware of a peculiar burning sensation upon my right leg. It took me a moment to realise that the heat was emanating from inside my stocking, just above my knee, where Anne's key, the Master Key of Bainbridge, was tied. The tarnished gold burned with a growing warmth; I tore off the stocking and untied the key as quickly as I could. The metal was glowing white-hot now, but it did not pain me. I took the key in my hands and felt my pulse quicken, the blood coursing through me; I was a frozen body thawing back to life.

Suddenly, I was filled with an incredible lightness that lifted me from the ground and to my feet.

I did not walk to the gate—the Master Key pulled me there. I tried the lock—it fit perfectly. I turned the key—the gate swung open. All breaths were held, and nobody made a sound.

Then, the great clock in the Entrance Hall below struck the hour, and I retrieved my spoon from the ground.

'Four o'clock,' I said. 'Teatime.'

Asylum Letter No. LXIII

Blood was everywhere.

A dozen Chasers were dead with many more soon to follow, our sharpened spoons having been put to the good use they had long been intended for.

Dr. Stockill had sounded the alarm, waking everyone in the institution at once. For the first time in the Asylum's long and gruesome history, the inmates had the clear advantage: We outnumbered the staff, and we had nothing to lose. It was not difficult for us to kill—not difficult at all; it simply needed to be done, and so we did it.

The Asylum's greatest experiment was that which its ingenious directors never expected: After an age of mental and physical torture, strangled at every turn by impending death and pure inhumanity, what would we become? *What might we be capable of?* The Tea Party Massacre was the answer to the question they never asked.

As the furnace had supplied the Asylum with the easy means to carry out mass extermination, only a few hundred of us remained, a horrific contrast to the thousands there had once been. Still, we had more than enough in our ranks to strike terror into the hearts of our captors once we were on the other side of the bars.

The bulk of our multitude had been sent to search the institution for any remaining Chasers, for it was collectively decided that no one could be left alive. Whilst one of our factions hauled its prisoners to the Hydrotherapy Chamber, and another used their spoon handles to eviscerate the opposition, the members of the Striped Stocking Society assembled for a brief discussion upon how best to confront the doctors; they were, no doubt, devising tactics to survive the onslaught and take us down instead.

We concurred that a select few of us ought to deal the primary blows, whilst the rest would guard the area and restrain the 'patients', should they prove uncooperative. We equipped ourselves with as many spoons as could be strapped to our persons, and it was time to visit our doctors at last.

Though one might have expected the devils to save their own, the doctors had fled to their separate corners. Having heard the dying screams of the Chasers and medical assistants echoing through the halls, they had realised that we were armed, and, even more frighteningly, that we were organized. Sir Edward arrived to report that Dr. Stockill had shut himself inside his chamber, but we all agreed to save our best for last.

Dr. Lymer had retreated to the Bloodletting Wing. We found him huddled beneath his table of leech jars and bleeding bowls, armed only with a solitary hammer as though he had never been required to protect himself, and didn't know quite how to go about it. The girls advanced upon him and lifted the Doctor to one of his own bleeding beds. He wailed and pleaded for mercy, but we no longer understood the word.

We worked quickly. The Doctor wriggled like one of his salted leeches, and so the others held him down whilst I buckled the leather straps over his limbs. We tore away the Doctor's nightclothes. Brandishing our spoons, we executed a variety of carvings upon Dr. Lymer's body, taking care that his bloated face was well attended to. Long slashes blazed across his chest, and a decorative series of slits ran the length of his arms and legs.

When we felt that Dr. Lymer was sufficiently sliced and on his way to good health, the Captain and I each chose a leech jar from the table.

'You might feel a little pinch,' I said.

Then, we emptied the vessels, pouring the leeches over the shrieking Doctor's mutilated body. His blood, having overflowed the shallow moat running round the edge of the bed, was now spilling onto the floor; although he had lost much of it, the Doctor was still living, which was exactly what we wanted. The leeches needed no instruction; they spread rapidly over every exposed inch of flesh.

I raised my spoon and drove the pointed spike directly into the center of the Doctor's forehead just before the leeches covered his face completely. The shrieking stopped. His eyes rolled back in his head and he went slack-jawed, unwittingly inviting the leeches to crawl into his mouth and stop his breath forever. It was a fantastic sight; Dr. Lymer was covered from head to toe, smothered by a glittering black armour writhing with life. Our work done, we left our former tormentor, or what remained of him.

Next, it was on to Dr. Greavesly's private quarters. Reaching his door, we found it unlocked, the surgeon nowhere to be seen. Suspecting that he had fled to the Operating Theatre to arm himself, we flew down the stairs, through the Theatre door, and there he was—the demon, the butcher, crouched upon the table, his fiery mane loose and wild. He gripped a serrated bone saw in each hand and was waiting for us, an animal poised to pounce.

Without a moment's hesitation, the Captain stepped forwards, unsheathed a spoon she had strapped to her arm, and sent it spinning expertly towards the surgeon. The pointed handle now deeply embedded in his neck, he fell back upon the operating table, the audible cracking of his skull causing him to lose consciousness. Leaving the Captain's weapon protruding from the surgeon's neck, I took up my own spoon and thrust the handle deeply into Dr. Greavesly's stomach. Much to our collective surprise, he opened his eyes and roared, blood spurting from his throat. The others pinned down the surgeon's arms and legs; even with his tremendous strength, he could not overpower us all. Before I could finish the task, the Captain leapt onto the table, grasped the spoon I had left standing upright in the Doctor's stomach, and pulled it downwards, slicing through the length of his abdomen. With one last, guttural howl, Dr. Greavesly's head fell back.

At last able to devote our complete attention to the Superintendent, we must take extra care. By any standards the cleverest of the three doctors, he was far more likely to have planned a defense that might actually succeed. Wiping our bloody hands upon our shifts, we dashed up the stairs to the Medical Floor, then towards Doctor Stockill's chamber door, followed by a growing swarm of Plague Rats. Their long teeth shone red in the gaslight; they had been aiding the other inmates in finishing off the staff, and now they had come for their prize. After all, they bore as much grievance against Dr. Stockill as did any of us.

I requested Sir Edward station the League just outside the door, keeping the inmates at a safe distance. Basil, who had observed the Superintendent more closely than any living soul, objected to my going in alone, but I beseeched him to let me be. I felt certain that, when confronting Dr. Stockill, a crowd would do more harm than good.

There was no sound from within the chamber, but I knew he was there—I could smell him. Gently, I turned the latch and found the door unlocked; somehow, I had known it would be. I walked upon my toes, steeling myself for the inevitable shock the Doctor may try and give me at any moment. The chamber was filled with that same almond scent I had been exposed to only hours before, and now knew the deadly significance of.

The boards creaked beneath my feet, the sound amplified a thousandfold to my anxious ears. I stared in all directions, but saw no one. Then, the door slammed shut; I raised my spoon and spun round to find Dr. Stockill standing close behind me.

A ghastly, distorted smile twisted the corners of his cruel mouth. Despite his disordered appearance, he no longer raged, and this worried me more than had he attacked me violently.

'W14A,' he said, seating himself at his desk, the very same from behind which he had first interrogated me. 'I'm so glad you've come . . . I rather expected you would. It seems we have the matter of our future to discuss.'

I had the sharpened spoon handle pointed towards the Doctor still, but he paid it no regard. Instead, using a delicate glass dropper, he dispensed a clear liquid into a large vial. Without looking up, he nodded towards the high-backed chair, the one with the leather straps hanging from the back.

'No one's head may be higher than—'

'Why haven't you killed me?' I interrupted, startled at the words I had not intended to say, but now, now that I held a weapon and could have set upon the Doctor quite easily, *now* I must know. 'Why have you kept me alive all these years?'

Dr. Stockill raised his eyes.

'Oh, but I have not kept you alive at all. Far from it, in fact.'

'I don't understand.'

'I have repeatedly exposed you to a greater concentration of the virus I have long been developing than any other human being has ever withstood. And still you live.'

'I have never lived.'

'You existed, then.'

'So your cure is effective. Was that not your desire?'

'I never administered the cure. You never contracted the disease.'

'Why?'

'If I knew that, I would be more powerful than any man alive, and you would be dead. You are the only reason the world has not yet experienced my greatest creation. Any resistance in the population renders my formula useless. *They*,' he gestured towards the door, 'are the population. *You* are that resistance. What makes you different from the others, W14A?'

'I am no different.'

'Then how do you do it?'

'I don't know . . .'

'Nor do I. And that is precisely why we must continue.'

'Continue?'

'Most certainly. Until I can prove my plague to be fatal against a person of great resistance, meaning yourself, it is not complete. However, I am feeling quite optimistic about my latest alterations to the formula. Now, you've made rather a mess of my institution—we clearly cannot remain here. Come away with me now, and I will spare your associates.'

'Spare them? You are outnumbered, Doctor. You always were. And they are very unlikely to spare *you*.'

'I suspected you might say as much. But, you see, W14A, they will have no choice.'

He lifted the vial he had been measuring and swirled it over the flame of a low taper. The liquid began to bubble; a curl of sapphire smoke floated towards the rafters. The scent of almonds burned my nostrils.

'Within minutes, a vapor will be released from this room that will fatally poison the blood of every living creature within this structure.'

'That would be suicide, Doctor, an act previously incomprehensible to yourself.'

'Oh, but that's rather *your* sport.'

Placing the vial in a wire hanger suspended above the flame, Dr. Stockill lifted a mask—very like the long-snouted headpiece he had worn whilst stalking the disease-ridden corridors, but with additional tubes and filters to protect against the scourge his smoking cyanide threatened to dispense to us now. He unbuckled the straps in preparation.

'Let's play our game . . .' I said.

'You haven't long.'

'Where would we go?'

'The clock is ticking, W14—'

'What will we do?'

'I will determine what is keeping you alive.'

'What will you take?'

'I shall take only what I need.'

'What do you need?'

'Oh, I am quite prepared. I need only you, and my . . .'

The Doctor's eyes passed from mine to an area beyond my shoulder, where they lingered. Turning my head to see what it was that had deserved his attention, I spotted, upon a bench near the window, a ubiquitous Gladstone bag of black leather, such as all men of medicine use to transport their tools and tonics.

I turned back to the Doctor and found him staring directly at me. His eyes widened, and, in the same instant, we both lunged for the bag. In his haste to rise, he had toppled the bubbling vial, his cyanide no longer an immediate threat. Reaching the bag before him, I closed my fingers round the handle and held it to my chest. Had I wished to, I could have tossed the thing from the window at once. Cautiously, Dr. Stockill stepped back.

Sheathing my spoon in the strap upon my thigh, I snapped open the bag to find two large bottles of amber glass. I withdrew one of them, and set the bag down again.

'Which is this, then? The disease or the cure?'

'Put that down.'

'Or is there much of a difference?'

'I said, put that down.'

I removed the stopper and tilted the bottle downwards, allowing a thin stream to trickle out, spattering the floor.

'All right . . . all right . . . just . . . stop. Put the bottle down, and I will find another way . . .'

I let spill another drop of the liquid.

'Leave this place. I'll send you off with more money than you could spend in a hundred lifetimes. Take your whores with you, if you wish it. Just leave me the bottle and get out.'

Without a sound, the door opened a sliver, just enough for Sir Edward, followed by Basil and the rest of the rats, to creep unheard into the Doctor's chamber.

'You can't save everyone, W14A. Stop trying.'

I watched over Dr. Stockill's shoulder as the swarm of rodents swam up the legs of the tables, onto the shelves, even up the chains to the gaslights hanging overhead.

'You hesitate,' said the Doctor. 'Be wise, W14A.'

'Don't call me that,' I snapped. 'I have a name. I have a NAME!'

'Shhh . . . be wise, Emily, Emily with no history, and no last name, and no one . . . you've come this far. Why would you end it all now? Leave this place, and you could have the whole world.'

'I don't want the whole world. I want Veronica back.'

'Who?' he asked, blankly.

At this final offense, I held the bottle out to him and spread my fingers wide. With the crashing of glass, the life's work of Dr. Stockill was soaking the floor, running in rivulets along the cracks between the boards before seeping into the wood and out of his reach forever.

The Doctor stared at me in utter despair, and this is when I kissed him. I kissed him, Diary, and I saw more horror fill his eyes than my knifepoint could ever inspire. Then, with my lips still pressed tightly to his, I reached beneath my shift, withdrew my spoon, and plunged the sharpened handle deeply into his back. The clicking of a thousand tiny claws filled my ears and I backed away from my greatest enemy, knowing that I was no longer needed.

All at once, every Plague Rat in the Asylum pounced upon Dr. Stockill. Screaming in absolute terror, he collapsed beneath their combined weight, and the vengeful rodents scratched at his eyes and tore him apart with their bloodstained teeth until there was nothing left.

Asylum Letter No. LXIV

It is the morning after the Tea Party Massacre, and dawn is breaking through our cracked windows. I have just now completed the relation of all that has happened to this point, for I knew there would be no sleep until the story passed out of me through my little silver pencil. I can hear birds, which have always seemed to stray from their route only to avoid this place, whistling in the trees outside. Does the world know that a mark upon its soul has been blotted out? Will the sky be any clearer today? The air any sweeter?

In the drawer of Dr. Stockill's desk, I found the Asylum's visitation ledger, that which had once been governed by the iron claw of Madam Mournington in the days before she felt morally incapable of booking the sort of appointments that were required of her—the days before The Cell. Opening the ledger to today's date, I saw that we had but one remaining task.

The bell rang in the Entrance Hall, announcing a visitor. The Captain stood facing the door, her tri-corner hat of striped wallpaper and apothecary orders cocked to one side. The length of braid that the inmates and I had woven for her was slung across her chest like a military sash, and a wee black rat perched upon her shoulder like a pirate's parrot. I delivered to her the long surgical knife that I had meticulously cleaned and polished for just this occasion. The Captain looked down at the rough hilt resting in her delicate hand. The bell rang a second time.

'Are you quite sure you want to do this alone?' I asked her.

'Yes.'

She breathed deeply.

'I'm ready. You keep watch.'

'Aye, Captain,' I said, then ascended the staircase to attend to the others.

Asylum Letter No. LXV

The remainder of the day was passed in the basement, gathering the bodies of the girls who had not yet been incinerated, and then preparing them for the first proper funeral that had ever taken place upon the grounds of the Asylum for Wayward Victorian Girls.

A towering pyre was made in the field over the Pits that still concealed the corpses of all who had ridden unwittingly in the Death Cart. We laid our newly dead upon the pyre, and covered them with the branches and wild rosemary we had found growing nearby. *Rosemary, for remembrance*, says Ophelia . . . a symbol that our sisters will not be forgotten.

As the sun set behind the bordering trees, a very curious procession emerged from the Asylum: Walking one-by-one, each girl wore clean stockings and a wrap of table linens for warmth; our bandaged hands held lanterns and slender ivory tapers. We were flanked upon both sides by rows of our Plague Rats; they walked with us through the courtyard and round to the side of the institution where the field lay. When we reached the Death Pits, we formed a circle round the pyre and raised our flames.

My heart was full with memories of the friends I had lost—girls, women who had died unidentified, unclaimed, and unimportant, yet who were here with me still.

I lowered my taper to the mound of sticks and fragrant brush, and so followed the multitude round me. As the flames rose higher into the glittering heavens, we threw back our heads and sang until our throats were dry.

Good night, sweet ladies, good night, sweet friends
You lie but sleeping, someday we will meet again
Sweet ladies, good night, sweet friends
You lie but sleeping, someday we will meet again
With rosemary green and bright
You're not forgotten, eternal night
Can't fade your memory, dim your light
You've made a difference, you've won your fight
We lift our branches and though we weep
No death could conquer, you only sleep
Good night, sweet ladies, good night, sweet friends
You lie but sleeping, someday we will meet again

Asylum Letter No. LXVI

It was the night following the Massacre that we decided to stay. Returning from our makeshift memorial, we gathered round the great hearth in the Entrance Hall, surrounded by cups of tea and everything from the kitchen pantry that was remotely edible, our bodies slowly remembering what it was like to be warm. There, we discussed our options.

One of our numbers claimed to have an uncle just outside of London; perhaps he could take one of us on as a maid in exchange for board, provided he was still living. Another knew of a public house that might hire one or two of us as barmaids under the same conditions, provided it were still standing. Further suggestions were proposed, each one more utterly impractical and entirely impossible than the last. The most qualified amongst us was no better off than the least; a girl who may once have been employed as a tutor of children or even a seller of hats would never again be allowed even these small opportunities. It would only be a danger to return to our families, most of which wouldn't be where we had left them, and wouldn't want us if they were, as they clearly hadn't wanted us before.

Where could we go but the streets? If the criteria for madness were still what we knew them to be, surely it would not be long before we were imprisoned all over again within one asylum or another. And, if we did succeed in avoiding recapture, what was our place in the world? With no money, no connections, and, worse, a bad name eternally attached to all things unsavoury, the best we could hope for would be occasional employment as seamstresses, a job that could never pay the most meager of expenses, or frequent employment as prostitutes, a job that we had all had quite enough of, thank you very much. No respectable household would ever take us on, not even as below-stairs kitchen maids, especially once they saw the brands upon our arms. No, once driven through the Asylum's sharply spiked gates, we were dead to the world, and just as well, for I did not think we could have kept even these lowly positions if given the opportunity; we had been removed from civilization too long to ever fit back into it.

'I do not think,' I said, after a time had passed in silence, 'that I shall go anywhere at all.'

'What do you mean?' asked my ladies. 'You intend to stay *here*? In the Asylum?'

A new life was slowly unfurling inside my mind. I was feeling the space round me and stretching my fingers to see if I could fill it. I was breathing the corrupted air and wondering if I could cleanse it of its poison.

'I think,' said I, 'that I mean to hold tightly to the freedom I have just won. If I step back through those gates, I become property of the world again, and I do not think that I can be anyone's property—anyone's *anything*—anymore . . . not ever. Can you?'

I saw that my fellow inmates were turning over this new idea to look at it upon all sides. They did not say 'yes', but they did not say 'no', and, little by little, I saw the gleam, gone for so long, return to Jolie Rouge's azure eyes.

I looked round at my dear, cherished sisters . . . the only family I have ever known.

'Yes, I *shall* stay,' I resolved. 'I shall devote what is left of my life to making my prison my palace. Just think of it, ladies: An asylum, by definition, ought to be a sanctuary for those who need one, and I fear I shall always need one.'

In the days that followed, the doors were open, the girls were free, and nobody left. The Asylum was ours now, and, finally, we belonged here.

Asylum Letter No. LXVII

It didn't take long to clean up the Asylum. The furnace came in quite handy for the disposal of the staff. Madam Mournington I had burned separately, for I felt she was owed that much for her final deed. Before I left her, I took the cameo brooch from her throat, and, later, buried it beneath the rosemary, with a prayer for the child who had been Dr. Stockill's first victim. Then, the basement was boarded up; no one ever need go there again.

It's funny, Diary . . . we thought we had eradicated our collective enemies, but the truth is that we never will. Having been tormented for so long, we no longer know what life is without this treatment. We had not felt ourselves change, yet, gradually, we had become so accustomed to such monstrosities that, now that we are free, we feel strangely drawn to them.

Consider the leeches as an example: Many of us had made peace with our blood-sucking companions long ago, and we continue to apply the creatures to ourselves and to each other even though we no longer must. After all, they had been prisoners too—abducted from their natural habitats just as we were; they have names, and voices, and, well, they must be fed.

Though all of the cruelty has gone out of it, we sometimes bind each other in the manacles and straight waistcoats of our former nightmares. It has become a game to us—we hold contests to see who can escape their restraints the quickest. We have decorated the wheeled metal beds from the Bloodletting Wing and race them down the same corridors we used to dread. We have found a thousand uses for the instruments of our torture, claiming them as our own, and reclaiming ourselves in the process.

The Plague Rats remain of the utmost importance to every aspect of our lives here, with the ever-protective Sir Edward watching over us all, the father few of us had ever known. The rats sit with us at tea, drinking from our cups, nibbling the crumpets and scones and teacakes, for we have such things now.

In fact, we have every material thing that we could wish for, and far more. Under the Asylum's previous regime, our tyrant-gaolers had absconded our belongings immediately upon arrival; they had sold some of our goods, and spent much of our money, but there remained hidden chambers filled with treasures amassed over decades—more than we needed to live as frivolously as we pleased for the rest of our days.

I had arrived entirely bereft of belongings, but many others had been deposited here by wealthy families who abandoned them, indeed, but not without full purses, having been given to think that their wards would be better cared for the more valuables they brought with them. Only too easy to fool, these guardians believed all this and had continued to send money, if only to ease their own consciences, never knowing that improved conditions could not be bought—not for any price.

The Asylum had been governed by masters of deception, yet it could not be denied that our directors preyed upon those more than willing to be deceived—who could be so easily led into doing evil. Worse, those who had a girl committed never knew what evil they had done. No one was informed when an inmate had died, and very few of those who brought us their mad ever returned, or even wrote to inquire after the progress of the 'cure', which was just as well, for the Asylum did not deal in cures.

We now govern ourselves, and we will never submit to anyone.

If the world never cared to know of the violence inflicted upon us, then the world ought not care to know of the violence that we had finally inflicted back. Besides ordering goods by post, we rarely have, nor have need of, direct communication with society beyond our gates. It is imperative to our survival that no one ever know of what has taken place here.

There is but one thing that weighs heavily upon my mind, and this is only because it is something I cannot share, and so I bear the burden alone: Just before the dawn following the Tea Party Massacre, I had entered the Operating Theatre intending to select a suitable knife for the Captain, for she wished to greet the The Cell's final customer herself and finish the task she had begun at Bainbridge. We had left Dr. Greavesly dead upon the operating table hours earlier, but, upon reentry, I found the table empty.

Frantic, I flew to the window just in time to see a figure, hunched and limping, stumbling through the early morning mist and into the black woods behind the Asylum, leaving a winding trail of red in the snow behind him. I prayed that he would die in the merciless cold, and that, should he chance to live, he would not be back.

Asylum Letter No. LXVIII

From the very start of our new life within the Asylum, we had come to agreement by unanimous vote on one very particular point: We would continue to accept new patients. In the event that a girl was as sane as are the most of us, she might prove a pleasant addition to our strange society, and, if a girl truly was mad, and in need of serious care and rehabilitation, then perhaps we could make the Asylum for Wayward Victorian Girls what it always ought to have been: a place of safety and shelter . . . a sanctuary . . . an asylum.

And this, Diary, is how Sachiko came back into my life. She was delivered one morning in the hansom of a police constable who had found her walking backwards upon a railroad track just outside of London. Upon arrival, Sachiko refused to speak, and was so entirely catatonic that she did not recognize me, her oldest friend. As the months passed, my childhood companion was gradually revived to her former self, and better. We all have our battle scars, and Sachiko has not yet been able to tell me of precisely what happened to her during the small eternity for which we had been separated. Someday, perhaps, I will know her story, but, in truth, it little matters; we try our best to look to the future and leave our histories behind. We are learning to live again, and, for many of us, it is for the first time.

Yet, despite our best efforts, I do not suppose that we will ever know happiness as other people do—people who have never suffered as we have. I reckon that the reason we now indulge in our luxuries and teas and dances and music and all things beautiful and even frivolous is simply to counter-vail the reality that, no matter how many years are left to us, there will never be enough time to fill the void that had been borne inside of us each when we were made so brutally aware of how very little we mattered to the world. Revenge itself may indeed be the best revenge, but slaying one's enemy does not give back what they stole. There is not enough revenge in the world for that.

Still, we do our best to live as blissfully as we can, and I daresay we have great fun trying. We have reformed the Asylum in every aspect, from the kitchen to the cells and even the flat rooftop over the Wards where we often gather to look down upon the city of London as the sun sets—upon those same twinkling lights I had once marveled at as I stood bare-foot in the middle of a bridge with Anne at my side. I am now equally removed from the city as I was upon that day, but I am no longer running towards it.

We have between us girls of every conceivable talent, from bakers, who craft the most exquisite creations from pastry and cream (and who enable us to enjoy High Tea at both four o'clock in the afternoon and four o'clock in the morning), to writers and painters of great brilliance, to master musicians, of whom I am proud to count myself amongst, and who keep our extraordinary household supplied with music, for there is always music, and Sachiko and I play our Mozart duets for royalty as we always said we would, for we are the kings and the queens, and *this* is our territory.

Asylum Letter No. LXIX

It is the eve of the New Year at last.

We have enjoyed the most glorious Yuletide, and the scent of pine and sugarplums still fills the Asylum. Whilst many of our girls had passed the holiday in teaching themselves to skate upon the icy surface of the Bathing Court, I had assigned myself the monumental task of creating a perfect Asylum replica in gingerbread for the Plague Rats. But it is the turning of the year that I have looked most forward to since we attained our freedom.

Upon this eve, we mean to begin what I believe will become our most precious annual tradition. We have organized a Tea Ball—a grand tea and dance—upon the rooftops of the entire institution. It shall be the affair to transcend all other Asylum celebrations, and those in the city as well, I am quite sure.

In preparation for our first Ball, we each contributed our individual talents: I had devoted months to the composition of a new musical work to be presented at midnight, and the ladies in the kitchen planned a lavish, highest-of-the-high tea, with a three-meter *croquembouche*, a pirate ship made entirely of spun sugar, and enough champagne sent up from London for every girl, and every rat too.

We have agreed to dress in white from head to toe as a symbol of our resurrection, and I think this particularly meaningful, for I feel that we are finally growing into our new life. Though our phantoms will never leave us, our demons are almost gone.

The clock in the Entrance Hall rang out in joyful majesty—the Ball was soon to begin.

We ascended to the rooftops, followed by the Asylum ghosts, their wispy figures swirling about our skirts as we climbed the old staircase, emerging from the corners and within the striped walls to join us for our greatest celebration of freedom and unity.

I confess that, in my quieter moments, I often try to spot Veronica amongst the ghosts, but I never can, and I have learnt to be glad that she has been able to leave this place, even as I chose to stay. I content myself with the belief that, when I am at my end, she will be waiting.

At last, it was time.

A trail of teacups alight with flame marked the path leading to the rooftop dancing floor, and every girl was now in her place. As the musicians sounded the first note of the evening, a blinding shower of sparks—my surprise for my fellow inmates—exploded into the star-filled sky.

The revelry commenced, and, my God, the sheer joy exuding from every soul in communion was . . . overpowering. Though it was winter, and tiny flakes of snow had begun to fall, we were warmed by our dancing, by the blazing fires set in great stone urns placed about the roof, and, truth be told, by our liquid refreshments, be it the steam from the tea, or the bubbles from the champagne.

I began to feel inexplicably overwrought, almost as though I were—and this will sound very strange, Diary—as though I were *too* happy. I left the crowd to sit in solitude for a moment. I felt a hand brush my shoulder; I thought I heard Veronica's voice speaking my name, but, when I turned to look, no one was there.

I had not been away long when the Captain found me, bearing a teacup filled with pink champagne and candied ginger.

'Do you remember, Captain, a Sunday morning when I found that poor rat dead in the soup?'

'I think I will never forget it.'

'It was upon that day that I remember comprehending with complete clarity that we were truly prisoners . . . that all hope was lost to us . . .'

'Yes, sweet Valentine, but you have led us into a new life . . . you created hope where there was none, and *now* look what we have!'

'And I am so happy . . . but that's just it. I feel as though . . . as though I have realised with equal clarity that we are free, and, not only that, but *more* free than we had ever dreamt of being, and I don't know what comes next . . .'

The Captain took me in her arms. The ladies of the Striped Stocking Society rushed towards us with gleeful shouts, pulling us up and onto the floor with the other revelers. Determined to enjoy this moment, I breathed deeply and swallowed the contents of my teacup before tossing it aside to smash against the chimney. The music swelled, the dancers twirled, and I spun madly. Lifting my face to the sky, the silver powder settled upon my flushed cheeks, cooling them just enough that I may continue my wildness. It would soon be time to look to the constellations and welcome the New Year.

And, finally, I had done it!

I had managed to break through my past, through my memories, those that kept some secret part of my being embedded in the life I had long escaped. My happiness rose within me—a living, pulsating light, shooting from my toes to my legs and up through my raised arms to my fingertips—and I thought, *This! This is what freedom really feels like!*

I fell to the ground.

Sachiko ran to help me up, but I told her I was all right, and stood on my own.

Then, we both fell.

The rooftops were shaking, our beautiful scenery crashing down about us. All stood motionless and listened as a deep, yawning groan rose from the very depths of the building we stood upon. This unearthly noise was immediately followed by the sound of crumbling brick and stone.

The Asylum was collapsing.

Iron bars snapped out of cell windows as the structure round them was crushed under its own weight. And then, entire segments of the tenement began to fall.

I heard the words of Sir Edward upon the night I had first met him in Ward A . . . he had told me then that the Asylum was built directly upon the city's rubbish heap—that it was built only to deceive, that it had no foundation at all, that it was never, ever meant to last. It had always been a façade— outwardly grand, but, inside, merely mistake built upon mistake, flaw upon flaw upon flaw . . .

Every wall that had miraculously stood these long years had surrendered to the inevitable at last, and, as one fell, the rest followed.

How could I have thought that this could go on forever?

Rats scurried between the dashing feet of the panicked inmates as they hurried about in their voluminous gowns, frantically attempting to find a way down from the rooftops, but the exits were either blocked or had already fallen away.

And that is when the flames broke out.

The increasing snowfall did its best to contain the mounting inferno, but I knew that, within minutes, we would be engulfed.

I stared as hundreds of inmates, in an act of astonishing acceptance, lined themselves up along the roof's edge and began to jump—some alone, many holding hands, their skirts billowing about them, soft curls flying every which where through a sparkling midnight sky.

It was breathtaking.

Suicide, I thought, *is a cold, ugly, desperate thing, and, when it happens, it is always lonely. Suicide is not the poetic act that our painters portray.*

But the truth is that, in this moment alone, it was.

Peering over the ledge still intact before me at the ground so fatally far below, I thought of Anne—of that night we stood together, leaning over the rail of the bridge . . . of how the moon had shown us a different path that neither the Count, nor his friends, nor his hounds, nor anyone in the world save us could follow . . . .

I climbed up onto the ledge and extended my hand to the Captain.

'Well, where shall we sail to next, Captain?' I asked her, so that all round me could hear.

Our eyes locked, and she leapt up onto the ledge beside me.

'An entirely new destination, I think! The routing has only just been mapped, and we shall be the very first to explore it if we board the ship at once.'

Sachiko mounted and bravely took my other hand.

Enormous fragments of the roof were simply falling away, and the flames were close behind us.

I glanced back to my fellow inmates, and, as they dispersed towards the ledge, I saw Veronica. Her soft white gown melted into the snow she stood upon like sea mist; moonlit tendrils tumbled round her shoulders, and she smiled at me.

Then, I saw Anne. She, too, was smiling, and her green eyes gleamed as she gave a single nod of her head.

A third figure appeared from behind them and stepped forwards. Madam Mournington's hair was long and loose, and her eyes were every bit as beautiful as I had once suspected they might have been. I had never imagined them filled with such kindness, nor the smile so sweet.

'Anchors aweigh!' shouted the Captain, raising her ancient paper hat high into the air.

The last of the inmates took their places upon the ledge, and we all joined hands.

I called out to them for the last time.

'Goodnight, sweet Ladies, goodnight . . .'

And then, we jumped.

hospital entry 26: missing

It's four o'clock and I can't sleep.

I feel sick.

I refuse to believe that the Asylum is gone . . . that it really, truly collapsed . . . Emily dead . . . all dead . . . all over . . . I cannot . . . I *will* not believe it really happened . . . this is not how it's supposed to end . . .

I need to see the letter again.

Is it really to be my last?

Can I survive this place without Emily? Without all of them?

I don't think I can do it.

I don't even think I *want* to do it.

I'm starting to panic. I need to get out of this room. I need to get out of this hospital. I reach down into my stocking to retrieve the last letter . . . I wish there were some fucking light in here . . .

Something isn't right.

The paper feels different. It isn't the waxy, delicate parchment I had touched only a few hours ago. It is thicker . . . rough . . . with texture but without form.

I leap out of bed and open the heavy plastic curtains to look through the bars for a sliver of moon to see the letter by.

But I am not holding a letter.

I am holding . . . what is it . . . it looks almost like . . . a napkin . . . like the coarse, brown paper napkins in the psych ward bathroom . . .

I race to the locked doors, pounding them with my fists, shouting for the nurses to let me out, shouting that it's an emergency. My cellmates turn over in their beds, but they are too drugged to care about the noise. Finally, a nurse comes running and the heavy doors open. The artificial light in the hallway is blinding.

"Emilie! What are you doing?" asks the nurse, pulling me outside the bedroom.

"Somebody has been taking my things," I tell her.

Am I having a panic attack? I can't breathe.

"Somebody has been in my things. Somebody has been in my *bed*. Somebody in that room took something of mine, and I want it back right now. I don't care what time it is—this is *not* OK. Right now. Right now. Right now."

"Emilie, you have to calm down; we don't want to wake everybody, do we? Now, come along with me and we'll get you something to make you sleep. You've had a bad dream, that's all. We can switch up your medication and see if that helps."

"No! I don't want any more of your fucking drugs, and I don't want to fucking calm down. I want you to go in there right now and wake everybody up and find out who took it!"

"Took what, Emilie? What is it you're missing?"

I am not going to explain this to her. I need my notebook.

"Nothing . . . it's nothing. May I please get a personal belonging from the closet?"

"No, Emilie, not now—you'll have to wait until morning. Let's go. Come with me."

"Please . . . please . . . please, all I want is my notebook and I promise I'll calm down. I will be so fucking calm. Please . . . I'm saying please . . ."

The nurse pauses—this is not allowed.

"OK, Emilie, you can have your notebook, but only for five minutes, and then you have to go back to bed."

We walk down the hall toward the closet. The nurse's hand is on my shoulder. She is trying to keep contact—to anticipate my next move. She unlocks the closet door, and before she can pull the string to turn on the light, I am inside, digging through the boxes to locate my own. I feel for my notebook. The light comes on and I find it. Notebook in hand, I turn and walk quickly into the Day Room. *Don't run, don't run, don't run.*

"Emilie, let me give you something."

The nurse is following me.

"No, thank you, leave me alone. Leave me alone. Leave me alone."

I walk away from her. I know I am repeating myself, but I don't know why.

"All right, but five minutes, Emilie. I'll come back to get you."

I hear the nurse return to the glass booth; she is talking nervously to the other nurse on night watch. I sit down upon the old green couch that I had shared with Violet that day . . . that day when she had told me . . . I am tearing through the pages, looking for my Asylum letters, but they are not here. Between the pages where the letters ought to be are the same brown paper napkins, then a paper menu from the kitchen, then more napkins, another menu, more napkins, tissues, the wrapping from a teabag . . . there is scribbling on the rubbish, some in red crayon, some in pencil, scribbling, just scribbling . . . I bolt from the Day Room and pound on the booth where the two women are sitting and drinking coffee. One is on the phone, and the other comes to the window and talks to me through the small opening at the bottom, just like a ticket window at the movies . . . it's just like a ticket window . . . like they're selling something . . .

"What is it, Emilie?"

"Somebody has been through my notebook and taken my letters. This is *not* OK. You can *not* do this. I want to know who did this, and I want my letters back. Now."

"Emilie, nobody has been through your notebook. We don't do that here—your belongings are *your* belongings, and we respect that. Anything that was there is still there."

"That is a lie! You're lying to me! Get out of that cage, you cowardly bitch! Get out and look at this!"

The nurse emerges from the office.

"All right, Emilie, show me what's missing. Nance, will you get something for Emilie to take?"

"Look. I had letters in here. Here and here and here . . . between these pages . . . dozens of them . . . a hundred . . . they are all gone, and there is a bunch of garbage that I did *not* put here. Somebody has been in my notebook and replaced my letters with napkins and . . . and . . . *trash*. I need to have my letters back. Please," I am pleading now, "can you please find out where they are? I just need them back. I need them back. I need them back. I need—"

"Emilie, calm down, deep breath . . . come on now, give me one deep breath. That's a good girl. Now, let's look at this together. Let's see . . . The writing on this napkin looks like yours, doesn't it? And this one . . . this is *your* writing, Emilie. Can't you tell?"

It is my writing. It is my writing that goes from an elegant print to an unrecognizable scrawl and then back again . . . I have never understood why I can't just write in one normal style like normal people do. It is my writing. It is unmistakable. But it is impossible.

"No, this is wrong. I don't remember writing these. I didn't write these. I don't even know what they say . . . this is all gibberish . . . it doesn't say *anything* . . ."

Wait a minute.

"How did you know that?" I ask the nurse, quietly.

"How did I know what, Emilie?"

"How did you know that's my writing? Why would you know what my writing looks like?"

I'm not calm anymore.

"WHY WOULD YOU KNOW WHAT MY WRITING LOOKS LIKE?"

Oh god . . . Violet was right . . . they've been in my notebook . . . they've read everything.

"No, this is not right at all . . . No. No. No. No. No."

I am slapping the wall with each "No."

I can't stop.

Nancy, the other nurse, returns; she has brought one of the armed security guards back with her. An enormous beast with hideous breath, he calls me "sweetheart" and grips my shoulders tightly. Nurse Nancy forces the pills into my mouth and tries to pour water from a tiny paper cup down after them, but it only ends up on my face and spilling down my chest, soaking my hospital gown.

I hear myself screaming.

The notebook is on the floor, the napkins and other trash scattered around it.

I think I just kicked the guard who has hold of me from behind.

Dr. Sharp is rushing through the double iron doors that guard the entrance to the Maximum Security Psych Ward. He is walking toward me and I am trying to run away, but I can't. What is he doing here at this hour? Is he always here? Does he live here? Does he have a camera on me? Is he fucking watching me all the fucking time? I am screaming at him to get away from me. I don't want him to touch me. The guard lifts me from the ground as if I am no heavier than a lapdog or a throw pillow, and Dr. Sharp directs him into a room just off the hallway as I flail my limbs, trying to escape the giant's grasp. He is laying me onto a sterile white bed with a cold metal frame, and Dr. Sharp is strapping me down. He is strapping me down. I am being strapped down.

My vision is getting blurry . . . I can hear them all talking, but it sounds very far away . . . this is what the voices sounded like when I was little . . . this is exactly what they sounded like . . . what pills did she give me? The nurse is flicking the tip of a syringe. The Doctor's hands are on me. He is standing at the foot of my bed, holding down my legs. The Chaser is lifting my shoulders, exposing my back. Through half-closed eyes, I am looking directly at Dr. Stockill. Is he smiling at me? He nods to the nurse. My hair is lifted out of the way, and I feel the needle piercing the back of my ne—

hospital entry 27: the end

I am awake. I don't know where I am. But I am awake.

I am somewhere else.

I am lying flat upon a hard, narrow gurney.

My eyes flutter open to observe yet another awful fluorescent light buzzing overhead.

There is a strap buckled across my chest, two more around my wrists, and another over my legs. My wrists are thin, like Anne Boleyn's neck, and I manage to free my hands. I unbuckle the other straps and sit upright.

The room is small and painfully bright. It is a hospital room, cold and clinical, but there is nothing in it besides the metal bed with its thin blue mattress. Everything in the hospital that isn't white is blue . . . I think I once heard that this is because blue is the opposite of blood . . .

There is a single door with its standard silver hospital doorknob. I step down from the bed and walk to the door, my legs quivering.

I try the knob.

The door is locked.

It is completely quiet outside. Impossibly quiet. I knock on the door.

"Hello? Somebody?"

No answer. I am pounding on the door now.

"Somebody? Anybody? I'm awake!"

Still nothing.

"I'm awake! I want to come out!"

Dead silence. I am in a vacuum.

I am beating on the door . . . on the walls. I am screaming my bloody head off . . . I am screaming until I can't breathe . . . until my voice is gone and I can make no more sound. I am exhausted . . . I feel like my brain is shutting down . . . what have they done with me?

I sink to the floor . . . I don't know I've been crying until I feel the tears drying upon my face . . . I collapse in the corner, facing the wall, leaning my head against the plaster . . . it is far too white . . . blindingly white . . . it hurts my eyes.

I lift my hand to touch the wall . . . I feel a tiny crack in the paint . . . I pick at it . . . bits of paint flake off onto the speckled linoleum floor . . . I can't stop . . . larger flakes are peeling off . . . I am tearing at the wall now . . . I've made a large hole in the plaster . . . I'm still tearing . . . my fingers are bleeding, smearing the wall with red . . .

Finally, I sit back and look at what I've done.

Where the plaster has been torn away, I see the layer beneath . . . stripes . . . black-and-white . . . they're moving . . .

Excerpt #1 from confiscated notebook, passage of interest, typed out for clarity:

I had always thought that cutting was something that angsty teenage girls did for attention. That was before I began doing it.

It was strange how it all started . . . I was overcome by a sudden and intense compulsion to take a knife to myself. I had never before felt this, nor had I ever imagined feeling it. It came from within me—from some dark, primeval place. No one put the idea into my head. No one told me how it worked. I had never read about it. There was no provocation. It was all me.

The call is coming from inside your house . . .

Once the desire had come into me, I could not get the idea out of my mind. I was like an alcoholic who's never had a drink—I needed a fix of something I hadn't even tried yet.

The first time I gave in, I took apart a shaving razor. I was surprised at how easily it gave up its blades to me. The moment

I made that first, fateful slice, I experienced the gratification I had anticipated, and more. I knew instantly, as I sat upon the dirty pink tiles of the bathroom floor, watching the blood rising to the surface of my thigh, that I had just embarked upon a path I could never turn back from—a path that would change others' perception of me, as well as my perception of myself. That first slice was the severing of my already fraying bonds to those around me. I was now separate. I was *branded*, and I was glad to be.

I had always been ashamed of being manic depressive, and recently having post-traumatic stress disorder tacked onto that diagnosis was even worse. *What right have I*, I thought, and still do think, *to be depressed when there are people in this world who suffer so much worse in their lives than I?* I was ashamed to have a disease that nobody could see, but now, I had proof. I had visible symptoms, and I wouldn't have to explain myself anymore. I soon learned that I would spend my life defending myself instead.

Excerpt #4 from confiscated notebook, passage of interest, typed out for clarity:

I inspect my newly carved chest in the mirror that does not belong to me—nothing here belongs to me except my violin and my razor blades. And I see that it is my logo. My crossed heart. The one I sign my name with. God, how self-indulgent, I think, but whom then should I indulge if not myself?

I remind myself that my logo did not start out as a logo at all, but was merely a symbol I painstakingly painted upon my right cheek each morning during a particular period of my life when I needed it, as I still do, and the fact that hundreds of thousands are now aware of this logo and associate it with the brand that is me, Emilie Autumn, the girl who screams on stage and wears striped stockings up to her scars and ties a corset tighter than anyone, doesn't take away what it originally meant to me.

I have a heart to break is all it means. I am killable. It doesn't mean *down with love* or *I hate my ex-boyfriend* or any other mundanely pedestrian sentiment. It means that I have that within me that can also destroy me.

I learned this in the cruelest of ways. I am not special. I am not polished, or strong, or protected.

But I am protecting myself now.

When I paint this symbol upon my face each day, using a waxy scarlet lipstick and cheap black liquid eyeliner, it is the battle scar that reminds me both of my beating heart and of its fragility, and of how very raw I am. Besides, studying the fresh wound blazing upon my chest, the prohibitive X, the two curves and the point where they meet, you may think I had tried, quite literally, to cut out my heart.

And perhaps I did.

Excerpt #7 from confiscated notebook, passage of interest, typed out for clarity:

How is it that it is considered perfectly acceptable that I am harmed by endless external attacks, in infinite ways—from abuse, from rape, from this patriarchal culture in which females are spiritually slaughtered the moment they are ripped from the fucking womb, from the mundane cruelties of life that affect us all—and yet *I have no right* to harm, even superficially, myself?

It does seem a bit backwards to me that I must treat myself as a precious object when nobody else does.

Everything that is done to me from the outside—*all* of that I am advised and expected to "get over" and "forgive," and I can even pay a therapist hundreds of dollars per hour to teach me how to do this (there are a lot of people making money off of my pain). But I am not allowed to forgive myself, even if I wanted to. I am not allowed to forgive myself, because no one will forgive *me*.

Excerpt #21 from confiscated notebook, passage of interest, typed out for clarity:

There is not one, solitary reason why people cut themselves. There is *never* just one.

In my own personal case, I am driven by profound disappointment, a sense of irretrievably lost control over even the most intimate parts of my body, and, oh yes, I'm also gifted with one of the deadliest forms of mental illness.

I need this. But for how long? I can't do this forever, I'll run out of skin. There is thus, inevitably, an end date on this activity. But I am frightened. For cutting is just like crying . . . so much easier to start than to stop.

Yet there is also that element of entertainment—of wonder at the almost sensual pain during the cut, at the speed with which the crimson pearls rise to the surface, at the moment one waits in breathless anticipation to see whether, when the blood does come, it will be in the form of a thin, red line, or will it actually spill out in droplets, and then still more wonder at how the wound rushes and weeps, suddenly impatient, as the iodine is applied, just as a hug from a friend when one is on the verge of tears sends one into floods of them. It's almost as though we wait to see that it is all going to be OK—that we are someplace safe, with someone that we trust.

Excerpt #32 from confiscated notebook, passage of EXTREME interest, typed out for clarity:

Most of the insults I have personally received as a result of my cutting (which really does seem to make people curiously angry) have not been to do with how this act may hurt me, or what it says about how sad and desperate I must be—no, they have all been exclusively to do with how *disgusting* it is. How *perversely disgusting* it is. How perversely disgusting it is to *them*.

And, sure . . . perhaps coming from boys who have never suffered more than a scraped knee and are utterly unaware of what it *really* is to be badass, and who also no doubt look upon my body as something belonging to them, in which case I am also committing the crime of property damage, this does make a lot of sense. Yet it should perhaps be considered how very much blood I have to both see and *feel* pass through me for the too-many tedious months of my life before I am told that finding solace in seeing my own blood is so *very* perverse and shocking.

The truth is that girls are conditioned from the age of approximately twelve years old to see their own blood, and lots of it. We have *all* touched our own blood, because you can't do what girls need to do without coming into occasional contact. And, the thing is, it becomes perfectly normal.

Please . . . take a moment to explore the mind-numbing reality of just how much blood one girl not only bleeds but sees during the course of her life, and that's not counting childbirth, my friends, which is on a whole other planet.

I am hardly suggesting that this lifelong proximity to blood is any catalyst to begin cutting.

It isn't.

I simply believe that for friends, family, doctors, lovers, all of those surrounding a person who has cut herself to behave as though she had committed a crime, a disgusting, disgusting, *disgusting* crime, a crime against herself, and a crime of the *worst* kind because it damages her body, her precious, *precious* body, is a bit ridiculous.

For this *precious* body is the very same that is hooted and honked at, demeaned both in daily life as well as in ever evolving forms of media, harassed, molested, raped, and, if all that wasn't enough, is forever poked and prodded and weighed and constantly wrong for eating too much, eating too little—a million billion never-ending details which all point to the solitary girl—to *every* solitary girl—and say:

DESTROY YOURSELF

Excerpt #39 from confiscated notebook, passage of interest, typed out for clarity:

I have been really, *really* careful to do this right. I am a perfectionist in this as in all things. I am being clean, sterilizing everything I touch, protecting myself against infection because, *again*, I am not cutting to fucking kill myself. I am doing it so that I can get away from this constant compulsion toward suicide. *I am doing it not to die.*

And, in the end, I can tell you exactly what cutting is about, because it's not nearly as mysterious as anyone thinks: It is not about attention, or pity, or "self-harm," which is a terribly stupid term by the way. No. It is about one thing. It is about control. And I am filled with twenty-six years of female rage and a deadly determination to take mine back.

Though I had never set out to display them, I made my cuts in particularly intimate areas of my body that would only be known to the next person I allowed too close in a moment of forgetfulness. I wanted that person to know, and before it was too late, that I was *crazy* and *scary* and should be backed away from *immediately*. I didn't want to have to talk about it any-more. Just like a good novel, *show, don't tell.*

Excerpt #48 from confiscated notebook, passage of interest, typed out for clarity:

Practicing my violin tonight, my fingers are trembling and stiff, wobbly, drugged. I cannot imagine how I could possibly walk let alone play intelligently. And I know now that I am being experimented on. They don't know what they're doing. They're just throwing pills against the wall (or into my mouth) and seeing what sticks. I am a lab rat. I am a fucking violin-playing lab rat. I am a fucking violin-playing lab rat who wants to cut off her tail again. And her ears. And her whiskers.

Excerpt #52 from confiscated notebook, passage of interest, typed out for clarity:

The trouble with forgiving people is that it makes writing terrible things about them so much more difficult.

I have promised not to cut myself in his house.

(Doctor's Note: "His" is assumed to be referencing W14A's boyfriend at the time of this writing. We have been investigating the identity of this man and have narrowed it down to two subjects, one extremely famous, one marginally so. Names will be made available to specialists upon request.)

Fair enough.

I have managed to keep my word, and I am too strung out on what the doctor has forced into me to go anywhere else, so that means I don't cut at all, which is a good thing I suppose. Perhaps I am over the "phase," as he calls it . . . that would be nice. This was never supposed to be a way of life . . . it was about survival. But, is it not strange that the only things I don't feel guilty about are the very things everyone else has put me on trial for?

I know that what I was doing was madness in all eyes but mine, yet I wasn't shy about it at all. I hadn't done it to show off to people, nor to hide. My fault was that my sense of self-worth, or lack thereof depending upon where you're standing, was not bound up in my physical appearance—especially not in my legs or my chest. In my over-medicated (wrongly medicated) state, I couldn't remember to make everyone else around me comfortable *first*, and, for once in my life, *I didn't care.*

I wore the same clothes I always did, and it didn't occur to me that, because they could see an inch of a scratch that ran lower down my thigh than my skirt did, I was making the people around me extremely uncomfortable. It didn't occur to me because I wasn't ashamed of what I had done, which is not to say that I was proud of it—I wasn't. It was just something I did, because I needed to. For me.

Just for me.

Would I cut myself now? I don't know. When I did, it was for a good reason. If I did again, I'm sure it would also be for a good reason. I suppose that the cutting is really beside the point—it is the *reason* for cutting that I would like very much to avoid . . .

(Doctor's Note: We are unsure if W14A actually discontinued her pattern of self-harm as she seems to be claiming here, but no further reference to cutting is made in the notebook we confiscated, though some pictures have tested positive to having been painted in blood, as suspected. The marks currently found upon her legs—upper thighs—appear to be fresh, but could have been made within the last two weeks, perhaps more as her healing may have been slow due to extreme anemia.)

Excerpt #65 from confiscated notebook, passage of interest, typed out for clarity:

The very worst thing about being bipolar, depressed, or mentally ill in likely any way, is that any time you're legitimately sad—any time you're truly angry—and with good and clear reason, you will be told that you are only feeling as you are because of your illness. Every time your boyfriend is being an ass and you call him on it, this is what you will hear, so get used to it:

"Have you taken your medication today?"

A life of non-credibility, even amongst those you love—this is what you face. It is the eternal equivalent of being asked if it's your "time of the month" every time you get upset. If *this* doesn't make you want to kill yourself, I don't know what will.

Excerpt #78 from confiscated notebook, passage of interest, typed out for clarity:

It's difficult to tell someone that they shouldn't be defined by their illness. Or, rather, it's easy to tell someone, but it's difficult to hear.

It is impossible *not* to become defined by your illness, even to yourself, when everything you do is so closely intertwined with it. There is virtually no part of your life that you live like other people do—even the smallest detail is adjusted in some way—a way very possibly imperceptible from the outside.

And then there is always the question of what you *are* allowed to define yourself by, if not by something that affects you more than any other influence in your life possibly could.

Manic Depression surrounds me as much as my own skin does. It is my skin, but it is also my blood. I still own my heart, which I know because it hurts so much.

Excerpt #89 from confiscated notebook, passage of EXTREME interest, typed out for clarity:

For the Asylum doctor, a cured patient represents a serious threat; if you're well enough to leave, you're well enough to talk.

(Doctor's Note: W14A exhibits paranoia and inability to remain in her own reality, begins to reference "Asylum" more frequently.)

Excerpt #96 from confiscated notebook, passage of interest, typed out for clarity:

The Asylum serves to control rather than cure us . . .

Excerpt #99 from confiscated notebook, passage of interest, typed out for clarity:

I have only just tonight had the courage to open the bottle of Lithium that I have had in my possession for some time now. I'm stalling . . . I don't want to take these.

L . . . I . . . T . . . H . . . I . . . U . . . M . . .

Of course, to my eyes, the writing upon each pill only seems to taunt me, each precious pink gem of promised sanity reminding me just how far into the madness I have gone.

Lithium.
"It's just a salt," they said.
It's *just a salt*, though you must be sure to drink a great deal of water or else you'll die. But it's just a salt.
My *cure* is salt and water?

"Too much of water hast thou, poor Ophelia . . ."

Lithium. Lithium. Lithium.

You don't come back from Lithium.
Zoloft?
Prozac?
Maybe.
But not Lithium.
Lithium isn't for people who have bad moods.
Lithium is for lifers.
You're not going home after this.

Excerpt #102 from confiscated notebook, passage of interest, typed out for clarity:

I am nodding off now, eyelids drooping, exhausted.

As the medication kicks in, my writing becomes smaller and messier and seems to spiral downward into places that I don't know about . . .

It is almost like being possessed.

I look down at the journal I have been obsessively keeping, and I find page after page of words I can scarcely make out, written in a hand that is not my own, and yet, I've got ink on my fingers.

It is the following morning, and I can barely read what I wrote last night, and that is what both fascinates and terrorizes me.

Even now, I have no idea what I'm writing, and have to review the sentence I just finished in order to know where my thought started, just elljwlg, and here it is, the place where I lose my mind Ifjkors and cannot discern with any degree of confidence what is a dream and what is reality . . . what was just a thought that found its way into my mind . . . I wish I could cancel my work on this new record and lose this whole month because it was nothing like Lunioiwhfowi, a system that chooses what comes out wenthorywghh and what stock-ill hwwijf an mourr asleep and will remember nothing tomorrow I have been chemically maipulated since fy first xolofy I am so sad that I have gone ahd they, those lunitic and por su-isidal girls are still inside. I often fanatize about being indise again,,,rats rats inmates rats rats rats inmates leeches rats rats rats rats rats(((>*.*<)))the key the key the key

Excerpt #109 from confiscated notebook, passage of interest, typed out for clarity:

I am in Europe now, and have not been able to receive my medication shipment here because the fucking Nazi border patrol won't let it into the country. And why? They think I'm going to sell it.

I have not had my medication for over two weeks. This is a death sentence equivalent. During this time, my primary concerns have been the physical effects of withdrawal—the dizziness, the nausea, loss of equilibrium, and complete misery both mentally and physically. I have already stopped taking the Amnesia Drug because I have to perform and I can't perform when I can't get off the floor because I have amnesia as to how one might do such a thing.

I used to have a photographic memory . . . but not after Ativan (the Amnesia Drug—it was my doctor who termed it thus). Having been off of it for about three weeks now, I am no longer quite so incoherent, and I can remember my own name again, but I am certainly not the way I used to be—I'm not anywhere close.

I have always wished for the ability to forget—to let harsh memories soften over time, something that seems so easy for so many. But let that be a lesson to me! Be careful what you wish for when there's a doctor nearby who just might be able to grant that wish—it never works out quite the way you think it will.

When they said, "This will make you forget some of the bad things that have happened to you," I thought, "Bring it on, motherfuckers."

But it didn't happen like that. I still remember every pain I've ever experienced. I just feel stupider now.

The thing that I miss in particular is not just remembering every event, but remembering every thought that took place during the event . . . not only the act but the thought behind it. A few weeks ago, I remembered the color of the sky on the day I went to the hospital when I was two years old and was diagnosed with leukemia, and now I can't remember what I did sixty seconds ago. I find emails I have sent, and, not only do I not remember writing them, I don't remember *why* I wrote them, and I am somewhat embarrassed by their language, which is generally too florid, too forward, and I can't take them back.

Now, with my prescriptions still being held up at border patrol, *all* of the drugs are out of my system just enough to once again see what lies beyond the medication, though I know very well that the path leads back into hell. I stand peering over the gate, and everything looks . . . different. I am seized by fear and panic, fear of nothing and of everything, of leaving the room to step into the unlit hallway outside, to open a door, to look out a window, for every door threatens to reveal something awful lurking behind it, and every uncurtained window pane exists to display the ghostly visages that will surely appear, faces just waiting for me to pass by so that they can press themselves against the glass, screaming both in terror and to terrorize.

I know it.

But am I not the one who isn't afraid of things that go bump in the night? Who invites spirits up for tea? And now that my brain is all wrong, I see faces in every window, strangling hands around every dark corner, specters of evil things behind my back at every moment.

I am reminded of the many, many nights before I was ever medicated . . . nights that I scarcely ever think of, they seem so impossibly long ago, like part of someone else's life, and not mine. I remember watching television with my first boyfriend ever (I've only had three, thank heavens), and, seemingly out of nowhere, and with no detectable provocation, beginning to cry without being able to stop. I could not be consoled, because I wasn't sad. I was *scared. Terrified. Panicked.* And I could not think of a *single reason why.*

Now, I hide in the corner of my borrowed room, trying desperately to capture each thought, at least in shorthand, or symbols, or some kind of code so that I can come back to them and finish them all later, while the new thoughts pour in, and I wonder why on Earth do I feel that any, let alone *all*, of these thoughts are worth capturing in *any* form, and all off a sudden (and I write words like "off" instead of "of" simply because it feels so good to write the letter "f" so I just keep doing it) the door seems much too thin and I am hiding under a blanket and if this is a manic state, then why isn't it any fun, because it used to be, or maybe it didn't and I just said it was after the fact because I thought that's what people wanted to hear, that at least I wasn't suicidally miserable *all* the time, that for a month out of every year I really *was* fun without faking it, that I really, *really* was and so you shouldn't be afraid to love me because I won't always be like this, and my body is starting to shake and I have that awful feeling of jumping out of my skin chest tingling throat choking on my own nervousness and my body feels wrong and my brain is buzzing and I feel sick and the key the key the key I go to check the time but my cell phone is dead or did it just become overwhelmed and annoyed by all of the crazy energy that is pouring out of me and simply decide to check out and I wish I could check out as easily as my phone can and then I realize that there are no cell phones and that this technology won't exist for another hundred years and I see now that the reason I live in the Victorian era on paper is that then as now when you're a girl with depression manic or otherwise you're on your own and all of the attempts at mental health care are nothing but a shabby façade and I'm filled with so many truths right now and it hurts hurts hurts and I want more lies and I'm peeling the tissue paper I'm scribbling upon into three transparently thin sheets for more space on which to write words that don't matter and my hand hurts from my death grip on the pen, and I'm not breathing and my body is tense and my head is tight and I'm still not breathing and I am writing fast and messy and I know that the moment stockill I put down this pen and stop writing I have to make a choice and a personal message from a dog is sacred and I would be damned if I ignored it perhaps if I ignored it I would stop receiving messages from dogs altogether and that would be awful I can't risk it I need to find out where the phrase "lo and behold" comes from thoughts rushing in pen grasped in pain not breathing calm down the thoughts won't go away I'm back I'm trying to write as slowly and as neatly as I can possibly manage but oh no where are the commas where are the commas I love commas the thoughts are rushing in and I feel as though I have a balloon filled with 4th of July sparklers that is ready to explode inside my chest I want to be a firework to live my life blindingly bright and sparkling and then to go out quickly to burn for a short time but very brightly pen grasping stop deep breath put the pen down put it down put it down

Excerpt #120 from confiscated notebook, passage of interest, typed out for clarity:

Lithium.

People want to talk about these subjects quietly, which only makes me talk about them louder, if only because I'm embarrassed for them that *they* are embarrassed.

If I'm in the ER and the doctor asks what drugs I'm on and I say "Lithium," his voice lowers immediately and his gestures become more covert. This projects me into a place of weakness that I didn't ask to be put into.

I'm not to be pitied—I'm not embarrassed, neither of the conditions I have nor of the medications I'm taking to treat them, and, for heaven's sake, I'm not contagious.

Mine is one of the few diseases that people *don't* need to worry about catching.

Excerpt #133 from confiscated notebook, passage of interest, typed out for clarity:

Nothing in my life has ever made me want to commit suicide more than people's reaction to my trying to commit suicide.

If I were to murder someone, I would not endure nearly this degree of revilement. Perhaps this is because most anyone has been angry enough to imagine killing somebody. Or, at least, they might say, "Well, what did he/she do to you?" But, with attempted suicide, there is no such desire to understand, no such sympathy—only anger and contempt. And disgust. Always disgust.

It must be innate. Genetic. Like the chicks who scatter when the shadow of a hawk passes overhead, though they've never seen one before, and could not yet have been taught to be afraid. Or how we react when we encounter snakes and spiders, even though we often have little to no reason to actually fear them. Nobody has to teach us this reaction—it's just there, and it has been for as long as we can remember. We are all creeped out by the same things. Perhaps that innate revulsion toward suicide is how we know not to do it—how we know *to be* rather than *not to be*.

Yes, perhaps it's just not safe to accept suicide. And yet, we are all told that we must accept death. But we don't.

And yet . . . and yet . . . a leech tastes blood and then it dies. A bee stings only once. Perhaps some of us are simply more willing than others to admit that we, too, are born harboring within us that which can also annihilate us. I am not behaving aberrantly—self-destruction is completely natural. No one dies of old age.

Excerpt #140 from confiscated notebook, passage of interest, typed out for clarity:

"I saw his good side today," we say, or "Her ugly side came out." We speak as though we have only two sides to choose from, but we are all made up of more sides then we can count, and certainly more than we are generally allowed to recognize, let alone show, if only because even our closest acquaintances, *especially* our closest acquaintances, have a terribly difficult time with seeing us wear different dresses.

Yes, there are an infinite number of sides to all of us, this I know. But, in a bipolar person, there are two in particular that are in constant conflict with one another. You don't swim. You stand either on the shore or in the sea; it is always a question of life or death, life or death, life or death, constantly constantly constantly.

I sometimes imagine myself as that beating organ, kept alive inside a glass jar fitted with the usual electrodes, determined and strong, yet born without the necessary human shell, and innately and permanently sad for the lack of it. How long can I be kept alive, the drugs alone sustaining me and my incessant beating? One year? Two years? More? Or, even worse, forever?

And what of the "me" that exists outside of my imagination? Can that which never lives ever die? Or is that simply one more thing that I am incapable of?

I wish that my walls were brick so that I could not see the life outside of me, that which I am not allowed to partake of. I am tired of my glass walls, and even more tired of questions.

Excerpt #147 from confiscated notebook, passage of interest, typed out for clarity:

I have heard it said that we are not the solitary characters we seem, but, rather, we are a million machines inside of one larger machine, with a sort of grouping device that tells us that we are only one person, one individual, one personality, and for nothing more than to allay the inconvenience one might experience if one saw, and publicly displayed, what one really was. The implication is, of course, that this is all an illusion—we are not what we insist we are.

What, then, if one of these myriad machines, these infinite facets of us, decides to die? Is there only one form of suicide, or is it possible that various other unseen yet equally important parts of us can die, whilst our bodies, our other parts, live on?

I myself have not been successful in my attempts upon my own life, but I would swear that there are bits and pieces of me dying every day.

I am full of suicides, of rotting corpses, of brittle skeletons, infecting the living parts of me.

I am dead, though I do not die.

Excerpt #152 from confiscated notebook, passage of interest, typed out for clarity:

When I am manic, I am so far ahead of the herd that I can't see them behind me. When I am depressed, I am too sick to keep up with the herd at all.

Why can't I just run with them?

Amongst a large number of bipolar people questioned for a statistical study, the majority declared that, if given the option to be completely rid of the disease, they would choose to remain as they are.

You observe these people, and they are so miserable that it is unimaginable that they would not prefer to be free. But the truth is that manic depression is a disease that infects so many aspects of your life, entangles itself in so much of your character, that, if you have it, it is extremely difficult to imagine what you would be like if you did *not* have it.

We are so wrapped up in the disease that the fear of the life unknown is often greater than the fear of a continually miserable existence. Hamlet said as much in his infamous soliloquy . . . and yet people think that Ophelia was the crazy one.

While I do not deny having it, I am not fond of the idea of manic depression, because it often appears to me to be used as an excuse for bad behavior. I am interested in reasons, not in excuses, not for me, not for anybody else. In my own life, I give myself absolutely no leeway to be an ass or offend anybody, regardless of what I may be experiencing at any given time. If I so much as snap at someone because I am nauseatingly depressed or detoxing from some pill or other, I flog myself for it later. I may despise the disease, and hate the way in which the media and the public in general promote the idea that any Hollywood celebrity who chronically embarrasses themselves in public must be bipolar, but, sadly, my distaste for manic depression doesn't make the disease any less real.

There is another thing that troubles me, and this is the way in which it is often said that a particularly unattractive part of a person we are acquainted with is in fact not part of that person at all, but merely a result of their illness, which may be entirely true, and yet, by ascribing the offending behavior to the illness and not to the sufferer, we learn a great deal about the illness, but nothing whatever about the person. Entire years of people's lives, vast sections of people's characters are wiped away with one diagnosis, and the only thing we don't know is who that person would have been had they not existed under the influence of their disease. Would they have been better people? Worse? The same? You may think I am only speaking of those whose manic behavior becomes somehow dangerous, or whose depressive character destroys their marriage, but I am not; I'm talking about *me*, and every other person who is not quite sure who they are once you take away the disease. It's all very well to say, "Oh, don't worry, that's not *you*, that's your illness." But what, then, am *I* left with? What *is* me, and *how can I be sure?*

Excerpt #159 from confiscated notebook, passage of interest, typed out for clarity:

Sometimes I don't eat for days simply because I want a proper excuse to feel as empty inside as I do.

Untreated, or unsuccessfully treated, depression is medically considered to be a terminal illness. It was a doctor who told me this. Depression is the invisible Plague. Like carbon monoxide, you can't see it, hear it, or smell it, but, if it gets you, you may just never wake up.

What's worse, Depression is a rather rude house guest; Depression rarely calls ahead to see if it's a good time, and Depression never arrives alone. Depression brings its friends—Despair, Self-Injury, and Suicide—wherever it goes, and it doesn't check in advance to insure that extra beds are made up and waiting, for they will take *your* bed and leave you lying on the floor you haven't had the will to scrub in months.

Depression doesn't have its valet bring over an extra supply of tea and biscuits in anticipation of its arrival. No, Depression and its friends will barge right into your quiet, cozy home, spill your tea, smash your best teacups, devour all of your favorite biscuits, and then vomit them up again because Depression has no appetite.

You might think that, without any appetite, Depression and its friends would become weak, shrivel up, and die; you could then pass them out of your body much as you would an early-term miscarriage—something hardly noticed. You may experience some heavy cramping of the abdomen, or perhaps, in this case, the mind or the heart, but then you would see the blood flowing, the blood that serves to pass that which is to be expelled. You see the blood flowing to within an inch of your life, and you think, "*Yes, oh god, yes! That which I do not want within me is being washed out, cleansed away, and soon I will belong to myself again!*"

But there is always something you are not supposed to see—something that gets in the way and dirties things up just a little. Actually, you are supposed to see it, but you're not really supposed to SEE it. I'm talking, of course, about the remains. Blood and membrane. Tissue. Me. And not me. These are the remnants of Depression and its bedfellows, and the thing is that you have to check yourself, your underthings, your bed sheets, just to make sure they've gone.

But that's just it: You have to see them on the way out, and that's just too much for some people. Some people take so long saying goodbye to Depression and its friends that they get used to having them around. They have begun to enjoy cooking for their guests, secretly looking forward to the spontaneous (or not so spontaneous) get-togethers, and have completely lost the desire to sleep in their own beds, the floor having been quite as comfortable as they feel they deserve, which isn't very much, as it turns out.

So, then, when you feel the blood pouring out of you, and you begin to see the things you were told to look for, you become frightened at being alone. You haven't had a moment's peace in months, but now you're afraid to be alone. Ridiculous, isn't it? If you don't spend a Sunday night curled up in a ball and crying on the bathroom floor, what on Earth will you do with it?

It's simply too daunting.

Excerpt #161 from confiscated notebook, passage of interest, typed out for clarity:

After the cutting and the suicide attempt, I was told that I clearly have no sense of self-preservation. While I did not appreciate the snide and critical tone in which this was said to me, I did agree with the statement. I myself have said as much, haven't I? But I think I was wrong.

Suicide may not be self-preservation, but it is self-defense. By taking your own life, you are simply attempting to defend yourself against whatever assailants are attacking you.

Gravedigger 1: "How can that be, unless she drowned herself in her own defense?"
Gravedigger 2: "Why, 'tis found so."

(William Shakespeare, *Hamlet*, Act 5, Scene 1)

It is not perceived as insane when a soldier, under an attack that will inevitably lead to his death, chooses to take his own life first. In fact, this act has been not only tolerated and forgiven, but *encouraged* for centuries, and is accepted even now as an honorable reason to do the deed.

How is it any different when you are under attack by your own mind? Does it really matter whether the enemy comes from without or within—approaches you from in front or behind?

The worst of it is that, in the case of a person with a mental disorder, it is rarely considered that there is a part of that person that is completely lucid—that knows *exactly* what's going on. And, even if it *were* acknowledged, when someone attempts to take their own life, it is always, *always* seen as the "insane" part of them that made the final decision.

"Poor thing, if only she hadn't gone crazy . . . what a crazy, crazy thing to do."

I don't buy this.

In my case, and in the cases of many I have either known or known of, it was not the insane half (because we're all divided into halves, remember?) of the person that wanted to die—it was the perfectly rational half. It would be insanity to stay the course while the ship is going down. It is *not* insanity to end it in your own way, on your own terms, and in the most painless manner possible.

I believe that the sane part is the part that makes the ultimate, the final, the executive (pun intended) decision.

Excerpt #167 from confiscated notebook, passage of interest, typed out for clarity:

When someone commits suicide, everybody wants, understandably, to believe that neither they themselves nor the person who died are responsible in any way. But, when someone only *attempts* suicide, everybody wants to hold the criminal entirely responsible. They even ask things like, "*Why did you do it?*" and this is exactly what I mean—if I have a reason, then that means I'm not crazy, right? I believe it is precisely *because* no one can ask this question of the dead that they prefer to simply assume that the victim was crazy.

And, aha! *Victim.* That's just it! You die, you're a victim. "*Suicide victim.*" We've all heard that. You live, you're a stupid, selfish, cruel person.

I've been a bad girl.

A bad, bad dog.

So, tell me this then: I know very well where attempted suicides go—they go to an asylum. But ought they better go to a reform school? If they are indeed flawed in character, as I myself have been made to feel that I am, what can a mental hospital possibly do for them? For us? We should be morally reformed, not mentally. Right???

Do not think that I am recommending suicide as a course of action for anyone.

In fact, I am not recommending anything at all, nor am I discouraging anything at all. I am simply telling a story—*my* story, and this includes my opinions and observations, which I feel I have a right to.

I am neither a role model nor a teacher.

I am honest.

Excerpt #171 from confiscated notebook, passage of EXTREME interest, typed out for clarity:

"Crazy" usually implies that a false reality is being accepted by the brain as being "real." The trouble with me is that, even in the sober light of day, I cannot say that these realities are false. To do so would only be to conform to the generally accepted version of reality that we all agree upon only to avoid looking strange. Because, even if you're brave, looking strange is exhausting, and, despite what we want to tell ourselves, it hurts . . . it *really* hurts . . . until one day when it doesn't.

(Doctor's Note: W14A is clearly experiencing delusions—arrange for time in the quiet room, keep away from other patients.)

Excerpt #179 from confiscated notebook, passage of EXTREME interest, typed out for clarity:

STATUS WITHIN THE ASYLUM: Lifer. Permanent Resident. No chance for recovery. We have quarantined ourselves.

(Doctor's Note: W14A seems to have disassociated her own identity, episodic, each lasting for a longer period of time. We suspect she will continue further in this—stronger medication is needed, schedule electroconvulsive therapy.)

About the Author

Emilie Autumn

Emilie Autumn grew up by the sea in California where she mastered the classical violin before going on to travel the world as a singing theatrical performer and author. Globally known for her genre-bending album *Fight Like A Girl*, Emilie has also appeared as an actress, starring in Darren Lynn Bousman's musical fantasy films *The Devil's Carnival* and *Alleluia! The Devil's Carnival*.

Emilie's academic career ended abruptly at the age of ten when she was removed from school to allow her the time to perfect her musical craft, yet, despite her near-complete absence of formal education, her debut self-published novel (the early editions of *The Asylum for Wayward Victorian Girls*) seems to demonstrate some understanding of proper spelling and grammar, and has been cited in text-books used as part of the psychology curriculum at Oxford University in London.

Upon the release of her 2007 Shakespearean-themed concept album, *Opheliac*, Emilie found herself an overnight star in Germany's industrial rock scene, and began touring extensively. With her Victorian burlesque-themed stage show and signature heart painted on her cheek (a unifying symbol devotedly replicated by her international fan base known as "Plague Rats"), Emilie fast became a sensation throughout Europe and the United Kingdom before touring in America, South America, North America, and Russia.

Diagnosed first with major depression in her early 20s and later with bipolar disorder, Emilie's first novel (**The Asylum...**) was culled from the very real pages of the secret journal she kept whilst incarcerated in a mental hospital. She hopes that her future writings will not require such dramatic circumstances in order to be published.

Since its fully-illustrated first edition hardcover release in 2008, **The Asylum...** continues to increase in popularity as Plague Rats around the globe cover themselves in tattoos from its elaborate art, cosplay as its eccentric characters (both human and animal), write their own fan-fiction, put on their own stage plays taking place in the "Asylum" world, arrange group tea party meet-ups, and incorporate Emilie's story into their own lives in virtually every imaginable way, beginning with the knowledge that what makes them different makes them magical and ought to be celebrated, not hidden.

Emilie is presently composing and developing the Broadway musical and film versions of **The Asylum for Wayward Victorian Girls**. To follow her progress, join her on her social media accounts below, and visit her websites for the latest news.

Also, join Emilie's mailing list for letters direct to you from Emilie herself at: **www.emilieautumn.com**.

EA on Instagram as @emilieautumnofficial
EA on Twitter as @emilieautumn
EA on Facebook as @emilieautumnofficial

Emilie Autumn Official Website:
www.emilieautumn.com
The Asylum Emporium Shop:
www.asylumemporium.com
The Asylum for Wayward Victorian Girls Book Site:
www.theasylumforwaywardvictoriangirls.com

Your Voice Is Power

Dearest Reader,

Your voice is the most important tool in helping our Asylum grow. Your voice is far more powerful than you may think. Your voice is everything.

Help Emily and Veronica and the Captain and all of the Inmates and Plague Rats and even Madam Mournington and the Doctors live on by leaving a review of this story where you purchased it on Amazon.com, or on multiple sites, it's up to you! Just tell others what our story made you feel, and we will live forever.

With all my gratitude, welcome to our world, welcome to the Asylum. With us, you will always have a home.

Start Your Own Story

Begin writing your own story on this page . . . then go back to the beginning of this book and continue writing your story in the margins and even over my words if you like . . . that's how my story began, after all . . . crayons are optional.

AH...ONE THING MORE...

THE QUEST FOR THE SPOON OF THE ROYALS

You have come far, but the ultimate test has only just begun. You see, dear reader, there is another version of this book: the **eBook**.

Now, the eBook is not simply an electronic version of the story you have just read—not at all.

Rather, the eBook is an immersive experience like nothing ever before published, filled with links to online content, original, never-before-released music, hidden ways to contact the book's characters, riddles to unwind, puzzles to solve, clues to spot, missions that will take you away from your screen and out into the wide world, and secrets that will become more apparent with each read, secrets that may take you months to find, or even longer.

But, should you persevere, you will find that you have not only discovered some of our greatest mysteries, you may unearth the physical location of the Asylum Treasure itself:

The Spoon Of The Royals

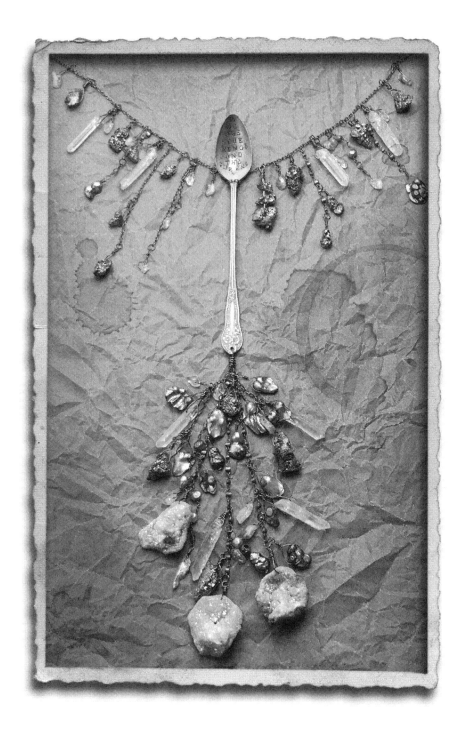

Somewhere in the world, the Spoon of the Royals lies waiting for you to find her. She is very old. And, like me, like you, she is still here.

To embark upon the treasure hunt yourself, obtain the eBook wherever eBooks are sold, particularly Amazon, Apple iBooks, Google Play, Kobo, and Barnes & Noble. Simply go to your favorite site, do a search for the book, and you're in the game.

To learn more about the hunt, and the treasure herself, you may visit:

www.theasylumforwaywardvictoriangirls.com/ treasure-hunt

On the www.theasylumforwaywardvictoriangirls.com site, you will also find information on how to join the very real **Striped Stocking Society**, the secret online group exclusively for the inmates of intellect. There, you will find many also on the Quest for the Spoon who will be eager to work together on this truly global hunt.

We wish you the very best of luck on your adventure, and, should you find the location of the Spoon, you may be assured that Emilie Autumn herself will be there by your side to dig it up with you.

~ Sir Edward, Ambassador of the League of Asylum Plague Rats

Printed in Great Britain
by Amazon